The

MARRIAGE BUREAU

for

RICH PEOPLE

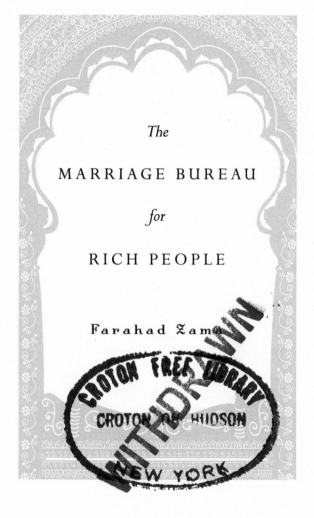

The

MARRIAGE BUREAU

for

RICH PEOPLE

Farahad Zama

AMY EINHORN BOOKS

Published by G. P. Putnam's Sons
a member of Penguin Group (USA) Inc.
New York

AMY EINHORN BOOKS

Published by G. P. Putnam's Sons

Publishers Since 1838

Published by the Penguin Group

Penguin Group (USA) Inc., 375 Hudson Street, New York, New York 10014, USA • Penguin Group (Canada), 90 Eglinton Avenue East, Suite 700, Toronto, Ontario M4P 2Y3, Canada (a division of Pearson Canada Inc.) • Penguin Books Ltd, 80 Strand, London WC2R 0RL, England • Penguin Ireland, 25 St Stephen's Green, Dublin 2, Ireland (a division of Penguin Books Ltd) • Penguin Group (Australia), 250 Camberwell Road, Camberwell, Victoria 3124, Australia (a division of Pearson Australia Group Pty Ltd) • Penguin Books India Pvt Ltd, 11 Community Centre, Panchsheel Park, New Delhi–110 017, India • Penguin Group (NZ), 67 Apollo Drive, Rosedale, North Shore 0632, New Zealand (a division of Pearson New Zealand Ltd) • Penguin Books (South Africa) (Pty) Ltd, 24 Sturdee Avenue, Rosebank, Johannesburg 2196, South Africa

Penguin Books Ltd, Registered Offices: 80 Strand, London WC2R 0RL, England

Library of Congress Cataloging-in-Publication Data

Zama, Farahad.

The marriage bureau for rich people / Farahad Zama.

p.   cm.

ISBN 978-0-399-15558-1

1. Dating services—Fiction.   2. Marriage—Fiction.   3. India—Fiction.   I. Title.

PR6126.A43M37   2009   2008046417

823'.92—dc22

Printed in the United States of America

1   3   5   7   9   10   8   6   4   2

BOOK DESIGN BY AMANDA DEWEY

To my parents, my wife, and my sons

For what do we live, but to make sport for our neighbors, and laugh at them in our turn?

JANE AUSTEN, *Pride and Prejudice*

Richness does not mean having a great amount of property; rather, true wealth is self-contentment.

PROPHET MOHAMMED (Peace be upon him.)

The

MARRIAGE BUREAU

for

RICH PEOPLE

Just Some of the Requirements
of a Perfect Brahmin Wedding

The mehndi henna patterning for "making the bride"

Austere clothes for the bridegroom to dress as a monk in the pre-ceremony rites

A palanquin for carrying the bride to the groom's house

Two banana plants cut off at the root with fruit still hanging on them

Mango leaf chains and jasmine, marigold, and kanakambaram flower decorations

A coconut for breaking before the bridegroom as he arrives

Two tall brass lamps

An idol of the elephant-headed god Ganesha

Rice flour and red dust for floor designs where the bride and groom sit

A sari that's held as a divider to keep the bride and groom apart in the early stages of the wedding

Hearth and small logs for fire; ghee and camphor to light it

Five types of fruits, and some betel nuts and leaves, crystal sugar, dried
   fruits

Garlands for bridegroom, his parents, and his sisters' husbands

Small photo of family deity and photos of parents of bride and groom
   if they are not alive

Cumin and jaggery paste, turmeric sticks, kumkum, plate of flowers

White pendants with designs for bride and groom's foreheads, made
   of Styrofoam

Rice to be used as confetti

Brass plate and tumbler for washing groom's feet

Bronze bell and idols of Krishna, Ganesha, and other deities for praying
   in new household

Silver tumbler with water and spoon for anointing and drinking

Sprouts of nine types of lentils for Gayatri Puja

Clear area to display household artifacts that the bride will take
   with her

Silver or gold toe-rings to be put on the bride by the groom

Grindstone on which bride will place her foot while the toe-rings are
   being put on

ONE

The honking started early. It was not yet seven in the morning and Mr. Ali could already hear the noise of the traffic on the road outside. The house faced east and the sun's warming rays came filtering into the verandah through the tops of the trees on the other side of the road. The curved pattern of the iron security grille was reflected on the polished black granite floor and halfway up the light green wall. Motorcycles, scooters, and buses went past in a steady procession, noisily tooting away. A speeding truck scattered other traffic out of its path with a powerful air horn. It was a crisp winter morning and some of the motorists and pedestrians were wrapped up in watch caps and woolen clothes. He opened the gate and stepped outside.

Mr. Ali loved the garden he had created in the modest yard, about twenty feet wide and ten feet long. He rubbed his hands to warm them up—sure that the temperature was less than seventy degrees. On one side, a guava tree spread its branches over most of the area from the house to the front wall. Under it grew many curry leaf plants, a henna plant, and a jasmine climber. There were also several plants in pots, including a bonsai banyan tree that he had planted eleven years ago. A well on his left supplied their drinking water, and next to it, there was a papaya tree and a hibiscus plant—morning dew shimmering silvery white on a perfectly symmetrical cobweb stretched between them. The low wall at the front continued around the house, separating his property from the road. He took a deep breath, taking in the fragrance of the jasmine flowers, and enjoyed the illusion of being in a small, green village even though his house was on a busy road in the middle of a bustling city.

Two maroon flowers had blossomed overnight on the hibiscus plant. They were high on the plant—above the height of the front wall. Mr. Ali walked up to them to have a closer look. The petals were bright and glossy; the edges fringed delicately at the end of a long fluted trumpet. The stamens peeked out of the center of the blooms, bright yellow pollen dotted among tiny, velvety, deep-red hair. Mr. Ali ran the back of his knuckle along one of the petals, luxuriating in the soft, silky touch.

Lovely, he thought, and stepped away to pick up some yellow guava leaves that had fallen down, and put them in a small plastic bucket with a broken handle that he used for a wastebasket.

He turned to the front and noticed a man reaching over the wall to pluck one of the flowers and shouted, "Hey!"

The man jerked his hand away, detaching the flower from the branch. Mr. Ali walked over to the front gate and opened it. The thief looked like a respectable man. He was wearing smart clothes. He had a mobile phone in his shirt pocket and he was carrying a leather briefcase in one hand. In the other, he held the bright blossom.

"Why are you stealing flowers from my garden?" Mr. Ali asked.

The man said, "I am not stealing them. I am taking them to the temple."

"Without my permission," Mr. Ali said angrily.

The man just turned and walked away, still holding the flower.

"What's happening?" asked Mrs. Ali from the verandah. Mr. Ali turned back and looked at his wife. Her hands were covered with flour and dough from the morning chappatis.

"Did you see that?" Mr. Ali said, his voice rising. "That man just—"

"Why are you so surprised? It's not unusual. These people want to lay flowers at the feet of the idol at the temple. It's just that normally you are not awake at this time. And anyway, don't start shouting so early in the morning. It is not good for your health," she said.

"There's nothing wrong with my health," muttered Mr. Ali.

"I heard that," said Mrs. Ali.

"There's definitely nothing wrong with your ears," he said, turning back to close the gate. "Hey!" he shouted. "Shoo . . . get out. Out . . ."

A white, skinny cow rushed back outside through the gate. It must have come in when his back was turned. Something red flashed in its mouth. Mr. Ali looked at the hibiscus plant and it was bare. Both its flowers were gone.

He struck his forehead with his hand in frustration and Mrs. Ali laughed.

"What?" he asked. "Do you think it's amusing to lose all the flowers from the garden before the sun has even risen fully?"

"No," she said. "But you are getting worked up too much over trivial things. After retiring, you've been like an unemployed barber who shaves his cat for want of anything better to do. Let's hope that from today you will be a bit busier and I get some peace," she said.

"What do you mean?" he asked.

Mrs. Ali rolled her eyes. "I have been running the house for more than forty years, and the last few years since you retired have been the worst. You keep interfering and disturbing my routine," she said. "You are not the first man in the world to retire, you know. Azhar is retired, too, and he keeps himself occupied quite well."

Mr. Ali said, "Your brother goes to the mosque regularly to spend a little time saying his prayers and a lot more time sitting around on the cool marble floor discussing *important* matters like politics, the Indian budget, the shameless behavior of today's youth, and the Palestinian problem."

"So what's wrong with that? At least he is not troubling his wife at home while he's at the mosque," said Mrs. Ali.

Mr. Ali knew that this was an argument he could not win, so he did not reply. Besides, despite Azhar's newfound piousness (he had recently started growing a beard), he actually liked his brother-in-law and got along well with him.

Mrs. Ali nodded as their servant maid opened the gate. Leela was a thin woman in her forties with a perpetual wide smile that showed her big teeth, and she was wearing an old, faded cotton sari that had once belonged to Mrs. Ali. She came into the yard.

"Start by sweeping here first," Mrs. Ali said to her.

Leela nodded and said, "All right, amma."

Mrs. Ali turned to go back into the house. She said to her husband, "Come in and eat your breakfast before the painter comes."

Mr. Ali took one last look at the bare hibiscus plant and shook his head before following his wife inside.

The doorbell rang soon after they finished their breakfast. Mr. Ali went to the verandah and opened the gate. The painter grinned at him and waved toward a large, rectangular package, wrapped in newspapers and lashed to a bicycle standing just outside the gate.

"All ready," he said. "I'll need your help to set it up."

"Okay," agreed Mr. Ali, going onto the street with the man.

They unwrapped the package, and a sign painted on a galvanized sheet with a wooden frame behind it came to light. They carried it to the wall outside the house. Mr. Ali held up the sign so it was square, and the painter hammered long nails through the wood and fastened it.

Mr. Ali was pleased with the way it looked, but out of sheer habit he said, "Five hundred rupees is too much for a simple sign like this."

The man's smile dropped. "Sir, we've already agreed on the price. I am doing this at a special rate for you. The cost of paints is going up day by day. See," he said, touching the edge of the painted metal, "I've used special galvanized sheets that won't rust after the first rains. I've also put it up for you on the wall. I didn't just dump it like so much junk on your doorstep, did I?"

Mr. Ali quietly handed over five hundred rupees and the painter left. He wanted a better view of the sign, so he started across the road. A thin cyclist in an ill-fitting brown pullover almost bumped into him; Mr. Ali had to move smartly aside to avoid a crash.

"Look where you are going," said the cyclist.

"You should have rung the bell," Mr. Ali said. "How will people know you are there if you don't ring?"

"I was right in front of you. Did your eyesight fail when you got gray hair?" asked the cyclist, shaking his head and pedaling away before Mr. Ali could reply.

Mr. Ali dismissed from his mind the rude man, who did not even know the rules of the road, and walked forward until he was in the shadows of the houses opposite. He stood under a tall gulmohar tree. Its crown was still green, with just a few hints of budding red. A crow cawed raucously in the tree's branches. Sparrows twittered and flew busily about on their duties. Mr. Ali turned and looked back at the sign hanging on the wall of his house.

ALI'S MARRIAGE BUREAU FOR RICH PEOPLE it proclaimed in big bold red letters on a blue background. Underneath in smaller letters, it said, PROP: MR. HYDER ALI, GOVT. CLERK (RETIRED) and PH. 236678.

Four-story apartment blocks overshadowed his small house on either side. His house was the only one with a garden in front. All the others had been built right up to the street. Two doors to the left, he saw the temple that was the bane of his garden. A tiny shop, already open, hugged the temple's walls and sold newspapers, magazines, fruits and flowers. Mr. Ali looked at the flowers outside the shop and scowled. Why did people steal flowers from his garden when there was a shop selling them right on the temple's doorstep?

Mr. Ali looked back toward his house and saw two boys walking to school stop to read the new sign. He was so pleased that he quickly crossed the road and asked the boys to wait while he got them guavas from inside.

Mr. Ali's house was built on a long, narrow strip of land about twenty feet wide, and the rooms were all laid out in single file. After the garden, there was a verandah at the front, sharing the roof with the rest of the building, open on three sides to light and fresh air but secure against people, with waist-high walls and an iron framework above it to the roof. The house proper started behind it—living room, bedroom, dining room, and kitchen. At the back, there was a little cemented yard.

Standing in the verandah, Mr. Ali called out, "Let's set up the office."

His wife came out, wiping her hands dry on the edge of her old blue cotton sari. She had brushed her hair and plaited it. The braid was not as thick as it used to be years ago and there were streaks of gray in the black hair.

"Let's clear everything first. There is a lot of junk here that's not suitable in an office," Mr. Ali said.

Mrs. Ali nodded and they set down to work.

"We should have done this yesterday," said Mr. Ali, picking up a lampshade. "What will clients think if they come in?"

"The ad in the paper is being published tomorrow, isn't it?" asked Mrs. Ali. "Anyway, you told me that our address was not included in the advertisement. Isn't that true?"

Mr. Ali looked at his wife and laughed. "Don't be so suspicious. Of course I haven't put our address in the paper. But what if someone looks at the sign outside and walks in?"

"I doubt if anyone will come in that soon. Come on, let's finish this. I want to start cooking. Remember, Azhar and his wife are coming over for lunch," said Mrs. Ali, gathering a bunch of old *Reader's Digest* magazines and taking them inside the house.

"Take that photo off the wall," said Mrs. Ali when she came back.

Mr. Ali looked at the picture of their son with a young couple and a three-year-old boy, which hung by a wire off a nail. He reached out and started to take it down, but then stopped. "Leave it," he said. "It won't look out of place in an office and Rehman put it up."

Mrs. Ali looked at him oddly and Mr. Ali said, "What?"

She shook her head and didn't say anything.

Half an hour later, the verandah was completely empty. Once Leela had swept away the cobwebs and mopped the floor, Mr. and Mrs. Ali surveyed the space.

"Wow!" said Mrs. Ali. "I had forgotten how big this verandah is."

"Let's look at it from a client's point of view," Mr. Ali said.

He stepped outside into the front yard and closed the gate to the verandah. He waited a moment, then pushed the iron grille gate and stepped inside. He stood just inside the gate in one corner and pointed left. "Let's put the table so that I will be sitting with my back to that wall and facing any customers walking in," he said.

He then walked to that wall and stood with his back to it, facing the width of the house. "Okay," he said. "I will sit here and the table will be in front of me. I will need a cabinet to hold the files and other stationery. Let's use the wardrobe for that."

Mrs. Ali nodded and said, "Let's put the sofa against the front wall so clients can sit here and talk to you without shouting. We can put a couple of seats against the other two walls, so other clients can sit down as well."

"All right, let's do it," he said.

They started moving the furniture from inside the house. The table and chairs were relatively easy to move, but the wooden wardrobe and the sofa proved much harder, especially at the doorstep between the living room and the verandah.

Mrs. Ali said, "We really shouldn't be doing this at our age. Let me call Rehman. He will help us. After all, what are sons for, if not to help their parents in their old age?"

"No!" said Mr. Ali firmly. "I've already told you. I don't want him here now. If he comes, we'll just end up having an argument. I don't want any fights today."

Finally, all the furniture was in place. Mrs. Ali looked around, breathing heavily, and said, "I will put up curtains to cover all the grille-work, so you have privacy. Also, keep the door to the house closed as far as possible, so people sitting here cannot see inside."

The next day, Mr. Ali sat on a chair in his new office and laid out the newspaper on the desk. He opened the paper to the matrimonial section. Sunday was the most popular day for this and it ran to one whole page of closely typed ads. Mr. Ali ran his finger from the top trying to find his ad. He could not afford a proper "display" advertisement, so he had paid for a classified advertisement. He had agonized over his ad many times to pare it down to the absolute minimum because the newspaper charged per word and he didn't want to pay more than was necessary. He skipped over a "fair, slim, 22 years . . . ," a "Christian Mala, 28 years old . . . ," a "software engineer working in Bangalore . . . ," and a "London settled doctor, caste no bar."

He was more than three quarters of the way down the page before he found his own ad—"For widest choice among Hindu, Muslim, Christian Brides/Grooms, contact Ali's Marriage Bureau for Rich People."

Mr. Ali knew that he was exaggerating just a bit when he promised a wide choice. *The biggest problem with a marriage bureau,* he thought, *is that the start is the most difficult time.* If he had wanted to go into the restaurant business instead, he would have done up a place, hired some waiters, a cook or two, and opened with as big a dhoom-dhamaka as he could afford; people would come to try the food. The restaurant may not run in the longer term, but if the money and inclination were there, it would have been easy for Mr. Ali to open one. A marriage bureau is quite different. When the first client walked through the door and wanted to see suitable matches before parting with the fees, Mr. Ali would not have any matches to show the client. To get around this problem, he had decided not to put his address in the ad, and to run the business over the phone.

He felt proud to see his name in print. He took out a red ballpoint pen and circled his ad. He called out, "Wife, come and see this!"

"What is it now? How am I supposed to get any work done if you keep calling me like this?" Mrs. Ali said, coming out into the verandah.

Mr. Ali showed his wife the paper. She read the ad and smiled.

"Very nice," she said, and then frowned suddenly. "There are so many ads in this paper. Will anybody notice ours?"

Mr. Ali had been having similar doubts, but he put on a brave front. "Of course they will!" he said.

Mrs. Ali went back into the house and Mr. Ali started reading the newspaper. He skimmed over the headlines: a terrorist incident in Kashmir, an interstate spat about the River Krishna's waters, and a new shopping mall that was being planned in the grounds of the old Central Jail that had been moved out of the town. After folding the newspaper neatly, he rearranged the still-empty files.

An hour later, Mrs. Ali came out with two cups of tea and gave him one cup. Mr. Ali came out from behind his table and they both sat on the chairs by the verandah gate, sipping their tea and looking at the people and traffic on the road.

"Did anybody call?" Mrs. Ali asked.

"No. But it is still early."

"Do you think anybody will ring?" said Mrs. Ali.

Just then the phone rang and Mr. Ali jumped up, grinning smugly at Mrs. Ali. He picked up the phone and said in his most professional voice, "Ali's Marriage Bureau."

"Salaam, bhai-jaan! How are you today? Did you get any customers yet?"

It was Mrs. Ali's brother, Azhar. Mr. Ali's voice dropped in disappointment. "Not yet," he replied.

"I am thinking of going to the Pension Line Mosque for the afternoon prayers. Why don't you come with me?"

"Why?" said Mr. Ali. "Today is not Friday."

"Where does it say in the Quran that you should only go to the mosque on Fridays?" asked Azhar.

"No, thank you," replied Mr. Ali, "I'm busy."

He passed the phone to his wife.

The business took off slowly, as expected. A few people became members and Mr. Ali advertised on their behalf. He forwarded the replies to his members but also kept their details, and as the weeks passed, his files steadily grew.

TWO

The smell of pomfret—his favorite fish—frying wafted from the kitchen as Mr. Ali sat down at the dining table. A month had gone by since he had opened the marriage bureau, and business was steady but slow. The fees Mr. Ali collected barely covered the cost of advertising and his other expenses. However, the work occupied his time and kept him out of his wife's hair, and that was the main thing. Today had been exceptionally quiet. He had not received a single call all morning.

The phone rang—once, twice, three times.

He was tempted to let it keep ringing, but got up because business had been so slow. The chair made a noise on the granite floor as he pushed it back.

"Where are you going? I'm just bringing out the fish," said Mrs. Ali from the kitchen.

"I'll take just one moment. Go ahead and serve the food," said Mr. Ali, going to the living room and picking up the phone on the extension there.

"Hello, Ali's Marriage Bureau," said Mr. Ali.

"I've seen your advertisement in the paper. Do you have any Baliga Kapu brides?" asked a male voice.

"Please give me some details, sir. I am sure we can find someone for you," he said, picking up a pen and pulling a blank piece of paper toward him to write down the details.

"My name is Venkat. I am looking for a bride for my son. He is a software engineer, currently working in Singapore."

"How old is he, sir?"

"Twenty-seven."

"What did he study?"

"Bachelor of Engineering."

"What is he earning?"

"One and a half lakhs, one hundred and fifty thousand, a month. We also have lands in the Krishna District, which give a good income."

Mr. Ali was impressed. Mr. Venkat and his son would make good clients. "How many other children do you have, sir?" asked Mr. Ali.

"None. Bharat is my only son."

"How tall is he?"

"Five feet, ten inches."

"Is he fair or dark?"

"He is fair, takes after his mother," replied Mr. Venkat.

Mr. Ali decided that honesty was a better policy, in this case, than trying to bluff it out. "I don't have any matches right now for you, sir," he said, "but for somebody like your son, I am sure we can find a bride very easily. If you become a member, we will advertise on your behalf and get you a wide choice."

Mr. Venkat was hesitant. "I am not sure. . . ."

"Don't worry, sir! We will take care of everything. Your name will not even appear anywhere. We will get the letters and forward them on to you. The fee is five hundred rupees and I will spend most of it on the advertisement itself."

"Okay, what's your address? I will come there in the evening," Mr. Venkat said.

Mr. Ali had still not advertised his address. He said, "No need to come personally. You can send me a check by post."

"No, no. I want to see you before I decide," Mr. Venkat said.

Mr. Ali gave in and told him the address. "On the main road to the highway, two houses up from the Ram temple. There is a signboard in front of our house."

At five in the evening that day, Mrs. Ali was in the front yard. She drew water for the potted plants from the well with a pail attached to a nylon rope. Once she had slaked all the plants' thirst, she opened the gate and stood there, watching the world go by. A few minutes later, she saw a thin, dark woman in her sixties walking past. She was wearing a sumptuous ruby-colored sari with the red vermilion bindi of a Hindu married woman on her forehead.

"Hello, Anjali, how are you?" said Mrs. Ali.

"Saibamma, Muslim lady, it's so good to see you. Is everything all right?" Anjali said.

The Alis and Anjali's family were neighbors many years ago when they both had been much poorer and lived in a rougher part of town. Anjali was from a lower caste—a washerwoman—and she never addressed Mrs. Ali by name, even after all these years.

"How are your boys?" asked Mrs. Ali.

Anjali and her husband had not studied past primary school, but they had made a great effort to give their two sons a good education. Their efforts had taken fruit—both the sons were now office workers and comfortably off. Anjali's elder son worked as a lecturer in a government college, and her younger son was the superintendent of orderlies in a local hospital.

"They are both doing well, by God's grace. How is Mr. Ali? Is he keeping well?" said Anjali. She came a bit closer and said, slightly less loudly, "Did you know that Lakshmi's son has thrown her out of the house?"

Lakshmi had been a common neighbor from the old district, a widow who lived with her married son.

"Really!" said Mrs. Ali, her hand to her mouth. "What happened?"

"His wife did not want her around, so he told his mother to leave, the poor woman."

"All that effort she put into raising her son, and this woman comes in and elbows her out. What a wicked woman. She is forgetting that she will also be old one day and a mother-in-law," said Mrs. Ali.

"You are right, Saibamma. What goes around comes around. But the son should also have some sense. How can he throw his widowed mother out of the house just because his wife said so?"

Mrs. Ali shook her head and asked, "Where is Lakshmi staying now?"

"She has gone to her sister's house. But how long can she be there?"

They both went silent for a while, contemplating the way the world was changing.

"Kali Kaalam," said Anjali, referring to the tenth age of the world according to Hindus. "In this age, people cheat and tell lies. They shirk their duty, and morality slowly seeps out of the world until God comes down to earth and destroys it."

Mrs. Ali nodded in agreement. The Prophet Mohammed had said the same thing—the world would turn very wicked before the Day of Judgment.

Anjali took her leave.

Mrs. Ali watched the traffic whizzing past in both directions for a while and was about to go in to start preparing dinner when she saw a white Ambassador car approaching slowly. It stopped at the shop by the temple and the driver came out and asked the shopkeeper a question. She couldn't see inside the shop, but the driver got his answer and went back into the car. The car came forward slowly and stopped in front of Mrs. Ali.

The rear window wound down and a dark, plump man asked her, "Madam, is this the marriage bureau?"

"This is the place. Please come in," she said.

Mr. Venkat wore white trousers, a crisp white cotton kurta and a slash of white sacred ash across his forehead. Two gold rings, one of them with a moonstone, adorned his fingers, and a thick gold chain hung around his neck. He was a big man, tall, fat, and dark-skinned with a big belly and the unconscious confidence, almost a swagger, of a man born rich who has become even richer in his own lifetime. He told Mr. Ali that his ancestors were farmers (caste: Kapu; subcaste: Baliga) and he owned large fields in the fertile Krishna delta and other properties in town.

"As I've already told you on the phone, I have just one son," he said. "He is a software engineer working for a big American bank in Singapore and earns a good salary. You might think it is easy to get a bride for somebody like my son, so you must be wondering why I had to come to a marriage bureau."

Mr. Ali, who had been thinking exactly that, was glad that Mr. Venkat was so choosy. It meant more business for him. He just nodded and kept silent.

"For one reason or another, every girl we've found is unsuitable.

I've asked my brother-in-law to find a match, but he is useless. He keeps bringing details of totally unsuitable candidates. Either they are too dark or too old or too short. Or they are not educated. I've told my wife to stop her brother from bringing any more details."

"Yes, finding the proper bride for a son is a very important duty for the parents," said Mr. Ali, in a soothing voice.

"That's right," Mr. Venkat said. "And now the matter has become urgent. My son is coming home for a holiday in two weeks. He will be here for one week and I want him engaged before he's gone."

"Not much time, then," said Mr. Ali.

"That's correct. Once he leaves, he won't be back until Deepavali, in the autumn. When a young son is far away from home, it is better to get him married off sooner than later. Who knows what temptations he might fall prey to otherwise? As it is, we can't get him married off this time, but at least if he is engaged, that will be something."

Mr. Ali nodded in agreement. He took out a form and said, "I've already filled this in with the information you gave me on the phone. Let's complete it and we can get started."

Mr. Venkat's demands for his son's bride were not many, thought Mr. Ali ruefully. She had to be fair, slim, tall, educated but not a career-minded girl. Her family had to be wealthy, ideally landowners, and from the same caste as Mr. Venkat. If they were from the same city, that was even better. They had to be willing to pay a large dowry, commensurate with his own family's wealth and son's earning capacity. Mr. Ali wrote it all down.

"Who will select the bride?" asked Mr. Ali.

"What do you mean?" Mr. Venkat said, waving his hand in front of him.

"Will it be your choice or your son's? Or, maybe your wife or your parents . . ."

"My parents are not alive, so it will be my choice. Obviously, my wife will have a say. And nowadays, boys want to see the girl and have a word too, don't they? It wasn't like that in our time. My father just told me one day that he had fixed my marriage with his business partner's daughter and that was that. Things have changed. I blame it on movies, myself. They teach these youngsters all the wrong things," said Mr. Venkat.

"You are probably right," said Mr. Ali. "But your son has gone abroad and probably seen how things are done there."

"Yes, I'm sure that doesn't help."

Finally, Mr. Venkat handed over the fees and left.

The next Sunday, Mr. Venkat's ad appeared in *Today*. Mr. Ali had outdone himself—the ad was small and to the point: *Baliga Kapu, six-figure salary, eight-figure wealth wishes beautiful same-caste bride . . .*

Mr. Ali's phone did not stop ringing from the morning till the evening. Several people complained that his phone was constantly engaged. They all wanted to find out about this wealthy man looking for a bride. They all had a daughter or a niece or a sister who was just the right match. Over the next few days, he also received almost a hundred letters. He forwarded them all to Mr. Venkat, who was very happy to see such a wide choice of brides for his son. All these people's details also went into Mr. Ali's files. He started writing to them that he had received many responses for that particular ad but he also had details of other suitable people in his files which he would share with them if they became members of the marriage bureau. He had to write to so many people that he typed out the letter and went to the shop by the temple. The corner shop not only sold loose cigarettes, bananas, candy for children, magazines, newspapers, and flowers and coconuts for the deity in the temple, but also had a photocopy machine. Mr. Ali asked him for a hundred copies of the letter.

"Sir, why did you trouble yourself? Here is my cell number. Just give me a call at any time and I will send my good-for-nothing son to come and pick up the work," said the shopkeeper, promising to deliver the copies in a couple of hours.

Mr. Ali left the shop, shaking his head in wonder. Corner shopkeepers with mobile phones! The world was truly advancing.

The next Sunday, Mr. Ali truthfully advertised, "Wide choice of Baliga Kapu brides. Grooms contact . . ."

Early in the morning, three weeks later, Mrs. Ali and her husband were in the front yard. Mrs. Ali was pointing out guavas and Mr. Ali was knocking them down with a long bamboo stick. Their servant maid, Leela, walked in. Two young boys were hiding behind the folds of Leela's sari.

Mrs. Ali said, "Come out, boys. Don't hide behind your grandmother. We are not going to eat you."

They slowly came out on either side of Leela. Mrs. Ali smiled at the two identical three-year-olds and asked, "When did you come to the city?"

"Last night," they piped in one voice. "We've come to celebrate the Big Festival in granny's house."

Mr. Ali stepped back and put the bamboo stick in the alley next to the house. Leela started moving the pots forward so she could sweep behind them. The twins moved with her like two planets around a star, not letting go of her sari.

Mr. Ali pointed to the boy on the left and said, "You are Luv, aren't you?"

The boys giggled and shook their heads. "No," said the boy. "I am Kush."

"Our granny gets confused too. Our mother is the only one who can tell us apart correctly," said Luv proudly.

"Even our dad gets our names mixed up," said Kush.

Mrs. Ali laughed and said to Leela, "The boys are lovely. Have you distracted the evil eye by giving it a sacrifice?"

"I have, amma. But whatever sacrifices we give, ultimately it all depends on God," she replied.

Mrs. Ali nodded and turned to go inside. Mr. Ali followed his wife toward the house. At the verandah, he looked back and said to the boys, "If you come inside, I have two identical twin guavas for you."

Half an hour later, the bell rang and Mr. Ali went to answer it. Mr. Venkat was at the front door with a huge smile on his face. Mr. Ali showed him to the sofa and sat down opposite him.

"Looking at your face, I would say you have good news," Mr. Ali said.

"That's right. Bharat got engaged yesterday."

"Fantastic. That's really good news," said Mr. Ali.

"Yes, and it is down to you. Fabulous match. They are perfect— wealthy, respectable. They are from Vijayanagaram," said Mr. Venkat, waving his left hand vaguely to the north.

"Not far, then," said Mr. Ali. "It's less than fifty miles from here. What did your son think of the bride?"

"The girl is beautiful. My son immediately liked her—so no problems there."

"That's great news. Thanks for coming and telling me," said Mr. Ali.

"Don't think I am an ungrateful man. I've got a gift for you and your family."

"There was no need," said Mr. Ali, as was expected of him.

"No, no. Allow me," he said.

Mr. Venkat got up from the sofa and went outside to his parked car. Mr. Ali followed him. Mr. Venkat said to his driver, "Take the bag into the gentleman's house."

The driver dragged a heavy jute bag out of the trunk of the car. Mr. Ali directed him to go by the passage on the side of the house and leave the bag by the rear door. The man nodded and heaved the heavy sack onto his back.

Mr. Venkat explained, "That's thirty kilos of black lentils from our fields. The harvest came in two months ago."

"Thanks, that's really generous of you. The lentils must be worth more than the fees—probably enough to make idlis and dosas for six months!" said Mr. Ali, smiling at the thought of the delicious rice cakes and pancakes to come.

Two months later, it was late March and the weather had turned warm. Even now, in the evening, the temperature was in the nineties and winter was just a memory. Mrs. Ali came out of the kitchen after making halwa, a sweet dish with semolina, sugar, clarified-butter ghee, cashew nuts, and raisins. She was feeling hot and sat in the living room under the ceiling fan. She actually wanted to sit outside in the verandah, but it was busy—several people, clients of the marriage bureau, were there. After cooling down for a few minutes, she picked up the phone to speak to her sister, who lived locally.

". . . the people are right here," Mr. Ali was saying to somebody on the phone, on the other extension.

Mrs. Ali put the phone down, annoyed.

The marriage bureau was now well established. It had become very popular with the Kapu community. It also had lots of members of other Hindu communities and Muslims. Mrs. Ali, however, was not happy.

The verandah at the front of the house was totally taken over by the business. Her husband had started printing his address in his ads, and visitors were continually streaming in and out—members, potential members, courier delivery men, advertising agents, and many others. If he was not in, she had to answer the door and deal with these people. The phone was also busy almost all the time, and she could not call up and have a chat with one of her sisters or brothers. They had also stopped calling her because they said the phone was always engaged.

Her husband had become very busy and neglected all his duties around the house. It had been almost a week since she had told him to fix the loose handle on the pressure cooker, and he still hadn't done it. What would happen if the handle came off while she was taking the pressure cooker off the stove? Also, she didn't think it was good for a man of her husband's age to be so busy. He was supposed to be a retired man, taking life easy.

As she was musing on all this, moving from anger to depression and back again, she heard her brother Azhar in the verandah greeting her husband. He pushed open the door to the living room and came in.

"Salaam, aapa," he said to his older sister.

Mrs. Ali stood up from the sofa and greeted him. "Sit down, Azhar. I'll get you tea. I've just made halwa. Do you want some?"

"No. I went to the doctor yesterday and he said my sugar level was up again. No sweets for me. In fact, reduce the sugar in the tea as well."

"Are you all right? Why did you go to the doctor?" said Mrs. Ali.

"I am feeling fine. It was just a six-month checkup."

Mrs. Ali got tea for Azhar and herself. "It's a good habit you have, going to the doctor regularly. It's best to find out and nip these problems in the bud."

They sipped their tea and everything was silent except for the whir of the ceiling fan and the noise of the traffic outside.

Mrs. Ali suddenly said, "He is always busy. See, even now, he cannot come and sit down with us—clients to look after or something. He is neglecting himself—no time for a siesta in the afternoon or a walk in the evening. I am worried. He is not a young man anymore. How long can this go on?"

"I know," said Azhar. "I met Sanyasi yesterday and he said that bhai-jaan has stopped coming for walks."

Sanyasi was another retired man and a common friend of her husband and Azhar.

"I don't know what to do," sighed Mrs. Ali.

Just then, Mr. Ali came in, smiling. "One more fish has fallen in the net!" he said, waving five one-hundred rupee notes.

"Congrats!" said Azhar. "But, bhai-jaan, seriously, how long can you keep this up? I met Sanyasi yesterday and he says it has been almost two weeks since you went for a walk with your old gang. I cannot phone my sister or you and have a chat anymore."

"You are right," said Mr. Ali, pocketing the five hundred rupees. "But what can I do? I cannot turn people away, can I?"

Mrs. Ali got one more cup of tea and gave it to her husband.

"I have to look after the clients, answer the mail, then compose the advertisements and prepare the lists. There just isn't enough time in the day," said Mr. Ali.

"The problems of success!" Azhar laughed.

"Don't laugh, Azhar. This is serious. Your brother-in-law is driving himself into an early grave, working like this," said Mrs. Ali, frowning and rubbing her knee under the sari. The arthritis in her knees had started acting up, as it always did when she was under stress.

"What a problem to suffer, eh?" said Azhar. "Most people invest loads of money into a business only to see it fail. Here, we have the opposite."

"It's a problem, nonetheless," said Mrs. Ali, cautiously flexing her leg. "You need to make more time for yourself and for me somehow. If it means advertising less and seeing fewer clients, then that's what you have to do."

"This business doesn't work like that," said Mr. Ali. "If I have fewer clients, then the clients I do have won't find any matches. This is a line where if you are not popular, you might as well not get into it at all."

"Then close the marriage bureau. We don't need the money and I cannot deal with all this hassle," said Mrs. Ali, feeling mutinous.

Azhar raised his hands in a placatory manner and said, "There's no need to go to such extremes. I have an idea. What you need is an assistant to help you, and a business phone so your current one remains free for personal use."

THREE

"Advertising is the key to success," said Mr. Ali. "How do you think my marriage bureau has become successful? It's because I spend a bigger portion of my revenues on advertising than any of my competitors."

Mrs. Ali did not reply. It had been a couple of days since Azhar's visit, and her husband had just told her that he had sent an ad to the local newspaper.

Assistant wanted for successful marriage bureau. Smart, typist . . .

There were several responses. The first girl who came could not speak a word of English; the second could not work after three in the afternoon, when her children came back from school. The third was a young man who was shocked that he would have to work on Sundays; the fourth was smart and suitable but did not want to work in a house. She wanted to work in a "proper" office.

Mr. Ali sighed and showed the eighth candidate out, saying, "I am sorry. We do not have air-conditioning. Yes, it gets hot in summer."

Mrs. Ali laughed and said, "Why don't you give up? You are just wasting money on these ads. They are useless. I will find an assistant for you."

"You?" said Mr. Ali.

"Why? Don't you think I can?" asked Mrs. Ali.

"Let's see you find somebody. If you get me an assistant, I will take you out for dinner."

"You are on!" replied Mrs. Ali. "But I am not getting fobbed off by a visit to a cheap snack parlor to eat idli sambhar. You will have to take me to a big hotel and feed me tandoori chicken."

The next day, Leela was late. Normally, she came to work before seven, but today they had finished their breakfast and it was well past eight and she was still nowhere to be seen. It was every housewife's nightmare—the dishes stacked up; the house unswept; the whole morning routine upset. Whenever Mrs. Ali met her sisters or friends, they always complained about their servants and she had to work hard not to appear smug. Leela was very reliable, and on the rare occasion that she couldn't come in, she normally sent one of her daughters to work in her place.

A nagging uncertainty gnawed at Mrs. Ali. Would Leela turn up? Should Mrs. Ali wash the dishes herself or should she wait? She decided to sweep the house. The thought of the house not being cleaned while the sun was halfway up from the horizon was unbearable. What if any guests turned up? What would they think of her?

Around eleven, Mrs. Ali heard a knock on the back door and un-bolted it to find that Leela had arrived.

"What happened? Why are you late?" asked Mrs. Ali.

There was no answer. Leela just went past Mrs. Ali into the kitchen and started taking the dirty dishes out into the backyard to wash. Leela was a tall, thin woman in her early forties but looked ten years older. She had a difficult life with an alcoholic husband and the general rigors of poverty, but she was invariably cheerful, always smiling and ready to chat any time. Today, however, she had a grim look on her face. Mrs. Ali decided to leave her alone for some time before trying to get an answer.

Mrs. Ali went to work scraping a coconut for the chutney she was making for lunch. When she finished, she washed her hands and took the coconut scraper outside to Leela, who took it silently.

Mrs. Ali threw the coconut shells into the wastebasket and asked, "Did your husband come back home drunk last night and beat you again?"

"No, amma!" said Leela. "I wish it was that simple. My grandson Kush is not well. Yesterday, they took an X-ray of the boy's head. There is a growth in his brain." She started crying.

Mrs. Ali was aghast. "There, there! Don't cry. I am sure he will be all right. Nowadays, doctors can cure so many diseases."

Slowly, Mrs. Ali got the story out of her. The three-year-old boy had started complaining of headaches. He also got tired easily and fell asleep frequently. The parents initially ignored his complaints until he started throwing up. They had taken him to a local doctor, who had given the boy a course of penicillin injections. It only made him worse. After a couple of weeks of worsening symptoms, the doctor had given up and asked them to take the boy to the city. In the city, an X-ray had been taken and showed a growth, but the doctors wanted to take a CT scan to be sure.

"The scanner was so frightening—like a big mouth swallowing the little child. My poor grandson, he was so brave," Leela said, her eyes watering again.

"Have you got the results from the scan?" asked Mrs. Ali.

"Yes, amma. The growth is definitely there and they said they have to operate to take it out. The doctor was very good. He explained everything patiently and said that the sooner we have the operation, the better."

"How much did the scan cost?" asked Mrs. Ali.

"Five thousand rupees, amma," said Leela. "My daughter says that all their savings are now gone. The operation will cost more money and I don't know where we'll get it from."

The next morning, Mrs. Ali, as usual, went outside at six to collect the milk. It was an old habit from years ago when the milkman actually milked the cow in front of the house and she had to stand there watching him to make sure that he did not dilute the milk from a secret water bottle. The cows were long gone and she now got a half-liter of milk from the dairy, but she still stood at the gate to collect it. Mrs. Ali also liked to stand by the gate while the day was still cool and watch the people who walked by her house—they all seemed to be in much less hurry at this time of day. As she grew older, she found that she was becoming more and more partial to peace and quiet. Most of the people on the road at this time were either thin pensioners or fat middle-aged people out for a walk.

It is interesting, she thought, *that you do not see any fat pensioners. Are they too poor to get fat or do fat people die before they become pensioners?*

She saw a young mother carrying a small child in her arms, and her thoughts went to Leela's grandson. She hoped he would be all right. The milkman came a bit early and gave her the milk, but Mrs. Ali did not go inside. She stayed outside, waiting. She had noticed a young woman in her early twenties who walked past the house every day, returning an hour later with rolled-up sheets of paper in her hand.

A few minutes later, the woman was walking past, and Mrs. Ali called out to her, "Hello! Do you have a moment?"

The girl looked around, appearing surprised at being addressed by a stranger.

"What's your name?" asked Mrs. Ali.

"Aruna," the girl replied.

"Are you going to the typing institute?" asked Mrs. Ali.

"Yes!" said Aruna, surprised. "How did you know?"

"I have seen you returning with rolled-up papers in your hand and I knew you must be learning to type. What's your speed?" Mrs. Ali asked. She had learned typing as a teenager herself, but it was many years since she had sat in front of a typewriter.

"Fifty words per minute," replied Aruna.

"That's good."

"Thanks." She smiled shyly. "I have passed my Lower and I am practicing for my Higher exam."

"Would you like a job?" asked Mrs. Ali.

"What job?" asked Aruna, looking suspicious.

She has every reason to be, thought Mrs. Ali. It is not every day that jobs are offered to people walking along the road.

"We have a marriage bureau," replied Mrs. Ali, pointing to the sign. "We need an assistant. I think it would suit a girl like you who lives locally."

"Oh!"

Mrs. Ali could see that the girl was tempted but not convinced. She said, "Why don't you go for your typing lessons and then come back later when the office is open? You can see for yourself then and decide."

Aruna nodded and went on her way. Mrs. Ali happily went inside. She knew the young woman would be back. Aruna always wore a simple cotton salwar kameez, trousers and a long shirt that reached down to the knees with slits at the sides. Her dress looked handmade. She did not wear expensive ready-made clothes. She always wore tiny earrings and the same thin gold chain around her neck. Her family was obviously not well off and she seemed like a modest, sensible girl—just the kind Mrs. Ali liked. She didn't think much of brash "modern" girls who wore T-shirts and jeans and spoke good English.

It was half past nine in the morning and it was hot but not yet scorching. Traffic on the road outside was still heavy and the road was noisy. The postman had just gone and Mr. Ali was busy working through the day's mail. There was a gentle cough and Mr. Ali looked up in surprise to see a young woman by the door—he hadn't heard the gate open.

"Namaste," she said, with folded hands.

"Namaste," he replied, distracted.

"May I speak to madam?" the woman asked.

"Madam?" he said, puzzled. His mind was still on the letter he was reading, and he couldn't figure out who she was talking about.

Luckily, his wife came out just then. She smiled at the girl and said, "Hi, Aruna! Thank you for coming. This is my husband, Mr. Ali. He runs the marriage bureau."

Mrs. Ali turned to him and said, "I've asked Aruna to come over and have a look to see if she wants to work as an assistant here."

"I see," said Mr. Ali, folding the letter and putting it to one side.

"Yes," said Mrs. Ali. "Aruna is a very good typist. She has passed her Lower typing exam and is preparing for her Higher exam. She lives locally as well."

Mr. Ali pointed to the sofa and said, "Please sit down, Aruna."

After she sat down, he asked her, "Do you want a glass of water?"

Aruna nodded and Mrs. Ali went inside to get it. This was traditional Indian courtesy—Muslim or Hindu. Feuds lasting generations had broken out when this simple courtesy was not observed. The Prophet Mohammed was reported to have seen a prostitute giving water to a stray puppy and to have said that the woman was sure to go to heaven. A traditional pooja, or prayer, among Hindus involves inviting God into your house as a guest, and one of the first steps in the worship is to offer the Lord a drink. Mrs. Ali came back with a glass of cool water from the fridge and gave it to Aruna.

Mr. Ali asked her, "Are you working now?"

"Yes, sir. I am a shop assistant in Modern Bazar," she replied, naming a new department store (the first multistory shop in the whole town). "I just started there three weeks ago."

"Why do you want to leave such a big shop and work here?" asked Mr. Ali.

"Oh! I was not planning to move, sir, but madam saw me outside and asked me to come in."

Mrs. Ali nodded. "That's right," she said, and turned to Aruna. "What hours do you work?"

"Really long hours!" the girl said, her hands tight in her lap. "The shop opens at eleven and we have to be there half an hour before that. It closes at ten in the night and we leave fifteen minutes later. It's very difficult to find a bus at that time of night and I get home after eleven."

Mrs. Ali was shocked. "Aren't you scared—a young girl like you traveling that late at night?"

"I used to be scared," said Aruna, shrugging her shoulders. "I don't mind now."

"What do your parents say?" asked Mrs. Ali, leaning forward.

"They don't like it, but what can we do? We are poor and need the money to survive. Until recently, I was doing my M.A., but our family finances have suffered lately and I had to leave my education and take up a job."

They were all silent for a moment, then Mr. Ali said, "We start at nine, close for lunch sometime between twelve-thirty and one, and open again at three in the afternoon. We stay open till seven. Sunday is our busiest day, so you have to come in for work on that day. You can take Monday off instead."

"Those times are very good compared to what I am doing. I don't mind coming in on Sunday, either. I work every other Sunday in Modern Bazar anyway. What is the pay?" asked Aruna.

"What do you get paid in Modern Bazar?" he asked.

"They pay me fifteen hundred rupees a month," replied Aruna.

"We can only pay you one thousand here," said Mr. Ali.

Aruna's face fell. "I like the hours, but I cannot afford such a big drop in salary."

Mr. Ali nodded and said, "I wouldn't expect you to. The salary is one thousand, but in addition, for every member who joins while you are in the office with me, you get twenty-five rupees bonus, and for every member who joins when you are on your own in the office, you will get fifty rupees as bonus."

Aruna looked skeptical.

Mr. Ali raised a finger and said, "At least one member joins each day, and sometimes two or three. You will definitely earn more here than you are earning in Modern Bazar."

Aruna was silent for a moment. Then she looked at Mr. and Mrs. Ali and said, "Thanks for the offer. I will need to think about this."

"Don't leave it too long. Another girl is coming for an interview this evening," said Mrs. Ali.

Mr. Ali watched Aruna close the gate and leave. He turned to his wife and asked, "Have you asked another girl to come in the evening?"

Mrs. Ali laughed and said, "You are such a buddhoo! Of course nobody else is coming for an interview. But the girl doesn't need to know that, does she?"

Mr. Ali was silent. He had often wondered how his wife would have fared had she run her own business. He was sure she would have been very successful.

Mrs. Ali said, "Why did you offer to pay the bonus? You might end up paying lots of money to her."

Mr. Ali smiled. "I want to pay lots of money. The more I pay, it means I am earning even more. . . ."

He could see the doubt on his wife's face.

"Do you remember when we were building this house, I went to the quarry to select the best granite stones for the floor?" he said, pointing his finger down toward the polished ground.

"Yes . . ." said Mrs. Ali, looking puzzled, no doubt wondering what granite tiles and quarries had to do with marriage bureaus and assistants.

"Quarries are difficult places to work and I was expecting a hard taskmaster driving the poor workers. Instead, I found a gentle-looking man with round glasses sitting in an office while the workers toiled away in the hot sun. I was surprised and I asked him how he got his people to work like that, and he told me that he paid his workers piece rate—the stonecutters, the saw operators, the haulers—each worker got a certain amount for every sheet. He said they managed themselves and if somebody was being lazy, they sorted it out themselves because it affected all of them. I don't want to be sitting here all the time looking over the girl's shoulder. I want her to work by herself."

Mrs. Ali nodded and said, "Imagine if the government had paid you by the number of files you cleared while you were in service. How much more efficient would you have been?"

Mr. Ali laughed and said, "I don't know about that, but I can tell you that Muthuvel, Rao, and Sanyasi wouldn't have come in at ten, gone to the canteen for a long tea break at eleven, lunch at one, an hourlong afternoon tea, and samosas at three before leaving the office at five sharp."

Fifteen minutes later, a potential client came in and Mrs. Ali went back inside the house. The man's name was Joseph. His grandparents were lower-caste Hindus who had converted to Christianity. He was looking for a groom for his daughter—caste or religion no bar.

In Mr. Ali's experience, it was actually more difficult to find a partner for somebody who said "caste or religion no bar." It was ironic, but true, thought Mr. Ali, that the more specific the requirement—a Turpu Kapu from Krishna District who owned at least twenty acres of land, for example—the easier it was to find a match. Also, Christians who were from higher castes looked down on the lower castes, calling them *converted* Christians.

"The fee is five hundred rupees, sir," said Mr. Ali, finally.

"Do I have to pay it up front?" asked Joseph. "Once I give you the money, what incentive do you have for finding my daughter a match?"

"We have helped many people. Look at our files. Why won't we help you?" said Mr. Ali.

"I've got a different idea. I won't pay anything now, but if my daughter's marriage is fixed, I will give you two thousand rupees. What do you say? Fair's fair," said Joseph, cracking his knuckles.

Mr. Ali stood up and said, "That's exactly the reason why marriage brokers are not held in much regard. As you know, they don't charge money up front, and ask you for payment when the marriage is fixed, either a fixed fee or as a percentage of the dowry. Then they push unsuitable matches just to get their fee and you cannot respect or trust them. That's not how we work. It takes money to advertise, print the lists, for postage and other things. Whether your daughter finds a match depends on a lot of things—including God's will, but my expenses still have to be paid. Please think about it and get back to me."

He showed Joseph out.

A few minutes later the gate opened again and Mr. Ali looked out through the thin curtains into the bright sunlight. Aruna and an older man were in the yard. The older man looked around the garden and said something to Aruna, and she smiled and nodded. Mr. Ali came out from behind his desk and called out to his wife.

Aruna introduced her father, Mr. Somayajulu, to both of them.

"Namaste," said Mr. Ali to Mr. Somayajulu. "Please sit down. Would you like some water?"

"No, please don't trouble yourself," said Aruna and her father together.

The sun was high, and it was very hot outside now. Aruna's father wiped his brow and tonsured head with a white cotton shawl that was over his left shoulder. Mr. Somayajulu looked like a typical elderly Brahmin. He was wearing a Gandhi-like dhoti loincloth and a long shirt. His head was shaven except for a small tuft at the back. Three lines of white ash were smeared across his forehead.

Mrs. Ali went inside the house.

"Your house is very cool," said Mr. Somayajulu.

"Yes, we are lucky," replied Mr. Ali.

Mr. Somayajulu said, "It is not luck. You have left the area in front of your house unbuilt and planted those trees. That's why your house is cool. In the past, all houses used to have trees around them, and they kept the houses comfortable. Nowadays, people bribe building inspectors and use up all the available land, with no place for trees or plants. No wonder it is getting hotter every year. You have done a very good thing, leaving some land aside."

Mrs. Ali came back with two glasses of lime juice for Aruna and her father.

Aruna said, "I would like to try the job for a week. If it works out, I will stay on permanently. Is that okay?"

Mr. Ali thought for a moment and looked at his wife. She nodded in agreement, and he turned to Aruna. "That's fine by us."

Mr. Somayajulu said, "I came to see where Aruna will be working. You obviously look like good people, and it is all right here. You cannot just let a young daughter go into anybody's house on her own, can you?"

Aruna looked embarrassed at her father's words, but Mrs. Ali nodded and said, "You are absolutely right. One cannot be too careful nowadays."

Aruna smiled and said, "I will take my father back now and go to Modern Bazar to take one week's leave. I will then come back to start work."

Aruna's father said, "Don't start the job today. It is amaavasya, the day with no moon. It is bad luck to venture anything new. Start tomorrow."

Aruna looked at Mr. Ali doubtfully. He waved his hand dismissively, and said, "That's no problem—tomorrow's fine. I was wondering why no new clients except that Christian called today."

FOUR

The next day, precisely at nine, Aruna walked in. She was wearing a simple, well-worn cotton sari. Her long hair was oiled and braided into a plait reaching to the small of her back. She had a bow of fragrant white jasmine buds tucked in her hair, a small bindi on her forehead, and a faint mark of white sacred ash on her neck. She had obviously gone to the temple before starting her new job. Mr. Ali pointed out an old wooden chair with a cushion, and two battens screwed loosely into its armrests. Once Aruna was sitting down in it, he showed her how to use the two battens to extend the armrests in front of her. Mr. Ali then placed a hardboard plank on the extended armrests. His assistant now had a ready-made table for working.

"You only need to use this chair when we are both here. Otherwise, just sit behind the table," he said.

Aruna nodded.

Mr. Ali opened his "filing cabinet"—the wooden wardrobe—and asked her to come over. He explained how the files were organized by caste, and how there were different files for brides and bridegrooms. There were quite a few photographs in the files as well. There were other files, one per active member, holding their correspondence.

The postman walked in just then—dark, tall, and lean. His bald head shone. He had been delivering letters for Mr. Ali since they had moved into the house. He lowered the heavy bag of letters from his shoulders and took out about ten letters from the bag and handed them over to Mr. Ali.

"Thank you, Gopal," said Mr. Ali. "I need some postcards. Can I come in today?"

"I don't know, sir. Let me find out and I'll tell you when I come in for the afternoon round," said Gopal.

Mr. Ali nodded and asked, "Do you want water?"

"No, I am all right, sir. Have you got a secretary?" Gopal said, looking at Aruna.

"Aruna is the assistant, just started today," said Mr. Ali.

She smiled at Gopal.

"How's your daughter?" asked Mr. Ali. "You won't need our services now."

"She's doing well. We got a postcard from her just yesterday. She's happy at her in-laws'. And what jokes you crack, sir. How can a poor man like me afford your services?" the postman said, laughing.

His white teeth gleamed in his dark face, showing his happiness— his daughter had been recently married. Mr. Ali knew that he just got by on his small salary. Gopal lifted the bag of letters onto his shoulder, nodded good-bye, and left.

"He is a good man, always cheerful, even though he has aged parents and a disabled brother to look after on his postman's salary," said Mr. Ali to Aruna. He tore open the first envelope, extracted the single sheet of paper, and said, "Every letter must be answered the day it arrives. That is the most important work we have to do."

He read the letter aloud: "I have seen your advertisement for Muslim engineer . . . fair . . . two older brothers . . ."

He gave the paper to Aruna and took out a slim file that listed all the ads that he had placed in both English and Telugu newspapers.

He said, "You need to figure out which advertisement the letter is referring to. I always put a code in my ad. See the address in this girl's letter? It says 'ME26' after our name. Look in this file, we advertised this last Sunday."

Aruna looked through the files and found one advertising a Muslim marine engineer, twenty-six, respectable family, seeks fair bride . . .

"We need to do two things with this letter," said Mr. Ali. "First, reply to them acknowledging receipt and inviting them to join our club. And second, put it in the client's file so that we can send them all off after a few days."

Aruna nodded, frowning with concentration.

"How do I reply, sir?" she asked.

Mr. Ali opened a drawer on the side of his table and took out a bunch of postcards. They had already been neatly handwritten. He took out one and showed Aruna where the letter began "Dear——" and the rest of the line was blank. "You have to fill in the person's name here," he said. "Then turn it over and write their address. Put the card in this basket." He pointed to a blue plastic-wire basket.

Aruna followed his instructions.

"You do the next one," Mr. Ali said.

Aruna opened the letter and scanned it. "Sir, this one does not have a code."

"This is where we have to use our intelligence. Is it somebody looking for a boy or a girl?" Mr. Ali asked.

"They are looking for a girl, sir."

Mr. Ali asked, "Which caste?"

"Brahmins," she said.

"I know the one. Look through the files, there is only one ad last week for a Brahmin."

Aruna found the advertisement, reread the letter, and nodded. "Yes, sir. That's the one."

"Good, you know what to do," said Mr. Ali.

Mr. Ali and Aruna processed the next couple of letters in silence before he left the table and walked into the house to see what his wife was doing.

That afternoon at about half past three, Mr. Ali went to the post office on his scooter. The post office was not far—just two blocks away, around a corner. Mr. Ali parked the scooter on its kickstand, took out the postcards, and went past the line of people waiting at the counters and into the office.

A few months ago, Mr. Ali and his brother-in-law Azhar had been in line outside the post office for stamps when one of the postmen came out and told them that the postmaster was asking them to come in. Slightly mystified, they both went inside. As soon as the postmaster and Azhar saw each other, they greeted each other like long-lost relatives. They finally turned to a bemused Mr. Ali and explained. Naidu had joined the postal service as a young man. His first posting was in the port town of Machilipatnam, and the postmaster there was Azhar's father, who had treated all the postmen and clerks in his post office like an extended family, inviting them for dinners and advising them when they got into trouble. Naidu had risen slowly through the ranks until finally he became a postmaster himself but, he said, he had never forgotten the old man's kindness to a callow youth away from his family for the first time. Since then, Mr. Ali never had to stand in line outside again for stamps or postcards. He didn't even have to use the letter box to post letters.

Inside the post office, at the back, there was a clerk with a big sack of letters, who was defacing the stamps on each envelope with a heavy round wooden block. The clerk was a seasoned hand at this task and the *thud . . . thud* of the stamp was quite fast. Mr. Ali went to the clerk and asked, "Have all the collections come in?"

The clerk nodded and took Mr. Ali's letters with his left hand while his right hand kept stamping the envelopes on the table. Mr. Ali's postcards were all defaced and pushed into another sack that was already half full.

Mr. Ali went to the postmaster's desk. It was a small post office, and the postmaster sat in one corner at a slightly bigger table than the other people in the office. The postmaster greeted Mr. Ali politely and asked him to sit down. Mr. Ali said, "Naidu, how are you? I need some more postcards."

Naidu replied, "Yes, I know. Gopal told me. There is a big shortage of postcards at the moment. But I rang the head post office and managed to get a few cards for you."

He turned and asked a clerk to get them out of a cupboard. While waiting for the cards to be brought out, he asked, "How is madam?"

"She is fine. Have you heard about the raid on the post office in the Agency village?" Mr. Ali said.

"Shocking, sir! Shocking! How can they raid a post office? Is nothing sacred anymore? I am telling you, sir, the world is not what it used to be."

Mr. Ali nodded. He knew that in Naidu's opinion, the whole country was held together by mail. Naidu had once told him that the British were justified in taking the Koh-i-Noor diamond for their queen's crown jewels because they had set up the postal department in India.

Mr. Ali paid for the postcards and made his way outside. The harsh sun made him blink as he emerged from the dark interior of the post office. As he made his way to his scooter, he saw a man selling papayas on a cart across the road. He went over and asked the fruit seller, "How much?"

"Fifteen rupees for a papaya, sir."

The papaya plant in his garden only gave small green fruit with lots of black pearl-like seeds. This new variety of papayas that had just started coming in the market in the last couple of years was different. They were big, and when cut, the flesh was deep orange; there were almost no seeds. They were also much sweeter than the traditional variety. Mr. Ali had heard someone mention that these papayas were hybrids from Thailand, but he didn't know if that was true.

"I don't need a full fruit. How much for half?" asked Mr. Ali.

The man replied, "Eight rupees. Fresh, sir."

Mr. Ali said, "Five rupees."

"You are joking, sir. Just cut today on the slopes of Simhachalam. Came straight from the sacred town," said the vendor. "Eight rupees is a very reasonable price. All right, seven rupees."

The temple town of Simhachalam is home to a famous Hindu temple and Mr. Ali wondered if the man would have tried quite the same sales pitch if he had known that his customer was a Muslim.

"Six," said Mr. Ali.

The fruit seller pleaded, "How can I feed my children if you drive such a hard bargain? Six-fifty, last offer."

"Six," said Mr. Ali, unyielding.

"All right, sir."

The fruit seller started packing one of the already-cut papayas in an old newspaper. Mr. Ali made him cut a fresh papaya, overriding the man's objections, and went back to his scooter.

• • •

When Mr. Ali came home, a family of three were looking at the albums in the verandah. The man and his wife were in their fifties and their daughter was in her early twenties. The man was short and pudgy with a thin, graying mustache. He had very little hair on his head, but what little hair there was, was well oiled and neatly combed. His wife was wearing a bright yellow chiffon sari with green dots. The girl was wearing jeans and a knee-length cotton kameez. Aruna introduced them to Mr. Ali.

"Mr. and Mrs. Raju, sir, and Soni. They became members about a month ago."

Mr. Ali remembered, and nodded to them. "Yes, yes. I sent you details of the chief engineer's son last week. You are also an engineer, aren't you? I thought it will be a good match."

Mr. Raju said, "That's correct, Mr. Ali. We even spoke on the phone, if you remember. After you sent me the details, I found out that my cousin's brother-in-law knows the bridegroom. They both went to the same college."

"Even better," said Mr. Ali. "If you know them personally, there's nothing like that. You can find out what kind of people they are."

"I know, Mr. Ali. They seem to be quite good people in all respects, but the match is for their eldest son. They have four other sons and one daughter."

"How does that matter?" asked Mr. Ali. "Nowadays, people don't live in joint families, do they?"

Mr. Raju said, "I asked my cousin to speak to his brother-in-law about that. The family definitely wants their daughter-in-law to stay with them."

"That will just be in the beginning. After a year or two, I am sure they will separate. After all, the groom is professionally educated, isn't he?" said Mr. Ali.

Mr. Raju said, "Probably, sir. But we cannot take the risk. Soni is our only child and she will find it difficult to adjust to such a big household. We were hoping that you might have some other match."

Mr. Ali stopped trying to convince them. He knew their minds were made up. They knew their daughter best, after all. He thought for a moment and said, "That is the best match among Rajus that I have at the moment. I've already sent you all the lists I had until last week."

He paused and continued, "I might have something for you. . . ."

He asked Aruna for the new forms folder—a hardboard pad with a strong clip on the top. It held all the forms that had come in the last few days and had not yet been collated into lists. He flipped through the forms until he came to the one he was looking for. "Here it is; this only came in three days ago. Chartered accountant, only one brother. Oh! He is too old for your daughter. He is thirty-four and your daughter is only twenty . . ." He tailed off, looking at Soni quizzically.

She replied, "Twenty-two."

Mr. Ali smiled at her and said, "Too much age gap."

Mr. Raju nodded, but stretched out his hand to Mr. Ali to look at the details. Mr. Ali handed the file over, open at the form he was reading. The three of them read through the form and handed the pad back to Mr. Ali.

Mr. Raju said, "Looks like a good match, but you are right—the age gap is too big. Also, he is only five feet, four inches. Soni is quite tall."

Mr. Raju's comment about his daughter's height reminded Mr. Ali of an old client. He asked Aruna to take out the first correspondence file. Mr. Ali opened it and went through the file until he found the section he was looking for.

"Here it is! Bodhi Raju—lawyer, twenty-seven. He is a six-footer and he wants a tall wife. He was one of my first members, and I don't know if he is still looking for a wife or if something has been fixed."

"How come he was not in the list you sent us?" asked Mr. Raju.

"He didn't want me to," sighed Mr. Ali, remembering. "He was one of my very first clients and it was a blow when such an eligible bachelor told me to keep his details out of our lists. I didn't have that many members then, you see. I told him that he would get a lot more responses if people saw his details in the list but he was adamant. So what could I do?"

Mr. Raju and his family nodded in understanding. Mr. Ali said, "Let me call him. I have his cell number here."

He copied the number onto a piece of paper and handed Bodhi Raju's form to the three people on the sofa. They read through it quickly and looked up at Mr. Ali. It was obvious they liked what they read.

The phone rang and rang until Mr. Ali was about to hang up, thinking, *Last ring.*

Just then, somebody answered the phone. "Hello."

It was a woman's voice and Mr. Ali's heart sank. He must have gotten married, after all.

"Is Mr. Bodhi Raju there?" he asked.

"The lawyer is busy with a client. Whom should I say is calling?"

"Who are you?" asked Mr. Ali, a bit rudely.

Luckily for him, the woman did not take offense. "I am the receptionist in his office. Hang on a moment, the client's just come out. Let me give the phone to the boss."

"Hello, who is speaking?" said a man's voice.

"Bodhi Raju?" said Mr. Ali.

"Yes, who is this?" asked the voice.

"It is Ali from the marriage bureau. How are you doing?"

"Hang on a moment, just a second," the man said, and Mr. Ali heard a door close. Suddenly it was much quieter on the phone.

"Mr. Ali, please go on. How can I help you? I hope you don't need my professional help." He laughed.

"No, thank you. I called to ask if you are still looking for a bride."

"Yes, sir. No luck so far."

"Good," said Mr. Ali unself-consciously. He gave a thumbs-up sign to the Rajus and said on the phone, "I have a very good match right in front of me. Very respectable family and well off. The girl is tall and good-looking too."

Soni blushed and looked at her feet.

"Why don't you give me your parents' details, and the bride's family will get in touch with them," said Mr. Ali.

"My mother is dead, but my father lives with me at the same address I gave you. You can speak to him on the residence phone. I remember writing the number in the form when I filled it."

"Thanks," said Mr. Ali. Just as he was hanging up, he remembered one more question. "How many brothers and sisters do you have?"

"Two brothers and one sister."

"Do they all live with you?"

"No, my elder brother and my sister live with me, but my younger brother has gone to America to do his Master's."

With mutual thanks, they hung up the phone and Mr. Ali turned to the anxious Raju family.

"He is not yet married," said Mr. Ali, giving the good news first. "However, he does have two brothers and a sister. One of them has gone to America, so only the three of them live together with their father."

"Oh, it is still a big family and they all live together, too," said Mr. Raju. Their faces fell.

Mr. Ali nodded and suddenly remembered. "Ha, ha!" he said. "There is one important detail I forgot to mention. His mother is no more. She has gone to heaven." He pointed a finger up toward the sky.

Mr. Raju was still frowning but his wife brightened up.

"You mean . . . ," she began.

"That's right," interrupted Mr. Ali. "Your daughter won't have a mother-in-law. You know what they say: A woman without a mother-in-law is a very fortunate daughter-in-law."

Mr. Raju was still not sure.

Mr. Ali said, "You must think like a chess player. Just as a rook might be worth two bishops, or a queen worth two rooks, how much trouble is a mother-in-law? Will she be less trouble than two brothers and a sister? I don't think so. Especially when you consider that one brother is abroad and the sister will get married and leave the house at some point."

Mr. Raju shook his head, still not convinced.

Mrs. Raju turned on her husband. "The gentleman is right. You don't know these things. I think it is a wonderful match."

Mr. Raju had to give in. They took the details, thanked him profusely for his help and left, promising to be in touch once they had spoken to the lawyer's family.

Mrs. Ali came out, bringing three bowls of chilled diced papaya, and sat down with Aruna and Mr. Ali. Mr. Ali savored the cool fruit, basking in the glow of a job well done.

As Mr. and Mrs. Ali were turning in for the night, the doorbell rang. They both looked at the clock. It was just past nine.

Mrs. Ali said, "Who can it be at this time? If they are members, tell them we are closed."

Mr. Ali picked up the keys from a hook just inside the living room door and went into the verandah. It was dark outside and he switched on the light in the yard. He was surprised to see his son, Rehman, standing outside with the trademark cotton bag slung over his shoulder, looking grim.

"Is everything all right?" Mr. Ali asked anxiously.

Rehman nodded. "Yes, abba. Everything is all right," he said.

Mr. Ali unlocked the verandah gate and they went into the house. Rehman was a couple of inches taller than Mr. Ali, but not quite six feet. He was wearing a long shirt made of khadi—rough homespun cotton cloth—and some nondescript trousers. The last time Mr. Ali had seen his son, he did not have the short, thin, slightly unkempt beard.

"Have you eaten?" asked Mrs. Ali.

"No," replied Rehman, "but, it's all right. I am not hungry."

"Nonsense," said Mrs. Ali. "It's past nine. How can you not be hungry? Come into the dining room. I have some rice and rasam. Let me make an omelette."

Rehman washed his hands and sat down at the dining table. Mr. Ali pulled out a chair and sat next to him. He looked at his son as his wife bustled about, quickly creating a simple dinner from the leftovers.

"When did you start growing a beard?" asked Mr. Ali.

Rehman looked up in surprise, rubbing his hand over his chin. "I was going from village to village the last few weeks and forgot to pack my razor," he said.

Before Mr. Ali could ask him what he was doing "going from village to village," Mrs. Ali came in with the hastily prepared dinner.

"I am so pleased you are here. You should have called us and let me know you were coming. I would have prepared a proper meal for you," she said.

"Ammi, leave it. This food is great. I don't need anything else."

"How can I leave it? Between you and your father, you don't give me a chance to feed you. You look so gaunt. At least if you were married I wouldn't worry so much. There'll be somebody to look after you."

"Not that again, ammi."

They all fell silent as Rehman wolfed the food down. Mr. Ali wondered when Rehman had last eaten. Finally, Rehman finished eating and got up to wash his hands. Mrs. Ali cleared up the dishes. Rehman sat down at the table again and Mrs. Ali came back into the dining room.

"Why did you come here at this late hour?" asked Mr. Ali.

"My friends and I are going to Royyapalem tonight," Rehman said.

Mr. Ali frowned. "I've heard that name . . . I remember. Isn't that the village where the Korean company is setting up a Special Economic Zone? That's great news—are you going to be designing any buildings there?"

"That's the place, abba," said Rehman. "But I am not going there to work. The villagers' lands are being taken away from them. My friends and I are going to protest."

Mr. Ali shook his head in disappointment. He said, "Silly me! Here I was, thinking that you were going to be working for a multinational. How long will you design latrines for villagers and houses for poor people? There's no money in working for people who cannot pay for your services. It's time you started working on big projects. With your qualifications, you can walk into any job you want."

"Abba, I am already working on projects that I want to do and I earn enough to get by. And it gives me time to do the things I really believe in, like protesting against people who want to take over farmers' lands."

"What's the point of protesting? How will it help?" asked Mr. Ali. "That's a big company. All the political parties are in favor of the zone. What can ordinary people like us achieve by trying to stand up to them?"

"We will protest. We'll try and get media attention. People have to know that an injustice is being committed by the government and the multinational company," Rehman said.

"Will it be dangerous?" asked Mrs. Ali, her face tense.

"No. It shouldn't be. We are not breaking the law. We will protest peacefully," said Rehman.

"Don't be ridiculous, Rehman. Of course it will be dangerous. The police will be there in strength. The company will have its own guards," said Mr. Ali. "Didn't you see on TV how badly the police beat those workers who were protesting near Delhi? It will be like that."

"The policemen who did that got punished," said Rehman.

"Foolish boy! Who cares if the police got punished? It didn't undo the workers' injuries, did it? You people are going to get crushed," Mr. Ali said, banging his fist on the table.

The sudden noise in the night made them all jump.

Mr. Ali lowered his voice. "Anyway, industries have to be set up somewhere. Our population is growing day by day and we cannot support everybody on the land. I think the government is doing the right thing. The zone will create lots of jobs. Besides, the farmers are being compensated. It's not as if their land is being stolen from them."

"Abba, how can you be so naive? The compensation given to the villagers will be a small fraction of the true cost of the land. The villagers are farmers. What are they going to do with the money? They cannot just go somewhere else and buy land. The whole community will be destroyed. The government could have created the zone on poramboke, empty government land. Why do they have to take over prime agricultural farms?" said Rehman.

"I still don't see what you and your friends are going to accomplish against the government machinery," said Mr. Ali.

"If Gandhi had thought like that, he would never have started the freedom movement against the British," said Rehman.

"Oh! So now you are comparing yourself to Gandhi. Who next? Jesus Christ?" snapped Mr. Ali.

Rehman raised his voice too. "How can you just sit there and watch injustice being committed? Whether we achieve anything or not, at least we can try."

"You got such good marks in school. You are an engineer from a top college. Take up a steady job. You will have a standing in society—people will look up to you. Now look at yourself. Almost thirty years old and you wear rough clothes, carry a tattered bag. You don't even know where your next meal is going to come from. It is not too late even now. Give up all this nonsense and get yourself a good job with a big company. You can still turn your life around," said Mr. Ali, shaking his head in frustration, not understanding why his son was so thick and couldn't see something that was so crystal-clear.

"Abba, you may not like it, but what I'm doing is important. If you don't agree, then I'm sorry. I can't do anything about it," said Rehman, lowering his voice.

"You are not sorry. You are just a stubborn fool," said Mr. Ali.

Mrs. Ali said, "Stop it both of you. Can't you both sit in a room together for half an hour without fighting?"

They were all silent for a moment after that. Then, Mr. Ali said, "The commercial tax officer called again last week. He is still willing to give his daughter to you. He says he will set you up in any business you want. I don't know why, but he is really keen to have you for a son-in-law."

Mrs. Ali added, "Yes, son. His daughter is very pretty. Think about the match. How long can you go on like this? It's time you settled down with a wife and thought about your future."

"Ammi, she is the most flighty and useless girl I've ever met. Do you remember, we bumped into them at Lori's wedding? I was bored stiff in minutes. She had no knowledge of the world other than fashion and clothes. And as for her father, we all know how he made his money. He is one of the most corrupt officials in his department," Rehman said. "Anyway, that is all for later. I just came around to tell you that I'm going to Royyapalem tonight. The protest might be over in days or it might go on for weeks."

"Don't go, Rehman. It sounds dangerous," said Mrs. Ali, looking miserable.

"Ammi, I have to go. Please don't stop me," he said, holding her hands in his own.

Mrs. Ali suddenly started crying. Tears rolled down her cheeks and she took one hand out of Rehman's and tried to dab the tears away with the end of her sari.

Mr. Ali lost his temper and shouted, "Now look what you've done. You've made your mother cry, you heartless brute. Go! Go and don't come back to this house again."

Rehman got up and hugged his mother. She held him tightly for some time and then let him go. Rehman looked Mr. Ali in the eye for a moment, nodded, and left. Mr. Ali followed him to the verandah and locked up the house, his anger turning to sorrow as he watched his son walk away into the darkness.

FIVE

The next afternoon, the temperature reached 104 degrees. Mrs. Ali sprinkled some water on the granite floor of the bedroom to cool it and lay down on the bed. She had her eyes closed but could not sleep during the daytime, especially when it was this hot and her mind was in such turmoil. Mr. Ali was fast asleep on the other side of the bed. She lay on the bed listening to the rumble of traffic and the occasional honking above the drone of the whirling ceiling fan, thinking about Rehman. He had doted on his father as a child. When did boys grow up and start defying their fathers? *Certainly not when their mothers were looking,* she thought.

She heard the rattle of the back door twice before she recognized the sound. She got up and opened the strong door made of mango wood. Light streamed in from outside and Mrs. Ali stepped back to let Leela in.

"What happened? Why didn't you come in the morning?" Mrs. Ali asked.

"We went to the doctor. He explained what the operation will involve," Leela replied.

"What will they do?" asked Mrs. Ali.

"Kush's head will be shaved and his skull cut open to make a hole at the back. They'll remove the growth through the hole," Leela said, her eyes watering.

"Poor little fellow. So much trouble at such a young age," said Mrs. Ali sympathetically.

"He has become very silent, amma. I don't know how much pain he feels anymore," Leela said.

"How much will it cost?" Mrs. Ali asked.

"Thirty thousand rupees," said Leela. "The doctor said that normally it will be a hundred thousand rupees but because it is a government hospital, they will pay for most of the things. The doctor was such a good man, amma. He took a long time and explained everything to us in simple language. Also, he is not taking any money for the operation."

"Do you have thirty thousand rupees? If they say thirty thousand, you will actually need to keep thirty-five or forty," said Mrs. Ali.

The fear that a family member might fall ill and require expensive treatment was the reason that they had saved so fanatically through the years. It was also why her husband was anxious that Rehman start a career. *But how can poor people save,* she thought, *when every broken cowrie shell they earned was necessary just to survive?*

"No, amma. That's what we've been counting all morning after coming back from the hospital. My daughter and son-in-law don't have any more savings after the scan and the tests. But she has the gold earrings I gave her at her wedding, and the mangalsootram."

Mrs. Ali nodded in understanding. "Is your daughter going to sell off her mangalsootram?" she asked.

The mangalsootram, a chain of yellow thread with two gold coins, is, along with the vermilion dot on her forehead, the symbol of a Hindu woman's married status. It is tied around the bride's neck by her husband as part of the wedding ceremony and is only removed on her death or when she becomes a widow. Mrs. Ali knew that for a Hindu woman to give up her mangalsootram is a sign of desperation only considered after the couple has exhausted all other possibilities.

Leela said, "Yes, amma. She says what could be more important than this? Her husband is taking it to the jeweler's now to sell it."

"A sad business, indeed—a husband selling his wife's mangalsootram," said Mrs. Ali, sighing. "What will your daughter wear instead?"

"She will tie two turmeric sticks on a string around her neck," replied Leela unhappily.

"How much will you get for the jewelry?" asked Mrs. Ali.

"The earrings are eight grams and the mangalsootram is twelve," replied Leela.

Mrs. Ali calculated rapidly, "Twenty grams . . . the jeweler will take some of it away as wastage. You will get about fifteen thousand rupees."

"I have ten thousand set aside for my second daughter's wedding. I don't know what to do. This is important, but I don't want to do injustice to my other daughter, too."

"What is your second daughter saying about using up the money saved for her wedding?" Mrs. Ali asked.

"She is a good girl. She says that we should spend the money and worry about her wedding later. . . . It took us fifteen years to save that money," said Leela, taking out the dirty dishes and sitting down to wash them. "In those days, my husband didn't drink so much. But now . . ."

Silence hung in the air for a moment between the women. A crow came flying and sat on the wall next to Leela, waiting for her to throw the leftovers.

Mrs. Ali asked, "What about the rest of the money?"

"We can sell off all our steel dishes and our TV, but because it is black-and-white, we will only get two thousand. We will have to go to a moneylender."

"How much will he charge?" asked Mrs. Ali.

"Three rupees," replied Leela, "per hundred per month."

"Once you fall into the clutches of the moneylenders, you will never get out. They'll suck your blood dry," said Mrs. Ali.

"What else can we do, madam?" asked Leela, and gave the pan she was washing an extra scrub with the bundle of coconut coir.

Mrs. Ali hesitated a second. She had already discussed this with her husband. She said, "So you have about twenty-seven thousand rupees. That leaves you three thousand short. We can give you three thousand rupees. You can keep fifteen hundred and work the other fifteen hundred off at half your salary over the next year."

"Thank you, amma. Thank you very much. May God keep you and your family always safe," said Leela, tears flowing from her eyes. She added, "In that case, we can go back this evening to the doctor and tell him we have the money. He said it is better to operate as soon as possible. I will ask the other people I work for, so we have some money to spare if the expenses overrun."

"Yes, do that. It will keep you out of the moneylender's greedy paws."

That evening, a short, stocky man came to the marriage bureau. Mr. Ali greeted him and asked for his details. He was obviously well-to-do, neatly groomed with a pencil-thin mustache.

He introduced himself. "I Mr. Ramana, civil engineer, Public Works Department. I looking for a husband for my daughter."

Mr. Ali asked him, "How did you find out about us, sir?"

"I seeing your ad for the last few weeks in *Today*," Mr. Ramana replied.

"Please fill up this form, sir. It will give us all the details we need. The fee is five hundred rupees," Mr. Ali said, and couldn't resist adding, "not that an amount like that will trouble an official in the PWD!"

The man smiled enigmatically and did not take offense. All infrastructure projects of the government are carried out through the Public Works Department, and the department is notorious for its corruption. Mr. Ali had heard rumors that contractors had to pay a fixed percentage of the contract value to PWD officials for every project. There were stories that the corruption was institutionalized, with every official getting a specific cut depending on his rank in the department, from the chief engineer down to the peon.

Mr. Ramana, Civil Engineer, took the form from Mr. Ali and slowly filled it in. Aruna and Mr. Ali continued working on the new list they were preparing. Mr. Ramana handed the form to Mr. Ali. Mr. Ali went through the form, making sure all the details were filled.

RELIGION: *Hindu*

CASTE: *Arya Vysya*

STAR: *Aswini (Gemini)*

AGE: *23*

BRIDE'S NAME: *Sita*

NATIVE TOWN/VILLAGE: *Vijayawada*

EDUCATION: *B.A.*

HEIGHT: *4'8"*

COLOR: *Wheatish complexion*

CURRENT EMPLOYMENT: *None*

APPROXIMATE VALUE OF BRIDE'S SHARE IN FAMILY WEALTH: *50 lakhs*

FATHER'S NAME: *Mr. Ramana Bhimadolu*

FATHER'S OCCUPATION: *Civil Engineer, Central Public Works Department*

BROTHERS AND SISTERS (MARRIED/UNMARRIED):
One brother, unmarried. Viswanath, 25 years, BE Civil, working as contractor

WANT TO MARRY IN YOUR OWN CASTE: *Yes*

FIRST MARRIAGE: *Yes*

DETAILS OF THE GROOM WANTED:

EDUCATION: *Graduate, preferably engineer*

AGE: *25-30*

HEIGHT: *5'10" or above*

ANY OTHER DETAILS: *None*

Mr. Ali nodded through all the details until he came to the groom's details. He looked up in surprise and said, "Are you sure about the height of the groom you want? There will be more than one foot difference between your daughter and your son-in-law."

"Oh, yes. That's an important requirement for me."

Mr. Ali nodded. "Okay, if you say so."

He took the money and handed the form to Aruna, asking her to give Mr. Ramana a list of Arya Vysya grooms. Mr. Ali explained how he advertised on his clients' behalf to get a better choice. Mr. Ramana nodded in satisfaction.

Aruna took out the list and gave it to him. She pointed out the membership number and said, "When you call us or come in again, please bring this number, sir, and we will be able to look up your details more quickly."

Mr. Ramana left soon after. Aruna smiled at Mr. Ali and said, "That was a very easy sale, sir."

Mr. Ali smiled back at her. "Maybe those stories about the Public Works Department are true. He's probably got so much money coming in, what's a few hundred rupees?"

A little while later, Mr. Ali went into the house and Aruna was alone in the office. A smartly dressed young man wearing a branded T-shirt and jeans came in. He had a full head of hair, well styled, and a neatly trimmed mustache. He wore shiny black shoes that he did not take off when he entered the verandah. He introduced himself as Venu.

He spoke good English and Aruna was not comfortable speaking just in English. As soon as the introductions were complete, she went to the inner door and called out to Mr. Ali.

Mr. Ali came out and said to the young man, in Telugu, "Hello. I am Mr. Ali."

He replied in English, "I am Venu."

Mr. Ali switched to English as well. "How can we help you?"

"I am looking for a bride," he replied.

"For whom?" asked Mr. Ali.

"For myself."

Mr. Ali asked him to fill out the application form. Venu took a few minutes to fill out the form and handed it to Mr. Ali. Mr. Ali looked through the form and gave it to Aruna. It was all pretty much what she expected, including "Caste no bar." An educated young man like Venu looking for a bride for himself wasn't likely to be fussy about the bride's caste. He was a service engineer for a computer firm in the city. He had completed his engineering degree from a small-town college and moved to the city for work. He was twenty-six years old and had an unmarried sister who was in the second year of her degree course. There was a surprise right at the end of the form, when she discovered that the young man in front of her had already been married and was divorced.

"So you are divorced?" Mr. Ali said.

"Yes," Venu replied. "I was married for six months. The girl was totally unreasonable. She was fighting every day with me and I could not find any peace at all in the house. So we got divorced."

"Please realize that many people do not want their daughters to marry a man who is a divorcé or a widower. Your choice will be limited," said Mr. Ali.

"I know that. That's why I am here," said Venu, handing over the fees.

Mr. Ali took the fees and Aruna put his application form in the new joiner's file. She went through the lists trying to short-list people who did not mind second marriages.

Mr. Ali told Venu, "We will advertise your details in newspapers as well. Because you specified that caste is no bar, the ads will actually be cheaper."

He seemed surprised. "Really? I didn't know that."

"Most newspapers in India charge less for matrimonial ads that do not specify a caste requirement. Also, they don't carry ads that specify dowry," said Mr. Ali.

"I am not surprised about the dowry aspect," said Venu. "After all, it is illegal—even though everybody does it. I just didn't know about the caste aspect."

"What about your parents? Are they still in your native place?" asked Mr. Ali.

"Yes," replied Venu. "They are not happy about the divorce. They have said that they will not look for another wife for me and I have to find one myself if I want to get married again."

"It cannot be easy for them. Especially if they live in a small town," said Mr. Ali. "Also, you have an unmarried sister."

Venu sighed and said, "They said the same thing: that it will be very difficult to get my sister married if I am divorced. But what can I do? I was not getting along with my wife and I refuse to spend my whole life with an unreasonable woman like her."

Aruna said to Mr. Ali, "Sir, there are only five matches that will consider second marriages—they are all widows and much older."

Mr. Ali skimmed through the matches and gave them to Venu. "The best bet will be to advertise for you."

He looked at the matches, nodded, and left.

After he was gone, Aruna said to Mr. Ali, "Such a selfish man, sir—he is only thinking about himself. What must his parents be going through? And his sister as well, how will she get married?"

Mr. Ali sighed and said, "The world is like that. It is full of all sorts of people and we see them at their worst here."

At seven in the evening, Aruna helped Mr. Ali close up shop and left for home, happy. Two days in a row, she had earned fifty rupees as a bonus.

A young man came in with his parents a few days later. His father was dressed in a shirt and a dhoti. His mother was dressed in a russet-colored silk sari. The young man, in a T-shirt and black jeans, had a thick mustache. Both he and his father were the same height—five feet and no inches. He introduced himself as Srinu.

Mr. Ali asked them all to be seated. He said, "Who are you looking for?"

"Me," said Srinu, as his parents both pointed at him.

"Good. Let me get some details off you," said Mr. Ali, and took out an application form. He asked, "How did you find out about us?"

"We've been seeing your ad in *Today* for the last several weeks."

Mr. Ali gave the form to Srinu and asked him to fill it up. A few minutes passed and Srinu gave the form back to Mr. Ali.

"Is the fee really five hundred rupees?" asked his father.

"Yes," replied Mr. Ali. "We do not charge anything more after the marriage is fixed. Our fee is all up front."

Srinu's father said, "How do we know if you can find us a match? It's a lot of money to pay when there is no guarantee of a result."

Srinu looked embarrassed.

Here we go again, thought Mr. Ali. "Nobody can guarantee a wedding, sir," he said. "That depends on God's will and how willing you are to make compromises. But we will make an effort. We will include your son's name in a list. We will advertise on his behalf. All this costs us time and money, and that's what you are paying for."

Srinu said, "That's okay, dad." He turned to Mr. Ali and said, "I don't want to marry a traditional girl from a village. I want an English-educated girl from a city."

"Hmph," his father grunted, and sat back with his hands folded across his chest, scowling.

"From the same caste," said Srinu's mother, speaking for the first time.

"Yes, mum," said Srinu. This was obviously an argument that had been going on in the family for some time. Mr. Ali understood why they had come to him for help.

Srinu took out a crisp five-hundred-rupee note and handed it over. Mr. Ali thanked him and put it in his shirt pocket. He skimmed through the application form. Srinu was an accountant in a nationalized bank, earning twenty-seven thousand rupees a month. The family were Vysyas—merchants.

Mr. Ali gave the form to Aruna and asked her to take out the Vysya brides list. Aruna took out the list and gave it to Srinu. His father examined the ceiling as if it was the Sistine Chapel. Srinu made a face and went to sit next to his mother. The two of them went through the list.

Srinu took out a ballpoint pen and made small tick marks against the names that looked suitable to him and his mother.

Mr. Ali went inside and came back with three glasses of water from the fridge for the clients. Srinu's father smiled for the first time since he had come in, and thanked Mr. Ali.

Srinu and his mother finished going through the list and handed it to Mr. Ali. He went through the list, reading the details of the selected girls. Three of them had numbers in brackets against them. These girls had sent in their photographs, and Mr. Ali told Aruna, "Please take out photos thirty-six, forty-seven, and sixty-three."

Aruna teased out the three photographs from the album and handed them to Mr. Ali. One of the girls was dark and a bit fat. The other two girls were quite good-looking. One of them had had her photograph taken professionally—he could make it out from the way she was posing in half-profile against a dark blue background. There was even a hint of lipstick.

He gave the photos to Srinu. He and his mother looked at them with interest. Srinu's mother took one look at the pretty girl's photo and said, "She is good-looking, isn't she?"

Srinu nodded numbly, and she turned to her husband and said, "Have a look at this photo."

Srinu's father grunted but couldn't resist taking the photo from his wife's hand. He looked at it for a few moments and handed it silently back to his wife. She evidently took his lack of comment as approval, because she turned to Mr. Ali and said, "Do you have any more details about this girl?"

Aruna efficiently handed the girl's file to Mr. Ali, before he even asked for it.

"Her name is Raji," Mr. Ali said. "They are a respectable family. Raji's father is a revenue officer with the state government. They have two daughters. Her elder sister is married and living in America. Raji has completed her B. Pharmacy. They are living in the city itself."

He gave them Raji's father's phone number and address. Mr. Ali said to Srinu, "Please bring your photo. We will keep it here and show it to any prospective brides who come here. You will get a better response that way."

The three of them took their leave.

Mrs. Ali came out and plucked a few curry leaves from the plants in the front yard. As she was going back, Mr. Ali gave her the five-hundred-rupee note and started telling her about Srinu and his family. She stopped him and said, "I've just put khatti-dal on the cooker. Let me put these curry leaves in it and turn the heat down. I'll come back again."

A couple of minutes later, Mrs. Ali was back. "Did you say the people who came just now were Vysyas?" she asked.

"Yes, madam," replied Aruna.

"Didn't a merchant family come in yesterday looking for a groom?" asked Mrs. Ali.

Aruna immediately looked up the new joiner's pad.

"Yes, madam. Arya Vysyas—the girl's father is in the Public Works Department," replied Aruna.

Mr. Ali looked up and said, "Yes, I did think of them, but the father was adamant that he wanted a tall son-in-law. Srinu is only five feet tall."

"It is worth trying, though. Why don't you give him a call?"

Mr. Ali nodded in agreement and pulled out their details.

"Mr. Ramana? Hello, sir, this is Mr. Ali from the marriage bureau."

"Hello, Mr. Ali. Do you having match for my daughter?"

"Yes," replied Mr. Ali. "A Vysya family just became members. They are a respectable family, sir. The father used to work in the state government. The son is working in a bank. Good salary and bright prospects. He is a very smart-looking guy and wants an educated girl like your daughter. It will be a very good match."

"Sounds interesting," said Mr. Ramana. "What other details do you have?"

"There is one issue, sir. The boy is five feet tall."

"I told you, Mr. Ali. I wanting a tall son-in-law. I not interested in somebody who is only five feet tall."

"Please think again, sir. It is a very good match in all other respects. They have already shown interest in another match but yours might be better. I can talk to them and convince them," said Mr. Ali.

"No, no . . ."

"Don't be so hard-hearted, sir. After all, your daughter is short, too. It will make a perfect match," said Mr. Ali.

"I not being hard-hearted at all. I being kind to my grandchildren. I don't want them to go through life being teased about their height. If I marry my short daughter to a tall man, hopefully, their children will be at least medium height."

SIX

Two days later, Mrs. Ali was making pesarattu, spicy mung-bean crepes, for breakfast, when Leela came in. She hadn't come to work the previous day.

Mrs. Ali asked her, "How is Kush? Is he all right?"

Leela looked tired. There were dark circles around her eyes as if she hadn't slept all night. She replied, "Yes, madam. I think he will be all right. The doctor told us that he couldn't say anything until Kush woke up. He was unconscious all day yesterday and woke up very early this morning. He recognized his mother and the nurses say that is a hopeful sign."

"Thank God," breathed Mrs. Ali.

"Yes, madam. The doctor told us that he would do his best, but in a case like this, involving the brain, it is ultimately in His hands," said Leela, looking up at the sky with half-closed eyes.

After some time, she told Mrs. Ali, "I can't come to work this evening again, amma. We are going to the Sitamma Neem Tree to thank Her and ask for Her blessings."

"I understand. I don't think I've heard you talk about going to that temple before," said Mrs. Ali.

"We normally pray to Ammoru. But when they wheeled my grandson out of the operation theater and he didn't wake for many hours, I was scared. So I went out of the hospital for a walk and on the way I saw a neem tree. I stopped in front of it and made a vow that if he woke up, we will go to the holy neem tree and make our offerings to Sitamma."

"I plucked a couple of hibiscus and some jasmine flowers from the plants today. You can take them to the temple if you want," offered Mrs. Ali.

Leela said, "Thank you, amma. In that case, I just need to buy a coconut and a few bananas."

She carried on with her work and Mrs. Ali continued cooking breakfast.

The days went past. As Mr. Ali and Aruna were packing up on Friday, Mrs. Ali came out to the verandah and said, "Aruna, you said that you will let us know after a week whether you will continue to work here or not. The time is up today. What have you decided?"

Mr. Ali looked up in surprise. He had got so used to the young girl working with him that he had forgotten that Aruna had said that she would try the job for a week before making up her mind. He could not believe that it had been such a short time since Aruna had started working in the marriage bureau. It felt as if she had been there forever.

It had been a good week, thought Mr. Ali. Sixteen people had joined that week and Aruna had taken home four hundred rupees in bonuses. If it carried on like this, she would earn a lot more than she did in Modern Bazar.

Aruna said, "Yes, madam. I really like this job. I will stay here. The hours are a lot better and the work is also more interesting."

Mr. Ali and his wife broke into smiles. Mr. Ali said, "Excellent. You won't regret it."

Aruna took her leave. Mrs. Ali turned to her husband and said, "You owe me a dinner."

"We can go to Sai Ram Parlor. They have a new family room which is air-conditioned," said Mr. Ali, half joking.

Mrs. Ali replied, "No! I told you before. I am not being fobbed off by idli sambhar; steamed rice cake and lentil soup is for everyday. Now, I want to go to a proper restaurant and eat chicken."

After dinner, Mr. Ali switched on the television in the living room and lazily flipped through the channels until he came to one showing the local news. The newscaster was saying, "The protest at Royyapalem has entered its sixth day . . ."

He sat up straight and looked at his wife, who stared back at him with big eyes. He turned back to the television.

An attractive young female journalist holding a microphone stood in front of a dark, stocky man with a vast belly, wearing white cotton clothes and a Gandhi cap on his head. She asked, "What do you think of the protests against the Special Economic Zone at Royyapalem?"

"The protesters are politically motivated and are acting against the interests of the people of Royyapalem and our state. We have negotiated the best possible compensation package on behalf of the villagers that is totally in line with central government regulations. The people were happy with it until outside elements came in and incited them."

"Will you negotiate with the protesters?" asked the interviewer.

"Absolutely not. These people are holding up the economic progress of our state. In the cabinet meeting earlier today, the chief minister has taken a personal interest in the matter. We will be ordering the police to take stern action against the protesters."

The newscaster cut in and said, "That was *Sun TV* talking to the state industries minister. Now let us go to Bhadrachalam, where—"

Mr. Ali switched off the TV and looked at his wife, who was holding her hand to her mouth. He said, "I told the fool. I told him . . . we both told him not to go. Now look what has happened. Why does he go against our explicit words? Did we make a mistake in bringing him up? Should we have been stricter when he was a boy?"

"Don't worry about that now," said Mrs. Ali. "What can we do to help Rehman?"

"You are right," said Mr. Ali, and thought for a moment. "Let's call him. He must have taken his cell phone with him."

Mr. Ali called Rehman's number. The phone rang several times before Rehman picked it up. "Hello," he said.

"Rehman. We just saw the interview with the industries minister on television. Is everything all right?" asked Mr. Ali.

"Yes, abba. It's going great here. The villagers are really supportive and we are attracting more attention every day."

"The minister said that they would send the police in to clear you all out. Your mother and I both think that things will get ugly. You've highlighted the problem as you wanted, now leave the place and come back," said Mr. Ali.

"Abba, I can't do that. The people are depending on us. Anyway, I don't think the police will dare to move against us. We've been here for almost a week and they haven't done anything."

"Don't be silly, Rehman. You are holding up a major project. It won't go on like that. Come back now and give up this foolishness," Mr. Ali said.

"No, abba. I cannot do that," said Rehman.

Mr. Ali gave the phone to Mrs. Ali and sank down into a chair, holding his face in his hands. After some time, he heard Mrs. Ali hanging up the phone. He looked up at her. She didn't need to tell him that she had failed to convince Rehman as well.

Aruna was at home, sitting on a mat in the kitchen, dicing brinjals into a bowl of water. Her mother washed three cups of rice and drained the water away. She measured four and a half cups of water into the rice and put it on the gas stove. She said, "It's good you got the vegetables. There were no vegetables in the house, and when I asked your father to get them, he shouted at me, saying that he didn't have any money."

Aruna smiled and said, "You know how naanna gets toward the end of the month. His pension is probably running out, and he must be getting worried about it."

Her mother nodded and replied, "I know . . . but the house still has to run—we have to eat. What's the point of shouting at me? It's not as if I am asking him to buy me jewelry."

Aruna sighed. Of late, as their financial situation deteriorated, her parents seemed to be arguing more.

They lived in a small house—one room, kitchen, and bathroom. The main room served as their living room in the day and bedroom at night. It held a bed against one wall and a tall, dark green metal wardrobe against another wall. She could see the wardrobe from where she was sitting in the kitchen. It had seen better days and was dented in a few places.

Not surprising, thought Aruna. It had come into the household as part of her mother's dowry and was older than Aruna. There were a couple of metal folding chairs next to the wardrobe. The framed picture of Lord Venkatesha that hung on the wall facing the front door with a garland of white plastic flowers around it was not in her view.

The tiny kitchen held a two-ring gas burner, three brass pots with water for cooking and drinking, and an open wooden cupboard that held their provisions. One of the shelves of the cupboard was closed with a fine mesh door and held milk, sugar, and ghee. Everything in the house was old but scrupulously clean.

Aruna's mother lit the second ring of the gas burner and put an aluminum pan on it. She poured a couple of tablespoons of oil into it. When the oil was hot enough, she took out an old, round wooden container. She slid the lid open on its hinge. Inside, there were eight compartments, each holding a different spice. She took a pinch of mustard seeds and put them in the oil. When they started popping, Aruna's mother dropped cloves, cardamom pods, and a cinnamon stick into the hot oil. She added a small plate of chopped onions to the pan. The lovely smell of frying onions filtered through the kitchen and into the rest of the house.

Aruna finished cutting and joined her mother at the burner. When the onions were brown, she lifted the brinjals, letting the water drain out of her fingers, and added them to the pan; they sizzled loudly. Once they had all been added, her mother stirred the vegetables around. Aruna got an old Horlicks bottle holding chili powder out of the cupboard. She took out a spoonful of the dark red powder and mixed it into the onions and brinjals.

She closed the bottle, put it back in its place, and said, "Amma, the chili powder is almost finished."

Her mother said, "I know. The chilies from Bandar are in season. I am waiting for your father's pension next week to ask him to buy five kilos. If we wait too long, the best chilies will be gone from the market and we'll have to buy late-season variety, which are not as good."

Aruna said, "I got some money today. We can go and buy them tomorrow."

Mr. Ali had given Aruna her commission for new members each day. She had not told her family about this money and had been feeling guilty about it as she watched her father getting more and more irritable as the end of the month drew nearer and his pension slowly ran out.

Her mother was surprised. "Where did you get the money? You haven't been there a month yet."

"This is not my salary. This is the commission for new members."

Aruna's mother nodded. Aruna could see that she didn't really understand but she didn't ask any more questions.

Aruna and her mother worked well in the kitchen together from long practice. They divided the work silently, without talking about it, and soon, dinner was ready. They went into the main room of the house and sat under the fan on the bed, which did daytime duty as a settee. Her younger sister, Vani, came home from college and changed. Her father was sitting outside and Aruna called him in. Vani unrolled a mat in the living room and her mother got the dishes from the kitchen. Aruna got the plates and glasses, and they all sat down for dinner.

"Vani, why did you come back so late?" asked Aruna's father.

"I went to the library with my friends. I told you this morning that I would come back late today," replied Vani.

"Hmph . . ." grunted her father, resuming his eating.

"Your sister got some money today," said her mother.

"Really, akka? Cool. How much did you get?" Vani asked Aruna.

"Four hundred rupees," replied Aruna.

"Wow. That's great. Can you give me a hundred and fifty rupees? I saw a great piece for a churidar the other day. Next-door—auntie said she will help me stitch it in the latest fashion if I get the cloth."

Aruna thought for a moment and said, "Okay . . . I will be getting three weeks' salary from Modern Bazar as well, so that's fine."

"Fantastic. Let's go tomorrow and buy it," said Vani, obviously excited. "I will go and tell next-door–auntie straight after dinner."

"Her husband will be back by then. Go tomorrow after he has left for the office," said her mother.

"Ohh . . . I can't wait," said Vani. Aruna looked amused at her younger sister's suddenly miserable face.

"It is such a waste of money. You have enough clothes," said her father.

"Leave it be. They are young girls and they are not even asking you to pay. What's your problem?" said their mother.

"Doesn't matter whose money it is. It is still a waste," her father replied.

"Naanna! All the other girls in the college wear different clothes for different occasions. I am the only one who wears the same clothes again and again," said Vani.

"You should have gone to the government college. There would have been other poor girls like you there. Who asked you to go to the corporate college?"

"But naanna, the corporate colleges are much better and they gave me a seventy-five percent discount because I got such good marks."

Her father turned to Aruna. "How come you've got money now? Have they already paid your salary?"

"No. Don't you remember? Sir said that he would give me twenty-five rupees for each member who joined. Well, it's been a week and sixteen members joined, so he gave me four hundred rupees," replied Aruna.

"You shouldn't waste the money on frivolous things," said her father.

Her mother replied, "Aruna bought the vegetables today and is getting Bandar chilies tomorrow for the house. Don't grumble."

She turned to Aruna and said, "When you get the money from Modern Bazar, buy clothes for yourself as well."

Aruna smiled and nodded in agreement. "Tomorrow, when I come home in the afternoon, I will go to Modern Bazar and resign and ask for my money."

"I will come back early and we can go to the shops," said Vani.

"No. I don't know how long it will take me to get the money from the store. Let's do it on Monday, because that's my day off," said Aruna.

Vani agreed, obviously deflated at the delay.

"Hmph . . ." grunted their father, but everybody ignored him.

While eating, Aruna looked covertly at her mother. She was thin and she didn't have any jewelry except her mangalsootram and two thin earrings. She was wearing an old cotton sari, much faded from repeated washing. *Just like mother herself*, thought Aruna. Genteel poverty had slowly ground her mother down, but Aruna could still make out the pretty woman she must have been at one time.

Aruna was surprised at how forcefully her mother was standing up to her father. This was unusual because she was usually quite docile. *Something about her daughter earning money was making her ready to stand up to her husband, thought Aruna.*

On Monday, Vani didn't feel well in the morning. By midmorning she was chirpy again. Aruna thought that her sister's illness was very mysterious—striking just in time to prevent her from going to college and then vanishing conveniently so they could go shopping. The girls got ready and left. They took a bus and went to the town center.

They spent some time looking through various shops but ultimately went to the shop where Vani had seen the cloth for the churidar, and bought it.

"Thank you, akka. This is going to be lovely. What shall we do now?" asked Vani.

"I was thinking of buying a sari for mother. She didn't buy one for the last festival because Vishnu-uncle died, remember?" said Aruna.

"That's a great idea. Let's go to Potana's. They have a good collection. We also need to buy something for you. Remember, amma told you to," said Vani.

The two sisters made their way to the sari shop. They left the bag with the churidar cloth with the girl outside the sari shop and were given a token. They asked for directions and made their way to the second floor. The floor was covered wall-to-wall with thick mattresses. They took off their shoes by the stairs and walked past the open wiring and disconnected water sprinklers onto the mattresses to a salesman who was free, and asked him if he could show them silk saris. The man nodded and indicated the floor in front of him.

They sat down on the mattress, folding their legs under them. The salesman turned to the wall and took out ten different saris without even speaking to them. He spread them all out in front of them, showing a bit of the border and some of the main part of the sari.

Aruna and Vani looked through them, whispering to each other.

"Which ones do you like?" asked the salesman.

Vani pointed out three. "We like the green color of this one, the blue border in that one, and the mango-seed motif on that one."

"Who are the saris for, madam?"

"One for our mother and one for elder sister," said Vani, pointing to Aruna.

The salesman pushed the seven saris that the girls had rejected to one side, and went back to the wall and selected ten more and spread them out.

This time they were much more to the girls' liking. The girls took longer to decide. Aruna discreetly looked at the price slips stapled to the bottom of the saris. They selected four in this round. The salesman cleared the ones they did not like, and took out five more saris from the wall, but Vani shook her head, not liking any of them. He turned to take out more, but Aruna stopped him. "Enough! I think we've seen enough. We'll decide on one of the ones here."

"No problem, madam. If you want to see more, just let me know," replied the salesman.

Vani went through them, saying, "Yes, no, no, yes, no, yes . . ."

He added the saris that Vani did not like to the big pile on the side. They were now left with four. Aruna and Vani talked about them some more and selected two—a plain light green sari with a dark green border and a reddish-brown one with a traditional mango print.

Aruna pointed them out to the salesman and said, "I like the plain green one for myself, but I am not sure about the other one for amma."

"Good choice, madam. The green sari is machine loom—easy to maintain for a young lady like you. The red one is slightly more expensive but it is a handmade kalamkari print from Bandar."

Aruna's ears pricked up at the name of the port town. "We cannot get away from that town!" she said.

"Pardon, madam?" he said, puzzled.

"Oh, nothing. We just bought Bandar chilies the other day."

"The best variety, madam. This is from the same place. Very traditional design. Your mother will like it very much."

The sisters looked at each other and nodded. Aruna said, "Okay, pack them up."

The salesman quickly folded the selected saris, pointed to Vani and asked, "Anything else, madam? What about for the young lady?"

"No, that will be all," replied Aruna.

The salesman took out a receipt book and wrote out a bill for them. As Aruna took the bill, she asked, "Do the saris have blouse pieces attached to them?"

"Not for the green sari, madam. You will have to buy that separately."

They got up and walked across the mattresses to the stairs. As she was putting on her shoes, Aruna saw the man folding all the saris they had rejected and putting them back in their place. She was glad she wasn't working in Modern Bazar anymore. Working on a shop floor was hard work. Aruna and Vani made their way down to the ground floor and went to the cash counter and got in the line. The cashier stamped the bill "Paid" and returned it to them. The girls then went to the next counter, where a security guard was standing. He took the bill, took out the saris that had made their way down, and put them into a bag, stamping the bill "Delivered."

The girls came out with the bag, exchanged the token for their earlier purchase, and made their way home.

SEVEN

The next morning, just after eleven, the sun was high in the sky and Mrs. Ali came into the verandah with a glass of water from the fridge. Mr. Ali had gone out and Aruna was managing the office alone. She offered the glass to Aruna, who drank it without letting the glass touch her lips.

"Thank you, madam."

"No problem," replied Mrs. Ali. "You've been busy all morning. I didn't hear you stop talking to clients since you came in."

"Yes, madam. It was really busy today. And sir had to go out, so there was no respite at all. Anyway, there are no clients now, so it is good to get a bit of rest," Aruna said.

Mrs. Ali sat down in one of the chairs. Aruna went back to her typing. After a little while, Mrs. Ali said, "Did you buy the clothes for your sister?"

"Yes, madam. We bought the material for a churidar. Our neighbor says she can help Vani make the dress."

"It's funny. Not that long ago, only Muslims used to wear churidars. Now even Brahmin girls like you and your sister are wearing churidars," said Mrs. Ali.

"Yes, madam. My sister wears half-saris sometimes, but she finds churidars more convenient."

"I agree. Did you buy anything for yourself?" asked Mrs. Ali.

"Yes, madam. I bought a machine silk sari for myself."

"What color is it?" asked Mrs. Ali.

"Green," replied Aruna. "I also bought one for my mother."

"Oh, that's very good of you. What kind of sari did you buy her?"

"A handmade silk one, madam. It is a reddish brown, kalamkari print."

"That's nice. I like those traditional designs. What did your mother think?"

"She was very happy," said Aruna. After a pause, she added, "Amma actually cried for a while."

"It is a big thing when your children buy you something. It is good that you care for your parents. So many children nowadays just ignore their parents."

Aruna blushed at the compliment and didn't say anything. She typed some more addresses into the list.

"Did your mum wear it?" asked Mrs. Ali.

"Not yet, madam. We are going to attend a cousin's wedding next month and she wants to keep it for that."

Mrs. Ali watched Aruna as she went about her work. *She is pretty,* thought Mrs. Ali, *but not actually beautiful.* Aruna had a light brown complexion. Her face was oval shaped and her hair parting was straight down the middle in traditional style. Her eyelashes were long and well defined. She had a pink bindi on her forehead. On one hand she had an old wristwatch, and on the other, she wore a dozen dark green glass bangles that clinked musically when she moved her hands. They were lucky to find an intelligent and hard-working girl like Aruna. Mrs. Ali knew that her husband would never see it, but Aruna also had an air of melancholy even when she was smiling and laughing. *There is a mystery behind this simple-looking girl,* thought Mrs. Ali. *I wonder what it is.*

"How tall are you?" asked Mrs. Ali.

"Me, madam?" said Aruna. "I am five feet, three inches."

"Your father is already retired, isn't he?" said Mrs. Ali.

"Yes, madam. My mother says we were born late. She was almost thirty-five years old when I was born, and it was another five years before my sister came along."

"It must have been such a shock to your mum to find out that she was pregnant at that age," said Mrs. Ali.

Aruna laughed and did not reply.

"It must be such a worry for your parents—having two girls to marry off after your father has left service," said Mrs. Ali.

"That's the big problem in our house," said Aruna.

Mrs. Ali nodded sympathetically, and slowly drew Aruna out of her shell as they made conversation until the next member came in and Mrs. Ali went back inside the house.

A few weeks later, Aruna was working alone in the office when a couple walked in. She recognized the couple and greeted them. "Hello, Mr. and Mrs. Raju. Have you come looking for more matches for Soni?"

Mr. and Mrs. Raju had been one of the first clients that Aruna had come into contact with after she started working here. They had been looking for a groom from a small family for their daughter.

The couple smiled and said, "No, we don't need to look anymore. The match that Mr. Ali found for her—Bodhi Raju, the advocate—was perfect. We finalized the engagement yesterday."

"Congrats!" said Aruna, pleased for them. "Sir had to go out. I will tell him when he comes back. He will be pleased too."

"Yes, it's unfortunate that he is not here. Anyway, here are some photographs of Soni's engagement function. Do you want to have a look?" asked Mrs. Raju.

"Of course," said Aruna, and took the album from her hand.

Soni was a good-looking girl, and she looked really beautiful in the bright orange sari. She was wearing a gold nose-ring with a chain that went over her cheek and linked to her left ear.

Aruna was surprised. She looked up and said, "I didn't think your daughter had a pierced nose."

Mrs. Raju replied, "It's a clip-on."

Aruna nodded and said, "It really suits her. She looks beautiful."

There was another photograph of Soni and her fiancé standing next to each other in a formal pose. Soni was holding a bouquet of red roses and Bodhi Raju was in a dark suit.

"Can we keep this photograph for our records?" asked Aruna.

Mr. and Mrs. Raju looked at each other for a moment. Then Mrs. Raju turned to Aruna and nodded.

"Thanks," said Aruna. She got up and looked through the files and took out a photograph of Soni that her parents had given Mr. Ali when they became members. She handed it back to Mrs. Raju.

"Thank you. Please tell Mr. Ali that it was a pleasure to do business with you all. We are very happy with the service."

When they left, Aruna looked at the wall which held the photograph of Mr. and Mrs. Ali's son with a couple and their son. An idea had been forming for a few days in her head—she took a strip of tape and stuck Soni and Bodhi Raju's photograph below that photograph. *It'll make a good collage and be a great advertisement tool,* she thought.

The next day, Aruna watched as a tall, smartly dressed young man came in, accompanied by two women. One of the women was older, dressed in a traditional Kanjivaram silk sari, and looked like his mother. She had at least ten gold bangles on each wrist. She had diamond earrings and a diamond necklace. Her mangalsootram had tiny diamonds that caught the light and sparkled. The other woman was younger and dressed less formally in a bright printed sari. She didn't have as much jewelry as the older woman, but what she wore looked expensive. She too had a mangalsootram with diamonds in it. The man turned and pressed a button on his key fob and the white car outside beeped once as it locked itself.

It was almost noon and Aruna wanted to go home. But she smiled and greeted them in the traditional Hindu way. "Namaste."

"Namaste, is this the marriage bureau?" asked the man.

"Yes, sir. Please take a seat. My name is Aruna. What can we do for you?" she replied, standing up behind the table.

The three visitors looked at each other, obviously at a loss about how to proceed. Aruna waited a moment and asked, "Who are you looking for?"

"It is for my brother," replied the younger woman, pointing at the man.

"That's fine, madam. You look like Brahmins, is that correct?"

"Yes, we are Vaishnava Brahmins. Do you have any matches in our community?" said the older lady.

"Oh yes, madam. We have lots of Brahmin matches. Please fill in this form, so we can find the right match for you," said Aruna.

The young man took the form from her and said, "Thank you."

He really is quite handsome, thought Aruna. The man was tall, as she had already noticed—definitely a six-footer. He was fair, had a strong chin, and a bushy mustache. His voice was soft, but rich. His eyes sparkled when he smiled.

The man filled in the form with a silver fountain pen and handed it back. His name was Ramanujam Prabhu Rao—twenty-eight years old and a doctor, a surgeon at the King George Hospital, the city's main government hospital. Their family was very well off, worth over five crores—fifty million rupees.

Aruna wondered why such a qualified man needed to come to the marriage bureau—especially as he wasn't old or divorced, either. He didn't raise a quibble about the fees and quietly handed over a five-hundred-rupee note to Aruna. She took out the list of Brahmin brides and handed it to the man's sister. The two ladies bent their heads together over the list and started going through it.

Mr. Ali came back home. He said, "Oh! You are still here. Go home for lunch, Aruna. I will look after these people."

"That's all right, sir. I will go a bit later. This is Mr. Ramanujam Rao. They are looking for a bride for the gentleman," she said, and handed him the filled-in form and the five-hundred-rupee note.

The ladies were still busy going through the list. Mr. Ali turned to Ramanujam and said, "Hi, I am Mr. Ali. Were you named after the mathematician or the sage?"

The young man chuckled. "Neither! I am named after my grandfather."

Mr. Ali laughed along with Ramanujam and said, "If you tell me what exactly your requirements are, we can help you better."

Ramanujam's sister looked up and interrupted. "As you can see, my brother is a very qualified man. We are looking for a beautiful, educated girl. She must be tall, fair, and slim. Good family. And they must pay a dowry of at least one crore."

Ramanujam looked embarrassed at the mention of the dowry, but didn't say anything.

Mr. Ali nodded and said, "I see. We have some matches that might be suitable. Let me show you one."

He stretched his hand out and asked for the list they were looking at. He skimmed down the list and pointed out one.

"These people are very well off. Her father is an IAS officer—a very senior bureaucrat. They are from here but they live in Hyderabad. I have seen the girl when she visited us, and she is really beautiful. But . . ." Mr. Ali's voice trailed off.

Ramanujam's sister looked interested. "But what?" she asked.

"I think . . . ," Mr. Ali muttered, and opened the wardrobe. He went through the files until he found the one he wanted, and took it out. He also took out a photo album and riffled through the pages until he found the one he wanted.

"Here, this is the girl." He handed the open album to Ramanujam's sister. All three of them looked at the girl's photo with interest. As Mr. Ali had said, the girl was really good-looking. She was photographed standing, in a dark maroon sari that really showed off her fair skin. She had an angular face with high cheekbones, full lips, artfully enhanced by lipstick. The sari was tied below her belly button and showed off her narrow waist. Aruna had seen the photo before and watched their reactions with interest. It was obvious that the girl in the photo was to Ramanujam's liking.

"Beautiful," said Ramanujam's mother. "And you said her father is an IAS officer?"

"Yes. But there is a problem," said Mr. Ali, who had been looking through the file. "I wasn't a hundred percent sure, but here it is. They are looking for a groom in America."

"Oh! We don't want to send our son abroad," said the older lady.

Mr. Ali said, "Why don't you have a chat with them? Your son is handsome and well qualified. The pair will look very good together. He is exactly what they are looking for in all other respects. It is worth pursuing this, they might change their minds."

"We will do that. Do you have any more matches?" asked Ramanujam's sister.

"Nobody that perfect. There is another girl whose father is a university professor. Very good girl but they cannot pay that much," said Mr. Ali.

"Let's have a look," said Ramanujam.

Mr. Ali pointed out the details of the professor's daughter in the list and said, "We do not have their photo. They wouldn't give it to us."

They talked for a while longer and the three of them thanked Mr. Ali and took their leave. Aruna helped Mr. Ali put everything away and went home for her lunch.

That afternoon, Aruna was again alone in the office. Mr. Ali had gone to the post office. A man in his late twenties came in. She had seen him before and remembered his name. She said, "Hello, Mr. Irshad. We sent you a list just the other day."

"Yes, I got the list. But what is the point? It is totally useless. I contact so many people but nobody even responds to my letters. I am now beginning to wonder whether the addresses are real or made up," replied the man.

"Of course they are real, sir. We don't make up any addresses here. See, we get letters every day and these are the addresses we put into our lists. Look at that photograph on the wall. Those two got engaged because of us. How can you say that we make up these addresses?" asked Aruna.

"I don't care what you say. I think you are all frauds. How is it possible that I do not get even a single response?" he said loudly.

"Sir, please don't shout."

"I will shout if I want to. I paid five hundred rupees, and it is all a waste. I have a good mind to complain to the police," said Irshad.

Aruna was getting upset, but before she could reply, Mrs. Ali came out.

"Aruna, what is going on?" asked Mrs. Ali.

"This—" started Aruna.

"I will tell you, madam. This place is a fraud. You just take money and have no intention of providing service," shouted the man.

"Please don't shout," said Mrs. Ali. "Remember that I am your mother's age."

Aruna was impressed by how calm Mrs. Ali sounded. The man looked a bit abashed but still had a mutinous look on his face.

"You will have to wait until my husband comes in. He will be about ten or fifteen minutes. You can take up your complaint with him. There is no point shouting at us ladies. If you wish, you can wait here silently, or you can leave and come back a bit later," said Mrs. Ali to the young man.

Irshad nodded and said quietly, "I will wait."

Mrs. Ali turned to Aruna and said, "Please get on with your work. Call me if you need me."

Mrs. Ali came back with a glass of cool water and handed it to Irshad. He nodded his thanks and drank half the water in a single gulp. Mrs. Ali went inside the house. Aruna didn't really have any immediate tasks, but she started going through all the old files so she could look busy. She avoided any eye contact with Irshad. Soon all was quiet except for the whir of the fan on full speed and the traffic outside. After a little while, she saw Irshad mop his brow with a handkerchief. He was slightly overweight and was perspiring. Mr. Ali returned soon, to Aruna's relief.

When he saw the young man sitting on the sofa, Mr. Ali said, "Hello, Irshad. Back again so soon? We don't have any lists of Muslim brides more recent than the one we sent you a few days ago."

Aruna was surprised when Irshad meekly said, "I don't know, sir. You send me all these lists and I write or call up quite a few of them, but nobody replies. When I joined, you said that I might get contacted by other people because my name will also be in a list, but that hasn't happened either. I just don't know what to do."

Mr. Ali asked Aruna to take out Irshad's file. She had already taken it out and kept it on top of the table, so she just handed it over to Mr. Ali. He smiled at her and sat on the chair across the low coffee table in front of Irshad and looked through it. He asked, "We have already advertised twice on your behalf. You got a few responses for the second ad. What happened to those?"

Irshad said, "Nothing. I wrote to about half of them, but except one or two of them, nobody even replied."

Mr. Ali looked up with interest, "Oh! What did those people who wrote to you say?"

"They said they were not interested," said Irshad.

"Hmm . . . So people responded to the ad but did not reply back after you wrote to them. What did you tell them?"

"The usual. I am a successful salesman with a salary of eight thousand rupees but earning twenty-five thousand rupees most months. I am an only son. My father is no more and I live with my mother. The house is our own, built by my father a long time ago—we couldn't afford to buy one in the middle of the town like that now."

"I agree. There is nothing wrong with any of that. You are not short or too dark, either. What about the girl? Are you asking for a lot of dowry or any other unusual requirement?"

"No. In fact, I don't mention any dowry at all, because it doesn't even get to that stage," replied a clearly frustrated Irshad.

"Yes, your case is unusual. I don't see any reason why you should not get any matches. Why are you doing all the running around? What about your mother?"

"Since my father died, my mother has just immersed herself completely in religion. She spends half her time in prayers and the other half reading the Quran. She has just been on a pilgrimage to Ajmer Sharif and now she wants to go to Mecca and never come back."

"Oh, dear! You do have lots of trouble on your head at the moment. Well, if she goes off to Mecca, it will help you settle in with your bride when you get one," quipped Mr. Ali.

"Yeah, when I get one . . ." Irshad muttered sourly.

"Just out of interest, what do you sell?" asked Mr. Ali.

Irshad's face shone with interest for the first time since he had come in. He said, "I sell valves—little tiny ones to control chemicals or huge big ones for use in the shipyard. I sell electric valves, pneumatic valves, manual valves—all types. I am the best salesman for our company in the whole of South India."

Mr. Ali asked, "Do you think valves are important?"

"Of course, sir. Without valves, modern life would be impossible. Running water, flush toilets—you name it. They all need valves. Forget modern conveniences—without them, your blood could not circulate in your body. Life itself would not exist."

Mr. Ali looked at his earnest face and asked, "Do you mention this when you speak to your potential in-laws?"

"Sometimes," replied Irshad. "If they respond and ask me what I do, then I tell them."

Mr. Ali sighed and said, "Okay, let me think about this. I will give your matter some consideration. Don't be disheartened. You are a young man earning a good salary, with your own property. You are not too bad-looking and you don't have seven sisters to marry off. I am sure a match will come soon. Don't you have any uncles or other family elders who can help you?"

Irshad said, "No. My father was an only son and my mother is much younger than all her brothers. They have all died. My father was transferred from place to place and we've lost all contact with any family."

Mr. Ali replied, "Yes. That's a big problem with modern life. Families get scattered like chaff in the wind. Don't worry, young man. We will do our best and find the perfect somebody for you."

Irshad thanked Mr. Ali and left. Soon after, they heard his motorcycle start.

Mrs. Ali came out after Irshad left. She said, "Before you came, he was shouting at Aruna. He even shouted at me, claiming that we were frauds."

"Oh," said Mr. Ali. "You should have told me. I would have made him apologize to both of you."

"That's okay," said Aruna. "I was scared at first, but Mrs. Ali really put him in his place. He was meek after that. I thought he would shout at you when you came back, but he must have cooled down while waiting." She laughed with relief.

Mrs. Ali laughed with her. "Yes, he was jumping up and down like a live prawn, but I was pretty good, wasn't I?"

"Yes . . . Before you came, he was talking about going to the police and everything," said Aruna.

Mr. Ali frowned. "But I do find it strange. Why isn't he getting any responses?"

Mrs. Ali said severely, "What do you mean by joking about his mother? She might go to Mecca or to Medina. What's it to you? You should not joke about these things."

"How did you hear that?" asked Mr. Ali.

"I was in the front room in case he started shouting at Aruna again," said Mrs. Ali. "And don't change the subject."

Mr. Ali nodded and said, "I could see he was upset and I was trying to calm him down."

Mrs. Ali replied, "You were lucky. He could just as easily have taken offense and taken off again."

They talked for a while longer about Irshad, and then Mrs. Ali went back inside. Mr. Ali turned to Aruna. "Let's have a look at those new members first and make their ads. The agent from *Today* will come in first thing tomorrow for the copy."

She gave him the list and Mr. Ali sat down and started making up the ads. This was one task he had not delegated to Aruna. Forty-five minutes later, he handed the pile of papers to Aruna and told her, "Please put them in the top drawer. If I am not here when the ad boy comes, give them to him and tell him I will pay him later."

Aruna quickly flipped through the papers and put them in the top drawer.

She turned to Mr. Ali and said, "Sir, I can understand somebody like Irshad using our help. He is an average-looking man in an ordinary job. He doesn't have a father or other family elders to help him, so it is not a surprise that he will come to somebody like us. But why would somebody like Ramanujam, the doctor, need a marriage bureau? He is a good-looking man, a surgeon, quite young, and his family is very wealthy. Why would he come to us?"

Mr. Ali laughed and said, "The world is full of all kinds of people— luckily for us. I don't know why they made that decision, but let me tell you something—as long as his sister is looking for a bride for him, he will never get married."

Aruna was shocked and asked, "Why do you say that, sir?"

"Call it experience, call it a sixth sense. His sister will keep looking for the perfect bride, but perfection is an attribute of God alone; it doesn't exist in this world. It is said that the Moghul emperor Aurangzeb's daughters never married because they could not find anybody who was good enough for them, and that's exactly how it will be for Ramanujam. A pity, because he seems like a good chap."

EIGHT

On Friday, about a month later, Aruna arrived home and went into the kitchen as usual to help her mother. She started chopping up ladies' fingers—okra—into little rings. Her mother was turned away from her, stirring the onions in the pan. She asked, "Monday is your day off, isn't it?"

Aruna looked up at her mother's back. "You know it is. Why?" she said.

"Shastry-uncle came today."

"He comes here almost every day," said Aruna, laughing. "What's so special this time?"

"He said he may have found a match for you," said her mother.

"Amma, I don't want to go through that hassle again. Just tell Shastry-uncle to drop it, will you?" said Aruna, pushing up with the back of her hand a fringe of hair that had fallen in front of one of her eyes.

"They seem like good people—he is a clerk in the Indian Bank.

His father was a bank employee, too. They are from the village next to ours."

"Amma, what's the point? You know——" started Aruna.

"Aruna, don't get disheartened. Maybe this time it will work out," interrupted her mother.

"You know it won't. I won't go through it again. I won't," said Aruna. She knew she sounded like a child having a tantrum but felt unable to change her tone.

Her mother said, *"Aruna-a . . ."*

Aruna knew that tone of voice. Her mother wasn't going to take a no from her.

Aruna went back to her chopping, sulking.

"Just because it didn't work out last time, it doesn't mean that the same thing will happen now. Forget the past," said her mother.

After a while, Aruna said, "Amma, our finances are not good. Naanna is only getting half-pension now. Why don't we wait another two years until his pension comes back to full strength before looking again?"

"The seasons don't wait for anyone, Aruna. Especially not for young girls who have come of marriage age. It is already very late. If God had shown us some mercy, you would have been married by now. We'll manage somehow. We cannot delay your wedding."

Aruna sighed. Her father had taught Telugu and math in government schools before he retired. Most teachers who got posted to schools in small, remote villages either bribed their way out of the posting or simply never turned up at school. Her father had never done either—he accepted every posting stoically and went about his duties. His students, as she knew because she had been one of them, groaned because alone among the government teachers, he was never absent. He marked his students fairly, but strictly. He never gave private tuitions, but if a student showed aptitude, he taught the student weekends at his home without charging any money.

Almost three years ago, Aruna's father retired and they moved to Vizag and settled in a small house. Aruna graduated and started her M.A. course at the university. Vani joined a local school. About a year and a half later, a bombshell had dropped on their family. The government wrote to Aruna's father saying that his pension had been calculated wrong and he had been overpaid since he retired. The letter said that his pension would be stopped for eighteen months until the extra money he had received was canceled out. Her father was not the only one who had been overpaid. The whole batch of employees who had retired that month were in the same position. Her father joined the other employees and protested until the government changed its mind. Instead of being completely cut, their pension would be reduced by half and the money recovered over three years.

The family already had financial problems and now found it difficult to manage on half of an already meager pension. Aruna stopped studying for her postgraduate degree, and as the financial troubles got worse, she took up a job to help her family.

A few days later, Mr. Ali was going through the Christian Mala list that Aruna had typed earlier in the day.

"This is good," said Mr. Ali. "But I think the next time you should fit more addresses in each page. Here, instead of saying 'Date of Birth,' just type 'DOB.' "

Aruna nodded.

Mr. Ali pointed out another address in the list and said, "Here, you've typed 'Andhra Pradesh.' We can just type 'AP' or not type it at all."

Aruna nodded again and said, "I'm sorry, sir."

"No, nothing to be sorry about," said Mr. Ali. "By the way, it's a good idea of yours to put up photographs of our successes. There are quite a few there already, and the other day, Mr. Konda became a member after seeing those pictures."

Aruna smiled and said, "Thanks, sir. I've been meaning to ask you a question. Who are the couple with your son in that photograph?"

Mr. Ali looked at the picture on the wall and sighed. "That's a sad story. That couple were classmates of Rehman who fell in love with each other. The boy was a poor farmer's son from a nearby village and the girl was the daughter of a rich merchant from town. They married each other against the girl's family's wishes. They had a son, as you can see from the picture, but the girl's father never relented. Then a couple of years ago, when the boy was five years old, the father died in a construction accident. The girl took her son and went to her parents' house, but her father insulted her and threw her out. The poor girl could not bear it and committed suicide. Rehman thinks it was with the hope that once she was no more, her parents would take care of their grandson, but they proved heartless. They didn't come to her funeral and never asked about their grandchild."

Aruna said, "Some people are so stubborn. What happened to the poor child?"

Mr. Ali said, "His paternal grandfather is bringing him up on his farm in the village."

He was going to add something more, but he heard footsteps outside and looked up. Aruna took the list and went back to her seat. Mr. Ali saw the salesman, Irshad, come in, and smiled. "Good you could come so quickly when I called," he said.

"Salaam, sir," said Irshad. "Thank you for thinking about me."

Mr. Ali had been mulling over the young man's problem for the last few days. That day at breakfast he had been listening to the news on All India Radio and an idea had clicked in his brain. He called Irshad and asked him to come over. Irshad told him that he had an appointment with the chief engineer in the port at one, but he would come in just after noon to meet him.

"Tell me," said Mr. Ali, "what do you tell your prospective in-laws about your salary?"

"I tell them my base salary is eight thousand rupees, but with commissions it goes up to twenty-five or thirty thousand rupees a month."

"Right, and what do you tell them about your job?" asked Mr. Ali.

"I tell them that I am a salesman, sir. I tell them that my company is the second-biggest distributor for valves in India. We have a collaboration with German manufacturers as well," replied Irshad.

"All right. Is your company a well-known brand?"

"No, sir. It is just like valves. Without valves, nothing could run, but just as nobody pays any attention to them when they are doing their job, our company is not really known to the general public."

"Are you a good salesman?" asked Mr. Ali.

"Yes, sir. I have already told you, I have the best sales in the whole of South India, better than any salesman covering bigger cities like Chennai and Bangalore."

"Do you talk about valves to your prospective in-laws?" asked Mr. Ali. He noticed that Aruna had given up working and was listening avidly to the conversation.

"Well . . ." demurred Irshad.

"Yes or no?" demanded Mr. Ali.

Irshad dropped his head and wouldn't meet Mr. Ali's eyes. Mr. Ali just stayed silent, staring at him. Irshad looked up after a few moments and admitted, "Once or twice."

"Do you talk about your mother spending all her time in prayer when you meet potential clients?" asked Mr. Ali.

"Of course not, sir. It is irrelevant."

"Exactly," said Mr. Ali. "You are talking about irrelevant things when people are coming to see you. Once you have met several times and got engaged or married to their daughter, then you can talk about valves all you like and nobody is going to be rude to you. After all, you will be their son-in-law. But until you get to that stage, no talking about things that absorb you greatly but are of no interest to them. You are a salesman and you are failing to sell yourself. Do you understand?" asked Mr. Ali.

"Yes, sir," replied Irshad softly.

"Think of yourself as a product—a valve, an important and unglamorous valve. The customer needs it but she doesn't know it yet. It is your job to convince her that you are just the right product."

Irshad was looking at Mr. Ali with his mouth open.

"Er—" he began.

Mr. Ali interrupted him. "No ers or bers. We have a product to sell and we are going to sell it. What's your salary?"

The young man was thrown by the sudden change of topic. His mouth opened and closed soundlessly. Aruna giggled. Irshad glanced at her and his face reddened. He said, "Eight thousand."

"Wrong," said Mr. Ali. "What is the minimum you've made in the last six months, including your commission?"

"Er . . . ," said Irshad, clearly thinking hard. "Twenty-two thousand," he said.

"Okay. Your salary is twenty-two thousand."

"What's your job?" asked Aruna.

Both the men turned to her. "Salesman," said Irshad.

"No. You are a sales executive," replied Aruna.

"Excellent. That's a very good suggestion."

"You own your own house in the center of town. Your mother is a pious woman who will be no trouble to her daughter-in-law. No sisters to marry off. All positive points that need to be made clear in your sales pitch. Let's look through the latest list of brides."

Aruna took out the list of Muslim brides. Mr. Ali and Irshad went through the list of brides and identified five potential candidates who were the right age, height, and of similar financial background.

"Have you contacted any of them already?" asked Mr. Ali.

Irshad pointed out two of the five and said, "I've contacted these two."

"Let's leave them out. You have three possibilities here. Let's see, Malkeen, twenty-two years old, five feet, three inches tall, father is an accountant in the shipyard and she has two brothers. Can you take out her photo, Aruna?" asked Mr. Ali.

Aruna looked up the reference number and took out the photograph from the file and passed it to Mr. Ali. He looked at it briefly and passed it on to Irshad, who glanced at the photograph and nodded. Mr. Ali then moved on to the next girl in the selection.

"Shameem, twenty-six years old, five-feet-two. Her father runs that famous department store near the old head post office," Mr. Ali said, looking up. "You know the one I mean—it is on two stories and sells all those wall clocks and pressure cookers."

"Yes, sir. I know the one you mean."

"Right . . . Now, the third one—Aisha, twenty-four years old, just over five feet. Her father runs a grocery shop in Kottavalasa. It is a small market town, about thirty miles from here on the road to Araku."

Irshad nodded.

Mr. Ali said, "She has two brothers and a younger sister who is in college. What do you think? Are they suitable?"

Irshad thought for a moment and said, "I know you said they are all of similar financial status to me, but really, I think the second family—the owners of the department store—are too rich for the likes of my mum and me."

Mr. Ali nodded and said, "Hmm . . . Maybe you are right. It is a big store—they must be afraid of the income tax department and don't want to tell us their real wealth."

Irshad said, "I think you are right, sir. I remember reading that there was an IT raid on them last year."

"Okay. Let's contact the other two and see what happens." Mr. Ali looked up at the clock on the wall and stood up. He asked, "Isn't it time for your appointment with the chief engineer?"

Irshad stood up as well and took Mr. Ali's hand in both his hands and said, "Thank you, sir, for taking so much of your valuable time to help me. I will write to both those families."

Mr. Ali laughed and said, "No, young man. You won't contact them yourself. Come again tomorrow at the same time. We are normally not busy at this time. We will contact the families together."

Irshad left and Aruna said, "How did you come up with the idea of the salesman selling himself? That was very clever of you."

"Oh! Nothing like that," Mr. Ali laughed. He was pleased, nevertheless. "This morning I was listening to the radio, and on the news they were talking about a police constable whose bicycle had been stolen. That got me thinking."

About twelve-thirty in the afternoon the next day, the door to Mr. Ali's verandah opened and he looked up. Irshad mopped his brow as he came in.

Mr. Ali looked at him and said, "It's hot, isn't it?"

"Yes, sir. I couldn't get parking under the tree on the other side of the road. I've parked my bike just outside, and by the time I leave, the black seat will be scorching."

Mr. Ali laughed and said, "Better sit under the fan so you can cool down for now at least. It's the Month of Fire according to the Hindu calendar, and there's no point expecting it to be cool. You are a bit late. I almost sent Aruna home and closed the office for lunch."

Irshad sat down on the sofa. He said, "Sorry, sir. My mother asked me not to leave the house before noon. She said it was not auspicious because Saturn was in the ascendant until then."

Mr. Ali said, "Don't you know that Muslims are not supposed to believe in astrology?"

Irshad was clearly embarrassed. He shrugged and said, "What can I say? She never does anything without consulting the Hindu calendar that hangs in our kitchen."

Mr. Ali nodded. He knew the calendar that Irshad was referring to. Besides normal dates, it had the phases of the moon and the rising and setting times of Mars, Jupiter, and Saturn. He said, "Anyway, let's start our work for the day."

Mr. Ali turned to Aruna and she gave him the files for the two girls they had short-listed the previous day. Mr. Ali dialed the accountant in the shipyard first. A woman's voice answered hello. It sounded like her mother. The prospective bride, Malkeen, was probably in college at this time.

Mr. Ali said, "Assalamu 'alaikum. Is Mr. Salman there?"

"Wa 'laikum assalam. Who is calling?" the lady asked.

"I am Mr. Ali, calling from the marriage bureau. I wanted to speak to him about a match for his daughter."

"Oh! Just one moment. Let me give the phone to my husband."

Mr. Ali didn't hear anything for a moment, and then heard a man's voice say gruffly, "Yes?"

"Mr. Salman? Assalamu 'alaikum. We have a match for your daughter that you might be interested in," said Mr. Ali.

"Sorry. We are not interested anymore. In fact, I was going to call you to take my daughter's name off the list," said the man's voice.

Mr. Ali said, "Oh! Did you find a match already? You came over for the new list just last month—the whole thing must have been sorted out very quickly."

"Yes," said Mr. Salman curtly. "Take my daughter's name off the list. Bye."

The phone was hung up. Mr. Ali slowly replaced the phone in its cradle, shaking his head at the man's manners.

Wonder what's got into him, thought Mr. Ali.

Aruna and Irshad were looking at him expectantly. He shook his head. "No, they wanted me to take the girl off the list."

Aruna said, "That's strange, isn't it?"

Mr. Ali said, "Yes, take them off the list. Make sure we don't give their details to anybody else. I think the girl has eloped, and that's why they are so touchy."

Aruna gasped and said, "That's a terrible thing to say, sir."

"Why else would they be so rude? He came here just last month and was all polite and friendly. If he had found a groom for the girl himself, there's no need to act shirty, is there?" he said.

Mr. Ali took up the second file. The girl, Aisha, lived in a small town on the road to the mountains of Araku—home to tribal people and magnificent million-year-old limestone caves. Her brother lived in the city, and he had come in and joined the bureau on behalf of his sister. Mr. Ali looked through the form filled by Aisha's brother and called him on the phone.

When Aisha's brother answered, Mr. Ali said, "Hello. This is Mr. Ali here, calling from the marriage bureau."

"Assalamu 'alaikum, Mr. Ali, how are you, sir?"

"I am fine. I have a match for your sister. I thought you might be interested," replied Mr. Ali.

"That's good of you to call. Where is the boy from, sir?" asked Aisha's brother.

"Irshad is from this city itself and he works locally as well. He is a sales executive earning twenty-two thousand rupees a month. They have a big house in the heart of town. Lives with his mother," said Mr. Ali.

"That sounds interesting. When can I come over to discuss this match?" asked Aisha's brother.

"Your office is near the main bus stand, isn't it?" asked Mr. Ali.

"That's right, sir."

"Can you come over now? Irshad is here at the moment and you are not far. You might as well meet straightaway. Never delay a good task, as they say."

Irshad looked up, evidently surprised at the sudden invitation. He self-consciously brushed his hair with his fingers and sucked in his stomach.

Aisha's brother was silent for a moment and then said, "That's a good idea, sir. This is my lunchtime, anyway. I will be there in ten or fifteen minutes."

Mrs. Ali got glasses of cold water for all of them. Mr. Ali emptied his glass and stood at the front door, looking out. The road had emptied as the heat increased. The leaves on the trees drooped down listlessly in the pitiless sun. The stray dogs had found tiny patches of shade and lay down with their tongues hanging out. The birds fell silent; the crows were not to be seen, and even the sparrows stopped zooming around. He thought about the ceaseless march of the seasons—this hot season broken by the monsoon rains, then winter, a brief spring, and then summer again. *We struggle so much,* thought Mr. Ali, *for money, power, and love, but the world doesn't care. It just goes round and round in its own cycle.* He wondered how his son was getting along in the Royyapalem protest.

"Just this one match, sir," said Irshad, from behind. "I hope it works out."

Mr. Ali turned away from the road. "Don't worry. I have a good feeling about this one. Remember, when God makes a creature, human or animal, He also makes its mate at the same time."

"That cannot be the case, sir. In almost all cases, brides are several years younger than grooms," said Aruna.

"True," said Mr. Ali, laughing. "I am sure God has a good memory. After all, what are a few years to Him?"

"Yes, sir. It is said that in the world of Brahma, the Hindu god of creation, a blink of his eye is several hundred years in our world," said Aruna.

They were all silent for a while. Then Aruna said, "He could have a good filing system instead of a good memory, sir."

Mr. Ali looked at her and smiled. "You are correct—a good filing system can remove the need for a good memory. My memory is pretty poor, but our files let us manage all our clients. Our Prophet Mohammed, peace be upon him, told us to write all agreements down. He said that the faintest ink is more persistent than the strongest memory."

Soon, they heard the noise of a three-wheeled auto-rickshaw stopping outside the gate. A young man came in. Mr. Ali recognized him as Aisha's brother and said, "Hello, Jehangir. Good of you to come over as soon as I called. This is Irshad." Mr. Ali's hand pointed him out.

The two men looked at each other, clearly appraising one another.

Mr. Ali continued, "Please sit down, Jehangir. Irshad lives with his mother in the city in their own house. His father is no more. He is a sales executive—earns twenty-two thousand rupees a month and has his own motorbike. By the way, we don't have your sister's photograph with us."

Jehangir replied, "I know, sir. My father didn't agree to the photograph being left here. He is a bit old-fashioned."

Jehangir turned to Irshad and gave him an embarrassed grin.

Irshad nodded in return. "I know what you mean," he said. "My mother spends all her time in prayers."

"You do not own a shop, do you?" asked Jehangir.

"No," said Irshad. "Why do you want to know?"

Jehangir took a deep breath and said, "My sister is a very good girl. She does a lot of housework and helps mum with the cooking. She is adamant about two things. First, she wants to marry somebody in the city. She reads a lot and has decided that she wants to live in a big place. She has rejected some nice matches because they are from villages or small towns, and mum is in absolute despair. We don't know that many people in the city—I only moved here last year. She wanted to move along with me and said that she would look after my house, but my father refused. Second, she doesn't want to marry a shopkeeper."

Irshad said, "That's good—because I don't have a shop."

Jehangir said, "She is a very sensible girl—not headstrong at all. She knows all the housework and normally doesn't go against anything my parents say. But she's stuck on these things."

Jehangir was obviously worried that Irshad might think that his sister was a "difficult" girl. He continued, "My father has set aside five lakhs—five hundred thousand rupees—as dowry for Aisha. All the traditional gold ornaments like a long chandan haar, necklace, anklets, and earrings have already been purchased. Also, my mother has been buying silk saris for a few years now. There will be no stinting on that side. We are not very rich, but we will spend freely of what we have to make sure my sister is married off in style."

Irshad waved his hand in a dismissive gesture—but he knew that his mother would set great store by all these things and therefore they were important. They exchanged each other's contact details. Irshad and his mother would formally visit Jehangir's family and take things from there.

Both of them thanked Mr. Ali and Aruna for their help and left.

Forty minutes later, Mr. Ali and his wife were sitting in the verandah, having eaten their lunch. Aruna had gone home. Normally, Mr. Ali would take a siesta after his lunch, but there was a power cut and it was too hot to stay inside the house. In the verandah, there was a slight breeze that provided welcome relief.

"It's eerie," said Mr. Ali. "Everything's so silent, no traffic, no noise of the fan, not even any birds chirping."

Mrs. Ali nodded. They both sat in companionable silence.

After a while, they heard a voice call out loudly, "Palm fruit . . . co-o-o-ol palm fro-o-ot . . ."

Mr. Ali immediately went to the gate. He saw an old man carrying a big basket of fruit and called him. The man walked over; he was thin—his bare legs all sinew and bone. His face was gaunt and he had white stubble on his chin. The man was wearing thin flip-flops that were almost worn to the ground, and the straps on the left slipper had been replaced with rope.

Mr. Ali watched as the man took the heavy load off his head and put it on the ground. He had rolled a towel into a ring and put it on his head as a cushion against the basket, and it came undone as he bent forward. The man used the towel to wipe his face and head and put it over his shoulder.

"Good fruit, sir. Just what you need in this hot weather."

The basket was three quarters filled with palm fruit. Each fruit was a round disk about the size of the palm of a hand.

"How much?" asked Mr. Ali.

"Six rupees a dozen," replied the man.

The fruit were certainly fresh. The brown covering on them was light cream—not dark. They looked plump and juicy—not dried out and thin. Mr. Ali did not have the heart to bargain with the poor man in the hot weather.

"I will take two dozen," said Mr. Ali, and went back into the house. He came back with his wallet and a steel vessel. The man picked out twenty-four palm fruit and put them in the steel vessel. Mr. Ali pointed to one of the fruit and said, "Not that one. It doesn't look tender. All the water in it must have turned to jelly by now."

The man quietly replaced the fruit with another. Mr. Ali gave him twelve rupees and said, "Why did you come out in this hot sun? You should have started selling earlier in the day."

The man put the money away in a pouch tucked into his waist, rolled the towel round and round into a ring and said, "What can I do, sir? The bus was late coming in. The police had established a checkpoint and were checking all the vehicles."

"Don't you have any sons who will look after you? Then you wouldn't have to roam the streets in such hot weather," said Mr. Ali.

"I have a son, sir. But he is an irresponsible wastrel who goes against all the advice my wife and I give. He spends all his money on drink the day he earns it. It's my karma that I have a son like that and I am forced to work hard even in my old age. Can there be somebody more unfortunate than a man whose son doesn't listen to him?" said the man.

He placed the towel ring on his head and, keeping his head straight, he bent down to lift the basket. Mr. Ali bent down with him and helped lift the bamboo basket onto the man's head. The man stood up, his legs trembling under the strain, and Mr. Ali looked at him anxiously, one of his hands half-raised as if to support the old man if he collapsed. Once he was up, the old man seemed all right and went back onto the street, calling out, "Palm fruit . . . co-o-o-ol palm fro-o-ot . . ."

Mr. Ali stood for a moment in the hot sun, looking at the departing old man. The old man's words rang in his ears and he couldn't get Rehman out of his mind.

Mrs. Ali got a couple of steel plates and knives from the kitchen and they both sat down in their chairs again to eat the fruit.

They heard the outside gate open and looked out, surprised to see Azhar come in.

"What brings you here in the heat?" asked Mr. Ali.

Azhar sat down heavily on the sofa. Mrs. Ali asked him, "Do you want to eat a palm fruit?"

Azhar shook his head and said, "I've just heard from my friend in the police. You know, the inspector in Three Town police station."

Mr. Ali felt a prickling of apprehension. He felt his wife's hand on his arm. "What happened?" Mrs. Ali asked.

"The police have moved against the protesters in Royyapalem. There's been a truncheon charge and they've arrested everybody."

"Rehman?" asked Mrs. Ali.

"My friend called his colleague in Royyapalem and he confirmed that Rehman has been arrested, too."

"Has he been hurt?" she asked.

"I don't know," said Azhar. "My friend couldn't find out how badly he's been hurt, but he said that several boys were injured badly. Some of them apparently have fractures."

"Allah show mercy," said Mrs. Ali. "We have to go there."

Mr. Ali nodded numbly.

"No point," said Azhar. "They are bringing everybody into the city. They don't want to hold them near the village."

"When will they be here?" said Mr. Ali. "Where will they be taken to?"

"They will be here by the evening. The ones with fractures will be taken to hospital and the others to police stations. There are too many to put in one station, so they will be distributed out. My friend said he will let me know where Rehman is being held as soon as he finds out."

"Thanks," said Mr. Ali.

"No need for thanks. I am his maama, you know," said Azhar.

Mrs. Ali was in tears as she looked at her brother. Mr. Ali said, "What's the point of crying? We told him not to go but he wouldn't listen to us. When we told him the police were going to move against them, he was so arrogant. They'll never move against us, he said. What an immature boy he is. Hopefully, he is only hurt a little, and a night in the police cell will bring him to his senses."

Mrs. Ali said, "How can you talk like that about your own son? He is in trouble and it is our duty to help him."

Before Mr. Ali could reply, Azhar said, "Aapa, don't worry. We'll get him out as soon as possible."

NINE

The next day, Aruna's house was thoroughly cleaned, and a fresh, colorful spread put on the bed. Two folding chairs were taken down from the top of the cupboard and four more were borrowed from the neighbors. She and her mum worked in the kitchen for several hours frying different snacks. A packet of sweets and a couple of soft-drink bottles were bought.

The house was brightened and looked festive. Her mother was wearing the new sari and her father was wearing a neatly pressed dhoti. Aruna was on her own in the kitchen, changing, when she heard her mother say in the other room, "Why did you come so late? I asked you to come early today. Go in and change quickly. Help your sister. Make sure she wears the red stones necklace."

Vani slipped into the kitchen and closed the door behind her. Aruna wound the long cloth of the sari around herself and tucked the folds into the waistband of her petticoat. She took the other end of the sari and placed it over her shoulder. Vani got down on her knees in front of

Aruna and adjusted the pleats of Aruna's sari so they fell straight. Then she got up and helped Aruna pin the end of the sari that was over her shoulder to her blouse.

Aruna opened the dark blue jewelry box. Nestling on the maroon velvet inside were a pair of earrings and a necklace. She put on the earrings, took out the necklace, and placed it around her neck. Her sister moved behind her and fastened the clasp. Vani then went into the bathroom to wash her face. Aruna just stood there blankly.

Vani came out of the bathroom and quickly put on a plainer sari. Aruna moved mechanically to help Vani. The two sisters had just got ready when there was a knock on the kitchen door and they heard their mother call out. Vani said, "Yes, amma. We are ready."

Their mother came in and said, "They will be here any moment. Vani, help me put the snacks on the plates."

Aruna moved to help as well, but her mother said, "No. You just stand there. Don't spoil your sari."

Aruna watched as her sister and mother bustled around the small kitchen getting everything ready. Soon, they heard voices at the front door. Aruna heard Shastry-uncle's voice and then her father answering.

What's the point of this charade?, she thought despairingly.

The door opened and Shastry-uncle came into the kitchen. He said, "Aruna, you are looking really beautiful. They will love you."

"What about me, Shastry-uncle?" asked Vani.

Shastry-uncle pinched Vani's cheek. "You are looking beautiful too, my dear." He turned to Aruna's mother and said, "Sister, take some ash and smear it on Vani's cheeks. We don't want them to prefer Vani, do we?"

Vani laughed at her uncle's words. Aruna refused to smile. He walked up to her and said, "Don't look so gloomy, Aruna. They have come here seeking a bride for their son, not a human sacrifice."

"What's the point, Shastry-uncle?" said Aruna, looking ready to burst into tears.

He quickly drew back. "Don't cry, Aruna. Your eyes will get puffy. Maybe things will be different this time. You mustn't lose hope."

Once upon a time, when life was innocent and light, Aruna had been similarly dressed and waiting for a young man and his family to come and see her. She had been nervous, obviously, but also very excited at this event that might take her to the next stage in life.

The young man who had come to see her, Sushil, was five years older than she. He was working as an accountant in a ship chandlery firm. He was fair, not very tall, and had a pleasant, open face with a ready smile. Sushil's family was quite small—just his parents and himself. Apparently, a younger brother had died by drowning in the sea several years earlier. The match was ideal in many respects—the age difference was just right; Sushil was taller than Aruna but not too tall; their horoscopes matched; he had a good, if not quite ideal, job; the families were distantly related; their economic circumstances were pretty much the same.

Both sides approved the match. Talks progressed over some weeks to dowry and other exchange of gifts, with Shastry-uncle acting as the mediator between the parties. Aruna was impressed by how Shastry-uncle (as he later told her) had convinced Sushil's family that the groom was not a civil servant, they couldn't really expect the dowry they were asking for, and then argued with her father that nowadays government jobs were not everything and private jobs were almost as good. Finally, these matters were all settled. Aruna's father consulted his calendar and pulled out two auspicious dates—one in a couple of weeks for the engagement and another in four months' time for the actual wedding.

A couple of months after the engagement Aruna's father fell seriously ill. The illness dragged on and the wedding was postponed. Her father got worse and the doctors were baffled. They could not diagnose what disease her father had contracted. He drifted in and out of consciousness. Months passed. The doctors—one junior and one senior doctor—came up with different theories and drug regimes. Nothing helped.

Sushil and his mother came to their house one evening and broke off the engagement. Aruna's mother protested that her husband would get better any day and they could proceed with the wedding.

"We have been very patient," said Sushil's mother. "But there are limits. Does the education department cover the cost of a retired teacher's hospitalization?"

"No, it doesn't," admitted Aruna's mother.

"We have savings," said Aruna.

"Didn't your parents teach you not to interrupt when older people are talking?" snapped Sushil's mother.

Aruna was shocked into silence. Sushil's mother had always been nice to her before. Aruna looked at Sushil, but he looked embarrassed and avoided her eyes.

"You agreed to give us two hundred thousand rupees as dowry, in addition to forty grams of gold and a scooter. Can you still afford that dowry and celebrate the wedding in style?" asked Sushil's mother.

Aruna and her mother were silent. Aruna had been handling the finances for the last few months and she knew they couldn't do it. More than half their savings were eaten up by the medical bills, and her father was still unwell and they didn't know how much more money would be needed for his treatment.

"One has to be realistic in these matters," said Sushil's mother to Aruna's mother. "I would be the last person to question a woman's marriage, but I cannot help feeling that your mangalsootram has come at the expense of your daughter's. If your husband had died quickly, his savings would not have been exhausted and your daughters could have been married off."

Aruna always regretted that she had been so shocked at the woman's words, that she had not made any response as a shamefaced Sushil and his brazen mother stalked out of their house.

Her father's illness continued for a few more months. Shastry-uncle found another house for them and helped them move. He said that just before Aruna's father fell ill, he had told Shastry-uncle that the vaastu of their house was wrong. There was no door or window facing east, and that was trapping ill energies in the house. The new house had correct vaastu. In addition, their new house was smaller and the rent was cheaper.

Her mother took a vow and went around the Kanaka Maha Lakshmi temple one hundred and sixteen times on her knees.

The junior doctor came to Aruna one day when she was at her father's bedside and said that he thought her father had a simple viral infection that had somehow attacked his liver. He asked her if she would consent to a new experimental drug that he had read about in a foreign medical journal. In desperation, she agreed.

The illness left her father as suddenly as it had come. Everybody had their own theory about why her father recovered from the mystery illness. The junior doctor told Aruna that the convalescence would be long and that her father would not be himself for months, if not years.

When he was strong enough, Aruna showed him their financial status. He wept and said, "I wish I had died. Then the money that has taken all my life to save would have been of some use to my family rather than be eaten up by doctors and pharmacists."

Shastry-uncle brought a few more matches after her father recovered. But they were all inferior to the first match—they were older, their subcaste was not as good; the jobs were worse, one boy had even been unemployed; the men were fatter, shorter, or darker, or all three. Aruna realized that in their changed financial circumstances, she didn't have much choice, but she sickened of the whole experience and started protesting at being shown off to various people like a prize cow at a cattle mandi. Shastry-uncle finally stopped bringing more matches. This was the first proposal in almost a year. Aruna hoped it wouldn't start another round like last time, as she didn't want again to feel she was part of a cattle market.

Aruna stood in the kitchen, still as a pillar. She became aware of voices in the other room. The guests had arrived. She heard Shastry-uncle saying, "Welcome to my sister and brother-in-law's house. We are a simple, respectable family. My brother-in-law is a retired government teacher. His forefathers are traditional temple priests of the large temple at Annavaram. In fact, his elder brother is still the priest there. The girls are both well educated. They have also read the holy Shastras in both Telugu and the original Sanskrit."

Aruna's mother gave her a tray of snacks. Aruna pulled the pallu of her sari over her head and walked slowly into the living room. She was barefoot and her silver anklets tinkled as she walked forward. Her head was bent as she kept her eyes on the ground in front of her feet. She walked to where her father, uncle, and the guests were sitting. She put the tray of snacks down on the low table in front of them and stood by her father. There were five guests—she could make out the groom and his parents. She didn't know who the others were, but they looked like the groom's uncle and aunt. All the guests were looking at her intently and she was embarrassed and self-conscious.

The silence in the room stretched on and Aruna was getting more and more uncomfortable. Just as she was planning to go back into the kitchen, the groom's mother asked, "Daughter, what did you study?"

"B.A., madam," replied Aruna.

"That's good. Where did you study?" asked the groom's uncle.

"SVN College," said Aruna.

The conversation spluttered to a stop. Aruna's mother came out of the kitchen with glasses of water on a tray. She must have left instructions for Vani to stay in the kitchen, because her sister did not come out.

"Namaste," her mother said. "Please, take some snacks. Aruna made them."

Everybody reached out and took a plate each. Aruna's mother made a small sign to Aruna to serve the water. Aruna took the tray from her mother and placed it on the table. She gave a glass to each of the guests. Shastry-uncle, who was sitting in front of the groom, stood up from his chair and asked Aruna to sit down in his place. Aruna shook her head in refusal but her uncle insisted and Aruna sat down delicately.

The groom's mother asked Aruna, "How did you get the pakoras so soft?"

Aruna told her that she had added a pinch of baking soda to the batter and made sure that the oil was really hot before frying the pakoras.

The young man asked her, "What's your name?"

"I heard you are working? Where are you employed?" said the groom's uncle.

"Do you plan to continue working after marriage?" asked the groom's aunt.

"What about . . ."

"Why did . . ."

"How much . . ."

The visit went on for another hour. Once they had left, Vani came out of the kitchen and asked her, "What do you think of him?"

"Okay," said Aruna. "At least he didn't leer at me like the last one."

Shastry-uncle came back after seeing the guests off. "Right," he said. "That went well. They are a good family. I know them from way before. They are also being very reasonable. All they want is a scooter and one lakh rupees. Where do you get bank employees for one hundred thousand rupees nowadays?"

Everybody looked at Aruna's father. He looked up and said in irritation, "Why are you all looking at me like that? The dowry is one hundred thousand rupees, the scooter is thirty thousand, and the wedding ceremony will cost at least seventy thousand. I do not have two lakh rupees and that's that."

Aruna gave a sob.

"Brother-in-law, I have a solution for that problem too. I went to Annavaram," said Shastry-uncle.

"What? Why did you go there?" asked Aruna's father, looking confused.

"I met your brother," said Shastry-uncle.

"And?" said Aruna's father.

"Your great-grandfather was granted land by the king of Rajah-mundry."

"Yes, and what has that got to do with this? It has been divided down the generations and only a small piece of it came to my father. And only half of that belongs to me. The other half belongs to my brother."

"I—" began Shastry-uncle.

"Anyway, how dare you go to my brother behind my back? What were you doing there?" interrupted Aruna's father.

"Relax, babu-garu. I am worried about my nieces' weddings. And I am not the only one. Your brother is a good man. When I explained the situation, he was willing to sell the land and use it for Aruna and Vani's weddings. He only has one son and he doesn't need the money. His wife wasn't too happy, but he promised me that if Aruna's wedding was fixed, he will sell the land and help you," said Shastry.

"How dare you?" said her father. His face was red with anger.

Aruna's mother had been silent all this while and now she spoke out. "My brother is trying to help our family. Your daughter is crying, and all you are worried about is your pride."

The two sisters watched their parents arguing, their eyes wide.

Shastry-uncle raised his hands in a placatory manner. "Relax. Everybody is trying to do their best for the girls. We are all family—this hasn't gone anywhere else."

"Even if my brother gives me the whole piece of land, it still won't be enough. It is in the middle of nowhere and it is not very fertile, either. You will be lucky to get twenty bags of rice in a good year from it," said Aruna's father.

"Brother-in-law, you don't go out enough. Land prices all over the state have gone through the roof. That piece of land will go a long way toward paying for Aruna's wedding."

"Even with the land, I cannot get Aruna married off. The money still won't be enough. We will have to find other money for the dowry. Once she is married, we will have other expenses—we have to spend money on treating our son-in-law properly. She might get pregnant, in which case we will have to pay for her childbirth expenses. Also, we need money to pay for Vani's education. We cannot do all these things without the money Aruna is bringing in as well," said her father, shouting.

Aruna and Vani were hugging each other, crying. Aruna's mother was horrified—she was standing still, with her eyes wide, her raised hand covering her open mouth.

"How can you say that, brother-in-law? How can you talk about living off your daughter's earnings?" asked Shastry-uncle, aghast.

Aruna's father just shook his head mulishly.

Shastry-uncle continued, "When will you get Aruna married, then?"

Aruna's father remained silent.

"Keeping a daughter unmarried after she's of marriageable age is a sin. It is against Hindu dharma and tradition," said Shastry-uncle.

When Aruna's father still did not reply, he continued, "Why am I trying to teach you the difference between morality and immorality? You are the teacher. You are older than me—both in age and in relation—being my elder sister's husband. You always taught us that money is not the most important thing in a man's life. Leading an upright life—a life of dharma—is much more important; this is what you have always told us, isn't it? What happened to that moral man? Why has money become so important all of a sudden, that you are willing to go against every convention, every tradition, against the Shastras, the holy books themselves, and keep a grown daughter in the house unmarried?"

He turned to go.

Aruna's father said, "Money is not important only when you have enough of it."

Shastry-uncle turned back. "Who among us is rich? Was my dad rich? Was your dad rich? Were we ever wealthy? We always had to look after every paisa. All of us. How many times have you bought jewelry for your wife? A lot less often than you wanted to, I am sure. When my wife died, she had just her mangalsootram and silver anklets. Everything else was gone—sold off to pay for my daughter's wedding. Forget jewelry for our wives—how many times did we deny some small thing that our children wanted because we couldn't afford it? What did you tell me when I used to get angry about that? You used to say that it was our karma—we had to bear it with patience."

Shastry-uncle's face was red, his chest heaving. Sweat poured off his forehead.

"You are right," said Aruna's father. "My daughter will get married when it is in her karma to do so."

Shastry-uncle raised his hands in disgust. He said, "This is truly Kali Kaalam, the age of evil. What the elders said is true. Honest men turn knaves. Teachers forget what they learned at their mother's breast. Rivers turn against their banks. Priests start loving money more than God. I cannot believe this of you, brother-in-law. You were the man I respected above everybody. If men like you get corrupted . . ."

He stood silent for a moment, then shook his head and continued, "When gold starts rusting, what can one say about iron?"

He stalked off, leaving Aruna and her unhappy family behind him.

Aruna turned to go into the kitchen to change back into her normal clothes. She heard a sob behind her and looked back. Her father had his face in his arms and he was crying. This was so unusual that she rushed back to him and knelt in front of his chair. She took his gnarled hands in her own hands and slowly pulled them away from his face.

"Naanna, don't cry. I don't want to get married now anyway," she said.

Aruna's father sobbed even more loudly.

"Naanna, please don't cry," she said. Tears were rolling down her cheeks as well.

"When I retired and got the letter confirming my pension, I knew it had been calculated wrong. I was a math teacher, after all. But I said nothing. I took the side of adharma, immorality, and all our troubles since then are a result of that wrong decision," said Aruna's father.

"You mustn't say that, naanna. You were not the only one who received that letter. More than a hundred employees retired at the same time as you, and they are all in the same boat," said Aruna.

Her father shook his head. "No," he said. "We all have to take responsibility for our own actions. I wouldn't have minded if the consequences of my deeds fell on me alone. But the burden of these consequences is falling more heavily on your young head, my dear daughter, than it is on mine. I don't know how to bear that."

He sobbed even more piteously. Aruna just held her father tight. She didn't know what else to do.

"Your son is causing a lot of trouble for the police department," said the inspector.

"I'm sorry . . . ," said Mr. Ali. He was deeply embarrassed that Rehman had been arrested and thrown in a police lockup; on the other hand, he was relieved that his son was not in the hospital, seriously injured.

"That's all right. It's better than going after thugs or pickpockets. A better class of prisoner, you know," said the inspector, and laughed.

It was evening and Mr. and Mrs. Ali and Azhar were in an interview room at the police station with the inspector and a constable. Mrs. Ali was holding a tiffin carrier with home-cooked food in it. Rehman had not yet been brought in.

Azhar said, "Can we give him food? Mothers . . ."

The inspector smiled and said, "I don't see a problem. He is only in lockup at the moment. He and his friends have not yet been charged. You can feed him if you want."

He turned to the constable and said, "Get plates and allow these people to serve food to their son later."

The police constable nodded. "Yes, sir. No problem, sir."

A heavily scratched table took up most of the available space in the small room. There were several chairs around the table. Rehman came in. He looked tired. His beard looked even more straggly and unkempt than before. There was a large contusion on his forehead and there were several purple bruises on his arms. He was tanned heavily and his eyes looked huge and startlingly white against his face.

Mrs. Ali gave a cry and rushed toward Rehman. He winced when she put her arms around him but he didn't say anything. She didn't let go of her son for several minutes. Finally, she stood a bit away from him, and Rehman greeted his father and uncle. They all sat down. Mrs. Ali sat next to her son and held his hand.

Azhar said, "What have you done? You are hurt so badly. You are causing so much distress to your mum and dad. Why did you get involved in this protest?"

Rehman said to his uncle, "Maama, if everybody thought like that, nothing would ever change. Didn't somebody say that for evil to happen, it is only necessary for good people to do nothing?"

Mr. Ali said, "But this is not evil you are protesting against, is it? The government wants to create industries and provide employment to our youth. You are stopping the economic progress of our country."

Rehman said, "You are right, abba. It is not evil, but it is still injustice. Poor farmers' lands are being taken away from them."

Mr. Ali said, "They are being compensated."

Mrs. Ali said, "Stop it, all of you. Don't start discussing your politics again."

Azhar said, "That's right. We won't have more than half an hour or so. Let's talk about what we can do. How many people were arrested along with you?"

"About thirty of us."

"I can ask my friend if he can somehow lose your papers and let you go. There is political pressure in a case like this, but I am sure they won't miss one person out of thirty," said Azhar.

"No, maama. That's ridiculous. How can you ask a police officer to break the law like that?" said Rehman, looking shocked.

Azhar said, "Don't be naive, boy. He won't do it for just anybody. But he and I go back a long way. He might do it for me. There's no harm in asking."

Rehman shook his head. "No way. I am not going to be a party to anything so disgusting. Anyway, I cannot leave my friends like that and go off by myself. This is a great opportunity to highlight the case to the media even more. If I do what you are suggesting, then everything we've done over the last week becomes meaningless. It will also be a betrayal of the villagers who've reposed their trust in us."

Azhar said, "What about your parents? What about their distress?"

Mr. Ali broke in. "Azhar, stop it. You are not going to convince him. What does our anxiety or shame mean to him? When I was growing up, it was considered a black mark against the *whole* community if the police even entered the village on a case. Now, my own son has been arrested and our feelings are nothing to him."

Rehman said, "I don't see anything to be ashamed about. I've not been caught stealing or lying."

Mr. Ali raised his hands. "He is in a police lockup, and he doesn't see any shame."

Rehman turned to Mrs. Ali. "Ammi, what do you say? You are silent."

Mrs. Ali started weeping. She said, "What can I say, son? As always, I am caught between you and your father. I don't know whom to listen to, or what is right and wrong anymore. All I can see is that you've been beaten badly."

Rehman held her hands in his and let her weep.

TEN

The next day, everybody was quiet in Mr. Ali's house. He knew why he and his wife were depressed, but he was surprised to see that Aruna was not her usual self, either. Mr. Ali eventually gave up trying to make conversation with Aruna. He went to the post office with the letters.

At the post office, Mr. Ali went past the lines at the counters and walked straight in as usual. He gave the letters to the clerk, who was busy defacing the stamps on the envelopes with a big round stamp. Naidu, the postmaster, was busy on the phone, but he signaled to Mr. Ali to sit down in the chair opposite.

Mr. Ali sat down and waited for Naidu to get off the phone. The summer was past its peak, but it was still pretty hot. It was also more humid, presaging the arrival of the monsoon. He heard the chatter of the sorting clerks, people wanting to buy stamps. He heard a young man asking a clerk how to fill a form to send money to his parents in the village.

The fan whirred away noisily above his head and the clerk stamped the envelopes with a metronomic *thud . . . thud . . . thud . . .*

Mr. Ali closed his eyes, shutting his mind to all the noises. He tried not to think about his son, hurt, in the police lockup. Instead, he wondered why Aruna was so quiet today. He hoped it wasn't anything he had said or done. His wife was always telling him not to make jokes about religion or caste, but he couldn't help himself. She had really settled in well and now he could not imagine running the marriage bureau without her.

"Sir, how are you? What can I do for you?" asked a voice, and Mr. Ali opened his eyes; he had fallen asleep. Naidu had got off the phone.

"Naidu, how are you?"

"I am fine, sir, with your blessings. I am sorry to keep you waiting. That was the Postmaster General's secretariat on the phone, and I couldn't hang up on them."

"No problem, Naidu. I am looking for more postcards. Do you have any?"

Naidu said, "I am really sorry, sir. We only have a few at the moment. I will place an order for them and I will send word through the postman when I get them."

"That's okay. I don't need them for a few days yet," replied Mr. Ali.

He stayed in the post office for a bit longer, talking about the weather and the news. Naidu asked, "Do you remember Gopal, the postman?"

"Yes," said Mr. Ali. "He's stopped coming to our house for the last couple of weeks. The new postman is not half as friendly. What happened to Gopal?"

"Do you remember he has a daughter?"

"Of course! When she got married, I joked with him that he did not need my services anymore."

"His son-in-law died," said Naidu.

"What? It's been just a couple of months or so since his daughter got married, isn't it?"

"That's right. Barely two months. She is Gopal's only daughter."

"Poor girl . . . poor man, such a tragedy," said Mr. Ali, shocked at the news.

They were both silent for a while, and then Mr. Ali asked, "How old was the son-in-law?"

"Twenty-nine."

Mr. Ali shook his head. "How did he die?"

"Accident. He was riding his motorcycle along the road past the cemetery one night. There were roadworks, and the workers had left a drum of tar in the middle of the road. The drum was covered with tar and black, and he didn't see it. He went smack bang into it. The doctor said he must have died instantaneously," said Naidu.

"What a shame. One silly mistake by one person, and such a tragedy results to a completely different person. I always thought that road was dangerous. But even if it was black, how did he miss the drum?"

"There was a power cut and all the street lights were off that night. And you know something? It gets worse."

"How can it be worse?" asked Mr. Ali.

"Gopal spent a lot of money on the wedding. He gave a big dowry as well because his son-in-law had a good job. He is still paying off the debts he incurred for the wedding. His son-in-law had an insurance policy for fifteen lakhs. Unfortunately, he had taken it out before he got married, naming his parents as beneficiaries and never changed it after the wedding. The insurance company is paying out the money to his parents. They have driven the poor girl out of the house without a single paisa to her name," said Naidu.

"What?" said Mr. Ali. "How can they do that? Can't she go to court?"

"Gopal has consulted a lawyer but the lawyer thinks the case will take a long time to settle. He has told them to try and settle it out of court but the in-laws are just refusing to talk to Gopal. They are claiming that their son died because of his daughter's ill luck."

"How ridiculous. . . . What a shame," said Mr. Ali.

They sat silent for some time, each occupied in his own thoughts. Mr. Ali took his leave, subdued.

When he arrived home, Mr. Ali saw Aruna dealing with a customer. She was saying, "We have members in America, sir. I am sure we can help."

The customer paid his fees and left soon after.

After the customer left, Aruna turned to Mr. Ali and said, "I can't believe these people, sir. That man who just left is fixated on getting a son-in-law in America and sending his daughter away. He is a well-off man, and looking at the photograph, his daughter is good-looking. He could easily find a son-in-law locally—his daughter will be close by, instead of across the seven seas. Why do people have such specific requirements? Why don't they compromise?"

He said, "I don't know why people don't compromise. But let me tell you a story. Did you know we used to have a cat?"

"A cat? No, I didn't know that."

"Oh, yes! This was several years ago. A white, fluffy cat with a lovely tail. It had one blue and one green eye. You don't get cats like that here."

Mrs. Ali came out and, noticing that there were no clients, sat down with them. "Do you remember our cat?" asked Mr. Ali.

"Of course," replied Mrs. Ali. "She was so lovely. She never stole any milk or fish at all; just waited patiently until I poured milk into a saucer or gave her a fish head. In fact, she used to drive away other cats from our kitchen."

"If it's not a breed that lives here, how did you get it?" asked Aruna.

Mr. Ali said, "One day I went to the market to buy some vegetables. As I was coming out, I saw this cat at bay against a wall being barked at by three dogs. They looked ready to tear her to pieces, so I threw a stone at them. The dogs ran off with their tails between their legs and I went up to the cat. Surprisingly, it didn't have any fear of human beings. The poor mite let me pick it up without any fuss. It was little more than a kitten and quite unlike any stray that I had ever seen. I brought it home with me."

"I remember when it came home. I don't like animals and we've never had a pet before. But she looked so pretty that I couldn't help falling in love with her immediately. I gave it a saucer of milk and she just lapped it up," said Mrs. Ali.

"That's right. Everybody fell in love with it as soon as they saw it. We just adopted it and the cat started living with us. After a couple of years, I started thinking about a mate for it. I searched high and low for another cat like that, but there wasn't one to be found. I had been looking for a few months without any success when suddenly it disappeared. Rehman was inconsolable. Both of us were quite upset. We thought that maybe it had died in an accident. We still missed it, but after a couple of months we had given up looking for it, and suddenly, it turned up again. It was heavily pregnant and went straight into a cupboard," said Mr. Ali.

He continued, "The next day, she gave birth to three kittens— mongrels. They were not white like their mother. They had dirty brown marks all over their bodies. But our cat loved them to bits. She groomed them, fed them, taught them all tricks, like climbing trees and catching mice."

"What did you do with the kittens?" asked Aruna.

"Once they had grown up a bit and could look after themselves, I took them to the fish market and left them there," said Mr. Ali. "I was looking for the perfect mate for our cat. But all she was interested in was a healthy male. She didn't mind that her kittens were mongrels. She loved them. That's the mistake people make—always searching for the perfect match, when they would be just as happy if they settled for somebody reasonably good."

"What stories you tell," said Mrs. Ali, laughing for the first time since the day before. "How can you compare human beings and animals? It doesn't make sense."

Mr. Ali shook his head and said, "It is true, though. Many men think that their daughters will only be happy if their son-in-law is a rich officer or a software engineer in California. That's not necessarily true. You need a man with good character who will respect his wife. If you have that, any woman will be happy, even if money is tight. If a husband comes home drunk or chases after other females, it doesn't matter if they live in a big house with lots of servants, she will still be miserable."

Mrs. Ali said, "What you are saying is true, but what if a woman could get a rich husband who didn't have any bad habits *and* respected her?"

Mr. Ali smiled. "Then they would live happily ever after."

Aruna said sadly, "And such stories usually begin, Once upon a time."

Some days later, Aruna and Mr. Ali were busy talking to a client. The client was not sure that the fee was worth paying and they were trying to convince him to join. Aruna gave the client a specimen list of suitable grooms, and the man started looking through it. The specimen list had all the details of the members but only incomplete addresses and phone numbers.

While the client was busy going through the list, Irshad came in.

Mr. Ali turned to him and smiled in welcome. "Hello, Irshad. What brings you back?" he asked.

"Good news, sir," exclaimed Irshad. He rummaged through his bag and took out two white envelopes. He gave one each to Mr. Ali and Aruna. The four corners of the envelopes were colored yellow with turmeric and the words "Wedding Invitation" were written in flowery cursive letters across the top.

They opened their envelopes and took out the invitation cards. The invitation was from Irshad's mother. At the top of the card, there was a picture of a crescent moon with a star above it. Under the moon and star, the words "In the name of Allah, most merciful, most beneficent" were written in small letters. The invitation itself read, 'Mrs. Ameena Khatoun, wife of late Janab Mohammed Ilyas, retired tehsildar, village officer, requests your gracious presence for the auspicious occasion of the wedding of her son, Mohammed Irshad, with Aisha, daughter of Janab Syed Jalaluddin, shopkeeper."

The invitation gave the address of the marriage venue and the time—ten in the morning on a Sunday in a month's time at the bride's house in Kottavalasa. Mr. Ali came out from behind his desk smiling.

Irshad extended his arm to shake hands with Mr. Ali. Mr. Ali brushed it aside and hugged him. "Congratulations. May you have a happy married life," said Mr. Ali.

"I owe it all to you, sir. If you had not taken a personal interest, it would not have happened," said Irshad, obviously emotional.

"Did you go to Kottavalasa to meet the bride and her parents?" asked Mr. Ali.

"Yes, sir. My mum and I went with the imam—the priest—at our local mosque. The whole match got settled in that one visit."

Aruna asked, "Did you talk to Aisha?"

Irshad blushed. He said, "For a few minutes, miss. She is quite a clever girl. She has written stories and published recipes in a weekly magazine."

Aruna asked, looking very innocent, "Is she good-looking?"

He blushed even more. "Yes, miss. She is very pretty."

Aruna continued, "What was she wearing?"

Irshad's body twisted in embarrassment. He hemmed and hawed for a bit and then said, "A sari."

"Obviously she would be wearing a sari at a formal occasion like that, but what color was it?" asked Aruna.

He thought for a moment, then said, "Orange, I think."

"Aren't you sure?" asked Aruna.

"Not really. All I noticed were her eyes. She had large, doelike eyes, they shone like marbles. . . . And I noticed that she was wearing fragrant jasmine flowers in her hair."

Aruna said, "If you want a happy married life, you should notice what your wife is wearing and you should compliment her if you think it suits her."

Mr. Ali said, "If you want an even happier married life, you should compliment your wife even when you think that what she is wearing doesn't suit her."

Everybody, including the client, laughed—Irshad, nervously. Mr. Ali turned to Aruna and said, "Stop it, girl. You are embarrassing the poor man."

He turned to Irshad and said, "Congrats again, Irshad, and thanks for coming and giving us the invitations. Most people would rather forget that their match was organized through a marriage bureau."

"How can I forget, sir? It is all due to you. You must definitely come to the wedding. In fact, you won't be just another guest; you will be a wedding elder. I will send a taxi for all of you to come to the wedding and bring you back again."

Mr. Ali said, "Okay. How can we refuse such an invitation? Mrs. Ali and I will both come."

Irshad turned to Aruna and asked, "What about you, miss?"

Aruna shook her head. "I am sorry. It is too far out of town. I won't be able to come."

"I understand. We may have a valima in town when we get back. You should come for that, at least."

Aruna looked blank. Mr. Ali explained, "We Muslims call the reception after the wedding a 'valima.' It is organized by the groom's side."

Aruna nodded in understanding. "I might come for that. If you don't hold a reception, you must bring Aisha here, so I can meet her," she said.

"Of course . . ."

Irshad took his leave.

The client had finished looking at his list a long time ago and had been following their conversation with interest. Once Irshad left, he said, "I will become a member. Here are the fees."

Mr. Ali pocketed the fee. "You won't regret it," he said.

As Aruna was packing up for the morning and leaving for lunch, Mr. Ali gave her the commission from the new member's fee. He said, "I didn't think he would join. He wasn't convinced that we could help his daughter. He must have changed his mind after seeing Irshad."

Aruna put the money away and said, "I am sure that helped, sir. Maybe we should hire an actor, and whenever there is a potential client who needs convincing, I can call him secretly and he can come in just like Irshad and tell us that we've done a great service and found a bride for him. 'Sir,' he could say, 'you are truly great. I had despaired of ever finding a good match but you people solved my problems in a jiffy.

Here is ten thousand rupees as a token of my gratitude.' You would refuse the money and he would reply, 'You must keep it. You deserve every paisa. I cannot tell you how grateful I am.' "

Mr. Ali laughed and said, "Aruna, you are wicked. Go home for lunch."

Aruna was at home, eating her lunch, sitting cross-legged on the floor in the kitchen. She chewed without interest, barely tasting the rice with sambhar and sautéed ridged gourd. Her sister, Vani, was away at college. Her father was lying down on the bed in the other room, with the ancient ceiling fan whirring noisily over his head. Aruna's mother was sitting in front of her on a four-inch-high wooden stool, silently swinging the palm-leaf fan so they both got a bit of a breeze.

For a brief time in Mr. Ali's house, she had forgotten the troubles in her life; but now they all came tumbling back on her. Shastry-uncle had come more than once and tried to talk her father around regarding her marriage, but he was adamant. He said he couldn't afford to get Aruna married and that was that. The last time, he had been quite rude to Shastry-uncle and told him not to come to their house again if that was all he could talk about.

Her mother had then picked a fight with him that had still not died down, and all the members of the household walked cautiously around one another. The tension was palpable. They didn't eat their meals together anymore. Aruna's father ate on his own in the living room, and her mother ate with Aruna in the kitchen. Vani had started coming home late from college, and when her father asked her why she was late, she gave monosyllabic answers.

Aruna's mother broke the silence. "We need to buy oil. I don't want to ask your dad for money. You know how he is nowadays."

Aruna nodded. "No problem, amma. I'll drop into the shop on my way back this evening and order some. I got my salary last week."

Aruna's mother sighed and looked unhappy. Aruna knew that if she had been a son, her mother wouldn't have minded asking her for money—in fact, she would have demanded it as a right. But Aruna was aware that her mother, a traditional Indian woman, felt that taking money from a daughter was just not right.

On Monday, Mr. Ali was sitting down at the table in his office, working. Mrs. Ali was going to see her old widowed neighbor, Lakshmi. Another ex-neighbor, Anjali, had told her that Lakshmi had been kicked out by her son and was now living with her sister. Mrs. Ali wanted to try and reconcile Lakshmi and her son. Mr. Ali would come down later and pick her up.

"I've kept lunch for you on the table. After you've eaten, don't leave your plate there. Put it in the kitchen sink and run some water over it," said Mrs. Ali.

Mr. Ali nodded his head.

"And don't forget to close the dishes after you've served yourself. Flies will sit on the food otherwise," she said.

Mr. Ali nodded his head.

"I've latched the kitchen door from outside. Leela said she will come late today. She will get into the kitchen from outside and do her work. Keep an eye out and make sure that the kitchen door is closed after she leaves. Otherwise, the cats will come in and drink all the milk."

Mr. Ali nodded his head.

"And don't leave the house and come down in a couple of hours and then hurry me back. I don't like that," she said.

Mr. Ali sighed and nodded. He said, "Okay . . . You'd better go, otherwise it will be time for me to pick you up even before you leave."

Mrs. Ali finally left, and Mr. Ali went back to his work.

He went through the lists and marked out those that were running low. Aruna would type out the details of the latest members to make up new lists. One of the ads had been printed incorrectly the previous day in the *Indian Express*. He called up the classifieds department and got them to agree to repeat the ad next Sunday free of charge. He went through the stationery cupboard to figure out if he needed to buy more supplies.

He was making a note to himself to buy envelopes and staples when a young woman in her early twenties walked in. She was tall, slim, slightly dark, and was wearing an elegant chiffon sari. She did not have a mangalsootram and did not appear to be married.

The woman brought her hands together and Mr. Ali did the same.

"Namaste, is this the marriage bureau?" she asked in a soft voice.

"Yes, miss. Please take a seat. How can I help you? I am Mr. Ali."

The woman sat down and stared at the floor, awkwardly twisting the end of her sari in her hand. Mr. Ali waited for a bit and when the woman did not proceed, he said, "It is okay, my dear. Don't be embarrassed. Who is the match for?"

"Myself," she said.

Mr. Ali took out an application form and gave it to her. He said, "Why don't you fill this in? We will talk after that."

The woman smiled at him and got busy filling in the form.

Mr. Ali went back to his work.

A few minutes later, she looked up and said, "Sir . . ."

Mr. Ali looked up from his work, took the form from her, and went through it.

Her name was Sridevi; she was from the Kamma community—a dominant caste of farmers and landowners who now owned aqua farms and software companies. She was twenty-three years old, a business graduate running a florist shop. According to the form, she didn't have any family money behind her, but was earning a good income.

Mr. Ali asked, "There aren't many florists in town. Where is your shop?"

Sridevi named a five-star hotel. "It is in the lobby," she said.

"Is it your own or do you just manage it?" asked Mr. Ali.

"It is my own," said Sridevi.

"The rent there must be quite expensive."

"No. They didn't have a florist, so I talked to the manager and convinced him to let me have a small place in the lobby for a percentage of the receipts. It has done really well and they've given me a bigger unit," explained Sridevi.

Mr. Ali nodded. It couldn't have been as easy as Sridevi said. She must be a formidable woman to achieve her success without family backing. Mr. Ali continued reading through the form. At the end, he found out why she had come on her own and had been so uncomfortable: she was a divorcée.

"How long were you married?" asked Mr. Ali.

"Fifteen months."

"What happened?" he asked.

"We had fights all the time—he was completely under his parents' control. They didn't want their daughter-in-law to work. I couldn't just stay at home all day but he wouldn't let me work. His family wanted us to have children as soon as possible and that's what he pushed for as well. It just became intolerable. After a few months, they even dragged me to visit a gynecologist, thinking that there must be some problem with me if I was not getting pregnant. I refused to talk to them after that and matters got worse," said Sridevi. She looked at him boldly, as if daring him to criticize her.

Mr. Ali said, "I am not judging you, Sridevi. You must have had your reasons. Didn't you tell your family what was going on?"

Sridevi didn't say anything for a moment. She took a deep breath and said, "I told them, but they said I was wrong to go against my in-laws' wishes. My father even said that it was a mistake to have educated me. He said it had given me *ideas*. Since my divorce, he refuses to talk to me."

"That's tough. What about your mother?" asked Mr. Ali.

"She comes secretly once in a while to meet me. She keeps asking me to go back to my husband, but I don't want to go through that again. I want to start afresh with somebody who accepts what I am."

"I must tell you right now, Sridevi. You are a young girl with no kids, but most guys who are willing to marry a widow or a divorcée will be much older and probably have kids as well," said Mr. Ali.

"I know that, sir. I am not in a hurry. I can wait until the right match comes along."

"Let's go through our lists," said Mr. Ali, turning to the cupboard that held the files.

He took out a list of Kamma grooms. It had only two men who were willing to consider second marriages—one was in his late forties and the other was fifty.

Mr. Ali said, "I will advertise your details in a couple of newspapers, and let's see if something turns up."

Sridevi said, "No, sir. For all that this is supposed to be a city, Vizag is just an overgrown town, and people in our community will guess it is about me if you advertise. Tongues will start wagging and I'd rather avoid that. As I said, I am not in a hurry and I can wait."

"Are you sure? There is no guarantee we will find anybody suitable," said Mr. Ali.

"There are no guarantees in this life, sir. That's one thing I've learned in the last couple of years," said Sridevi, standing up to go.

"Have you talked to anybody else about this? If not your family, then your friends . . ." said Mr. Ali.

Sridevi shook her head. "Not really. It is very difficult. People don't understand. It was very difficult even to find a place to live, because nobody wanted to rent their house to a divorced woman. Luckily, I found a good lawyer, and she made sure I got a flat as part of the divorce settlement. It is very strange—as a florist, I go to so many parties and functions, decorating the halls and stages. But I cannot go to any functions in my own house. My cousin got married last month and I didn't get an invitation. It is almost as if I am a widow—even worse, in fact: I've become invisible."

ELEVEN

A few days later, Mr. Ali was at his seat working with Aruna. It was midmorning, and suddenly the light changed. The harsh, bright light mellowed and took on a more brownish hue. Mr. Ali looked up and said, "I think it is going to rain."

He got up from the table and went to the door. He could smell the earth and knew the rain wasn't far away. Behind him, he heard Aruna shout, "Madam, it is going to rain."

As the first drops fell, he was shoved aside as Mrs. Ali ran past him, almost athletically, to a cotton sheet on which tamarind was drying. Aruna came out as well and helped Mrs. Ali collect the four corners of the sheet together and move it indoors.

Mrs. Ali said, "You shouldn't have just stood there looking at the rain. If Aruna hadn't told me, the tamarind would have got wet and spoilt."

Mr. Ali, who had not actually noticed the tamarind, even though it had been right in front of him, did not say anything. Aruna and Mrs. Ali went inside.

He was more interested in the rain. It was not the proper monsoon season yet. This must be a pre-monsoon shower. He looked on as the fat raindrops fell on the dry earth. Azhar came running out of the rain, opened the outside gate, and rushed to stand by Mr. Ali, out of the wet.

"Why did you come in the rain?" asked Mr. Ali.

"I didn't know it was going to rain, did I? It was perfectly sunny when I left the house," said Azhar.

Mr. Ali said, "Do you remember the old verse:

When the Bronze-winged Jacana shrieks,
When the Black Cobra climbs trees,
When the Red Ant carries white eggs,
Then the Rain cascades. "

"You have a good memory," Azhar said. "I haven't heard that for years. My grandmother used to sing it when I was a boy. Mind you, if I saw a cobra climbing a tree, rain won't be the first thing on my mind."

Mr. Ali laughed.

"I wonder if the monsoons will be good this year?" said Mr. Ali.

"I hope so," said Azhar. "That's what the meteorologists are predicting, so let's see."

"Yes," said Mr. Ali reflectively. "So much of India relies on the monsoons. Not just farmers, but birds, animals, and trees, too."

They were both silent, looking at the way the parched earth was soaking up the water and releasing its pent-up heat.

"You didn't tell me why you came here, anyway," said Mr. Ali.

"It is the first of the month, isn't it? I am not like my brother-in-law who earns so much money from the marriage bureau that he doesn't know what date it is. I am going to collect my pension," Azhar said.

Mr. Ali laughed and then became serious. "Any news of Rehman?" he asked.

"My inspector friend said they will be charged soon, in another day or so," said Azhar.

"What charge?" asked Mr. Ali.

"He thinks it will be breaking the peace," said Azhar.

"That doesn't sound too bad," said Mr. Ali.

Azhar looked carefully around and lowered his voice, "Don't tell aapa, but my friend says that the police in Royyapalem have been asked to find some evidence—any evidence—so they can be charged with something more serious, like criminal damage," he said.

"I was afraid of something like that. Do you really think they'll make up something just to get them?" he asked.

"Didn't you read the papers today? The boys have kicked off something big. The protest has been picked up by the media, and the whole village is up in arms. The government has declared Section One Hundred and Forty-four in that whole area."

"Section One Forty-four? That means a curfew, doesn't it?" asked Mr. Ali.

"Not quite," said Azhar. "At this stage, they've just banned any gatherings of more than five people. But I think it has gone past that. I think the whole project is in trouble."

The rain stopped and Azhar said he had to go.

"At least come into the house and have tea," Mr. Ali said.

Azhar said, "No, I'd better go. If it gets any later, the lines will build up in the bank. By the way, what are you doing this evening? A few of us are going to the beach. Do you want to come too?"

"In this rain?" asked Mr. Ali.

"This is just a squall. It has already stopped. By evening, it will be pretty hot again," said Azhar.

"Who is coming?" asked Mr. Ali.

"About ten or fifteen people—Sanyasi will be there," said Azhar, naming a common friend.

Mr. Ali thought for a moment and then said, "It's been a while since I've gone out with you guys. Let's go."

That evening, Aruna was looking after the office on her own. Mr. Ali had gone to the beach and Mrs. Ali was busy inside the house making dinner. A young man walked in and Aruna looked up from her typing.

He said, "Hello, Aruna."

Aruna saw the handsome doctor who had become a member a few weeks ago. "Hello, Mr. Ramanujam," she said. She was surprised that he had remembered her name.

"Is Mr. Ali here?" he asked.

"No. He had to go out," said Aruna.

"Oh! Apparently, my sister called him yesterday and he asked her to come today because there was a new list. My sister couldn't come, so she asked me to collect it."

"Yes, something came up just this morning and he must have forgotten that he asked your sister to come in. Anyway, I can help you," said Aruna.

"Thank you," he said with a smile.

"I remember, you are Brahmins, aren't you?" she said. Aruna knew Ramanujam was a Brahmin, but she asked anyway.

"That's correct," he said.

Aruna stood up and went to the cupboard that held the lists. She took out the correct list and handed it to Ramanujam.

As he took the list from her, Aruna noticed that he was wearing a golden watch that looked very expensive. His nails were neatly trimmed and he had long, tapering fingers. She was suddenly conscious that her dress was old and faded.

Ramanujam looked through the list.

"Do you want me to put it in an envelope?" asked Aruna.

"No need," he said, smiling at her.

"Does your sister live locally?" asked Aruna.

"Yes. She is married to an industrialist in town," Ramanujam said. He laughed. "I don't know exactly what he does, but the steel plant is one of his big customers."

Aruna nodded. They were obviously a rich family and his words just confirmed it.

"What about you?" asked Ramanujam. "Do you have any brothers or sisters?"

"I have a younger sister. She is still in college," said Aruna.

"What about you? What did you study?" he asked.

"I have a B.A. degree in Telugu and social science."

"Oh! A scholar," said Ramanujam.

Aruna shrugged. "I actually wanted to study for a master's degree, but I had to leave my studies," she said. As soon as the words left her mouth, she cringed internally. She wondered why she had said that.

"Why did you have to leave your studies?" asked Ramanujam.

"We couldn't afford it anymore. Also, my wedding was almost fixed and I didn't want to start something when I wasn't sure I would be able to continue it."

She tried to speak lightly but Aruna couldn't keep the tremor out of her voice. She picked up a piece of paper from the desk and turned to the cupboard.

"What happened to the wedding?" he asked. He must have noticed her hesitate because he added, "You don't have to tell me if you'd rather not."

Aruna sighed. "It's very simple. My father fell ill and he was in hospital for a long time. Most of our savings were exhausted."

Ramanujam said, "If he broke off the wedding because your father was not well, then maybe he wasn't such a good guy. You will probably find somebody even better."

Aruna shook her head. "No," she said. "He was—is—a good man. He married a distant cousin of mine. They are very happy. My cousin is the mother of a lovely boy," said Aruna.

Aruna thought that her heart would break. Sushil was the first match that had been proposed to her. The match had been perfect in almost every way and Aruna had fallen in love with him at first sight. At least, she thought it was love. She wasn't sure if what she had felt was love; she just knew that she had never felt those emotions before. She met him thrice—each time she had felt breathless when told that he and his family were coming over; each time she was almost tongue-tied when actually face to face with him. She had taken great care of her appearance—wearing her best saris, now sold for household utensils; plaiting her long tresses with a colored ribbon; wearing her gold necklace and earrings; and applying just a touch of talcum powder to her face and neck, to appear fairer than she really was.

She had been ecstatic when he had brought a string of jasmine flowers for her hair the third time he had come to visit her. He came without his mother or any other family—straight from work. Her father had been out and Aruna could see that her mother was scandalized that Sushil had turned up at their house without his family. Aruna's mother sent Vani over to their neighbor's house and had gone into the kitchen and left Aruna and Sushil in the living room talking to each other. Aruna and Sushil had talked for over forty-five minutes about all sorts of things. He had told her that he liked a particular South Indian film actress and she had teased him that the actress's nose was too wide. She told him that she had never been out of their state, and he had told her that he would remedy it as soon as possible after the wedding. He had told her that he would take her to Chennai and the hill station of Ooty. He had mentioned the word "honeymoon" and she had blushed furiously and gone into the kitchen to see if her mother needed any help. Her mother didn't need any help, of course, and so she had come back into the living room in less than five minutes and started talking again. He had apologized profusely for talking like that and she had prettily accepted his apology.

Sushil had asked her if she liked any film stars. She had shaken her head no. "Not even Chiranjeevi?" he had asked, naming the most popular Telugu film star.

"No. Anyway, boys like him more than girls, because he acts in all those action movies," she replied.

They even talked about serious topics: Why did he think the weather was getting hotter every year? What did she think about coalition governments? Should Naxalites—Maoist guerrillas—be supported when they burned down liquor shops in tribal villages?

They agreed on some subjects but not on others. Their agreements brought them closer—conspirators against the world; their disagreements added passion to their chat.

The talk had moved on to careers. He had asked her if she wanted to work after marriage, and she had replied that she would like to work somewhere if she could find a job and it was all right with him—and his family.

"I don't mind," he had replied. "My mother might not like it—let us see."

She truly hadn't minded, either way. She knew his mother would be difficult to get along with, but she was confident that in time she would win her over. She was in love with her fiancé. The sun shone in the heavens, the world was bright, anything was possible.

Vani came back from their neighbor's place—and Aruna had never hated her sister so fiercely. Her mother brought some boorulu from the kitchen. Sushil had taken a bite into one and burnt his tongue on the hot jaggery core. He had waved his hand in pain from the hot sugar, and Aruna had rushed into the kitchen to get a glass of cool water. She had hovered over him and had asked if he was all right at least three times, until he had assured her that he was fine and it was just a momentary shock. She had looked anxiously at him and their eyes had met—almost like a scene from a movie.

Her father had returned soon after Sushil had gone. Aruna and her mother kept quiet about the visit, but Vani thoughtlessly revealed it to their father. Her father was not happy at this unchaperoned visit but he didn't say anything. After all, the man was practically his son-in-law.

Aruna had gone to bed extremely happy. All night long, she had had vague dreams of Sushil and herself visiting a very atmospheric mountain valley with rolling fog. It was cold in the mountains and the two were walking down a mountain path wrapped in a single blanket. Delicious feelings tingled through her. She had woken up happy—hugging the memories of the previous evening tightly in her mind. She had remained in that state of mind for three more days, until the night her father had cried out from bed, unable to get up, and the dreams had slowly faded away as color was leached from her life, from her clothes, from her soul.

Aruna had never spoken about these events and feelings to anybody, not even to her mother or sister. She certainly couldn't tell the whole story to Ramanujam. But she couldn't hold it all inside, either. She now related some of it—just the bare facts.

Aruna and Ramanujam kept talking. He talked about his college days—he had done his Bachelor of Medicine in town at the Andhra Medical College, but his postgraduation as an M.D. in neurosurgery had been at the premier All India Institute of Medical Sciences in Delhi.

Aruna was impressed. "AIIMS? Isn't it supposed to be difficult to get into?" she asked.

Ramanujam shrugged. "It's a great institute. The campus is lovely and you get the best professors there. But for all that I learned at the college, I think I learned just as much staying in a hostel away from my family."

"I've never stayed away from my family. The only times I stayed away from home was when I stayed at Shastry-uncle's house for the summer holidays when I was younger," said Aruna.

Ramanujam said, "There were girls too in AIIMS. We boys were not allowed inside their hostel but they could come and visit us. If we wanted to meet one of the girls at the hostel, we had to stay in the front lounge and wait for somebody to walk past and then ask them if they would take a message for you. Some girls were pretty nosy. They wanted to know why we wanted to meet the girl; they asked all sorts of questions and then refused to take the message."

"It must have taught you patience," teased Aruna.

"It was frustrating. While we stood there, the milkman would walk past, the postman would walk past, the washer man, the canteen boy, the gardeners—in fact, all sorts of guys would be walking past, but we students couldn't cross the line in front of the lounge," said Ramanujam.

"Like a Lakshman Rekha," observed Aruna, referring to the line drawn by Lakshmana to keep his brother Ram's faithful wife, Sita, safe from all danger in the Hindu epic *Ramayana.*

"Exactly like a Lakshman Rekha, though some of the girls in the hostel did not exactly take Sita as their role model," laughed Ramanujam.

Aruna asked, "So how many times did you stand outside the ladies' hostel waiting for somebody to deliver your message?"

Ramanujam replied, "Not often—just three or four times."

Aruna laughed. "Yeah! Right!"

"No, really," said Ramanujam. "Besides, it was more fun to meet the girls in Singh's tea shop."

She laughed at his naughty grin.

Mrs. Ali suddenly called out from inside the house, "Aruna, why haven't you switched on the lights?"

Aruna realized with a jolt that it had grown quite dark. She replied to Mrs. Ali, "Sorry, madam. I am switching the lights on now."

She got up and switched on the light. The long white tube flickered a couple of times and then came on. Aruna closed her eyes, said a small prayer, and touched her forehead with the tips of her fingers.

Mrs. Ali came out and saw Ramanujam. "Sorry," she said to Aruna. "I didn't realize you had a client."

She went back into the house. Aruna felt guilty. It was very unusual not to have any clients visiting them in the evening. Had anybody left without coming in because the lights were not on and the front of the house was in darkness?

She turned to her files and said to Ramanujam, "We received one match that might be of interest to you. It came yesterday by post and it hasn't gone into the list yet."

She copied the details of the match—the daughter of a member of the Legislative Assembly—on a piece of paper and gave it to Ramanujam. "We don't have a photo of the girl. Her father writes in the letter that he will come by and have a chat with us when the Assembly breaks up and he comes back from Hyderabad."

She didn't need to say that the bride's family was wealthy. Everyone knew that politicians were all rich. Ramanujam looked through the details. "Thanks," he said. "I am not sure I really want to marry into a politician's family."

He looked at her and said, "It's time I was leaving. Do you know what time Mr. Ali will be back?"

Aruna shook her head. "I don't know what time sir will be back," she said.

Ramanujam nodded and made no move to leave. "Normally, I run my private clinic at this time, but not on Tuesdays, because that's the day I have two surgical sessions at the government hospital," he said.

Ramanujam told Aruna about the surgery he had carried out that day. A young man had been brought in from a village with epileptic fits. The fits were so violent that he could not travel in a bus or train. The family had tied him up on a string bed and had brought him on a bullock cart. The young man had been recently married and his wife had come along, as well as the man's parents. He told Aruna how the man's parents were ill-treating the poor woman, blaming her for their son's illness.

Aruna sighed in sympathy. If a man fell ill or lost his job soon after getting married, everybody blamed the poor bride for bringing bad luck into the family. Strangely, it didn't work the other way around—it wasn't the man's fault if the woman fell ill after marriage. In fact, the woman was scorned for not being a healthy bride.

"How did the operation go? Is he cured?" she asked.

"Well, we took the tumor out. He still hasn't woken up from the anesthesia. We'll know in the next few days."

Ramanujam looked at his watch. "I've got to go," he said.

Aruna smiled at him. She said, "I hope I didn't bore you."

"Not at all," replied Ramanujam. "I had a very pleasant evening. I hope I didn't keep you from your work. Thanks for giving me the list."

"No problem. I hope you find a proper bride in the list," she said, smiling.

Ramanujam rolled his eyes and got up.

Aruna stood up as well. "It's time for me to go, too," she said.

She put the papers away and closed the cupboard doors. She had already tidied the table away while talking to Ramanujam and she was ready in a minute. She put her handbag—a new purchase—over her shoulder, peeked into the house behind the curtain, and called out to Mrs. Ali, "I'm going, madam."

Mrs. Ali was on the phone. She covered the phone's mouthpiece with her hand and smiled at her. "Please close the door behind you," she said.

Aruna and Ramanujam left the house together. Aruna closed the door and closed the bolt through the iron grille. She put on her shoes and they walked out onto the road. Ramanujam's gleaming milky white car was parked outside. Aruna didn't know much about cars, but she could tell it was an expensive model. He clicked on the key fob and the car beeped and flashed its indicator lights twice. Ramanujam opened the door and turned to Aruna. "Do you want me to drop you off?" he asked.

"No, thanks," replied Aruna. She was tempted, but knew that if people saw her getting out of a car driven by a stranger, they would talk.

"Are you sure?" he asked.

"Yes, it is not far and I have to pick up vegetables on the way," she replied.

"All right, then. See you soon," he said, and turned to sit down in the car. Aruna stepped away from the car and started to walk.

"Aruna," he called out, and she turned.

"Yes?" she asked.

"Here's my card. It has my mobile number on it. If any suitable Brahmin girls become members, please call me," he said.

She looked at him quizzically.

"I want to check out the details before my sister or my mother sees them," he said.

"Are you afraid they'll force you to marry somebody you don't like?" she asked, laughing.

"No, nothing like that. But it is easier if they don't even see somebody I don't like; I won't have to keep refusing them," he said.

Aruna nodded. "No problem," she said, taking the card and putting it in her handbag.

TWELVE

The next day, Mr. Ali and Aruna were going through their lists to identify nonmembers. These were people who had responded to ads but had never become members themselves. Mr. Ali wanted to write to them reminding them to become members. They had been at this task for over an hour when Mrs. Ali finished preparing lunch and came out with three glasses of cool sherbet and sat with them. She used the end of her sari to wipe her brow and brought the chair a little forward to better catch the breeze from the fan. Mr. Ali saw the drinks and called a stop to their work.

"Let's take a break," he said. "This is hard work."

The three were silent for a few minutes while they sipped the dark red drink.

"What is this, madam?" asked Aruna. "I've never had this drink before."

"This is Rooh Afza. I suppose you can call it rose syrup. It is an old cooling drink used by Muslims. Most young people don't know about it now—they all drink Coke or Pepsi," said Mrs. Ali.

After some time, Mrs. Ali asked her husband, "So, what did all you oldies do on the beach yesterday?"

Mr. Ali laughed. "The usual—we walked along the beach, talked about our aches and pains and how much money our sons are earning or how much our little houses are now worth."

Mrs. Ali asked, "How many of you were there?"

Mr. Ali thought for a moment and said, "About eight of us. Oh, one more thing happened . . ."

Mrs. Ali frowned. "What happened?" she asked softly.

"As Azhar and I reached the beach, a Christian missionary stopped us. He started telling us how the Bible was the one true book and we should follow it if we wanted to go to heaven," said Mr. Ali.

"I bet Azhar walked away from him and you didn't," said Mrs. Ali.

"How did you know?" asked a surprised Mr. Ali. "I looked around and Azhar had disappeared. I told the missionary that it was a miracle, the way my brother-in-law had disappeared, but I don't think he had a sense of humor."

"Poor man," said Mrs. Ali in a sympathetic voice.

"Yes, I know. Here I was, ready to join my friends on the beach and this guy stops me and wants to talk religion," said Mr. Ali.

"Not you. I meant the missionary. Poor man, that he encountered you. You must have destroyed his confidence," said Mrs. Ali.

Aruna laughed. Mr. Ali looked at her severely and she bent her head, studiously looking at the lists.

"What do you mean?" asked Mr. Ali, turning to his wife.

"Did you or did you not exchange words with him?" asked Mrs. Ali.

"Yes, but—" said Mr. Ali.

"What exactly did you tell him?" said Mrs. Ali.

"Well, he showed me a pamphlet that he said proved the truth of the Bible. The pamphlet talked about how the Bible gave the order of creation of animal life—fish, reptiles, birds, land animals, and finally, men. He said that the probability of getting such a sequence right was one in many billions—that it proved the Bible must have been divinely inspired. He asked me to come to their church to hear more about the Bible and save myself from eternal damnation."

"What did you tell him? Did you insult him?" she asked faintly.

"Insult him? No! That was your brother who insulted him by rudely disappearing as soon as he opened his mouth. I did the courtesy of listening to his spiel and responding to him," he said.

"That's what I'm afraid of," said Mrs. Ali.

"I pointed out to him that the Quran had the sequence the same way. I asked him if that didn't mean that the Quran was divinely inspired too. He said that he didn't know the Quran, so he couldn't say," said Mr. Ali.

"Did you invite him to our house to study the Quran?" asked Mrs. Ali.

"No, don't be silly, woman," said Mr. Ali, exasperated. "I said, fair enough, you don't know the Quran, but surely you know about the Dusavatar of Hindu mythology. He said yes. I asked him if he knew the order of the ten avatars of God that came down to earth to destroy evil."

Aruna looked up in interest.

"I said the order of the ten avatars started fish, tortoise, boar, then half man, half beast. . . . Isn't that correct?" he asked, turning to Aruna.

Aruna nodded. "That's correct—the Dusavatars start off as Matsya, Koorma, Varaha, Narasimha, and the rest are human avatars," she said.

"I said to the guy, What a coincidence. Wasn't Hindu mythology divinely inspired, too? And since all our religions are saying the same thing, why go through the hassle of converting from one religion to another? I was born a Muslim and I am happy to remain one."

Mr. Ali looked at both women, as if expecting applause at his cleverness.

Mrs. Ali shook her head from side to side. She said, "Husband, one day somebody will bash you up. I just don't know if it's going to be Hindus, Christians, or Muslims."

"It is true, though. You ask almost any illiterate villager in India and he will tell you that God is one and religions are man-made. So why do all these so-called educated people with degrees create troubles in the name of religion?" said Mr. Ali.

"You cannot talk like that. People take these things seriously. I'm telling you again, somebody will beat you up one day," said Mrs. Ali.

Aruna nodded in agreement. "Madam is right, sir. You have to be careful about these things."

They went back to work. Mrs. Ali sat with them reading the Telugu newspaper. After a little while, she stood up and said, "Aruna, tomorrow we will be busy. We have to go to court. You will have to look after the office yourself."

"That's all right, madam. But why do you have to go to court?" said Aruna.

Mrs. Ali sighed and said, "It's a long story. Maybe sir can tell you."

She went inside the house.

"Akka, I got first class!" shouted Vani as soon as Aruna entered the house that evening after leaving the office.

Aruna broke into a smile and gave her a high-five and hugged her. Their mother was smiling proudly and so was their father. The whole family felt close and Aruna's heart almost broke when she realized how long it had been since they had all been happy together.

Somebody knocked on the door and her father opened it. They all looked out, and Aruna said, "It's the shopboy. I ordered rice on the way home."

She went to the door and made sure the rice was the same variety that she had ordered. She gave the boy a small tip and sent him away.

Her mother asked, "Have you paid for the rice?"

Aruna said, "Yes, amma. I paid for it at the time of ordering."

They all sat down on a mat in the living room for dinner. Their mother served steamed rice and the thin tamarind rasam with fried eggplants and cauliflower in a masala sauce. They finished their meal with rice in buttermilk. From her bag, Vani took out a packet of khova made with pure ghee from Sivarama sweet shop. She gave each of them a small square of the milk-based sweet, decorated with extremely thin silver foil. The khova melted in their mouths.

"Sivarama sweets, eh! How much did it cost?" asked Mr. Somayajulu.

"I didn't buy it, naanna. One of the boys in the class passed, and he gave everybody a packet as a gift," replied Vani.

"You must go to a temple and give your thanks to God," said their mother to Vani.

"Both of you should go to Simhachalam temple," suggested their father. "Aruna, you haven't been there since you started your job, either."

Aruna nodded, but Vani protested, "Naanna, that's far away. It will take almost the whole day."

Simhachalam temple was on a hill, quite a few miles out of town.

"Do it on Monday," proposed their mother, because it was Aruna's day off.

"Yes, this Monday is a good day to visit the temple. It is a full-moon day," said their father.

"Take a picnic," said their mother.

"Done," agreed Vani.

"You changed your mind quickly when mother suggested a picnic," said Aruna, laughing.

Vani pouted, then laughed as well.

After dinner, Aruna's father switched on their old black-and-white television to watch the Telugu news. The TV showed the king of Bhutan laying a wreath at Raj Ghat, Mahatma Gandhi's memorial in Delhi, then the king meeting the prime minister and other officials. The next item on the news was about the Reserve Bank's decision to keep interest rates unchanged. After that, the newscaster said, "At Royyapalem, police opened fire after protesters ignored Section One Forty-four and gathered for a public meeting. Two people are reported killed and eight injured, three of them seriously. The state home minister appealed for calm . . ."

"Oh, my God!" said Aruna, shocked.

"What happened?" asked her mother. All three of them were looking at Aruna.

"Sir and madam's son was one of the protesters," she said.

"Do you want to find out if he is hurt?" asked her mother.

"No, he wasn't at the village today. He was one of the first protesters. He and his friends were struck with lathis and brought back to the city under arrest. He is due to appear in court tomorrow."

"What a trial for such nice people," said her father. "Children just go gallivanting without realizing how it affects their parents."

The next day, Mr. and Mrs. Ali and Azhar were at the district court by ten. The court was a hundred-year-old stone building, built during the British times. It had the typical colonial look of buildings its age, with wide verandahs on all sides and faded green louvered doors and windows. It was surrounded by a large open area, dotted with gulmohar and laburnum trees. Under the shade of each tree was a lawyer in white clothes and black coat, surrounded by litigants and their families.

Rehman and his friends were being defended by a team of two hot-shot lawyers who had specially flown in from Hyderabad, the state capital. Mr. Ali had expected to pay a share of the costs, but Azhar told him that a lot of money had been collected to pay for the defense. There were police everywhere carrying lathis—iron-banded bamboo canes. There was even a TV camera crew by the entrance to the court.

"You don't see so many police at the court normally," said Azhar.

"It must be because of the shooting yesterday at Royyapalem. I am sure that the TV camera is also here because of that," said Mr. Ali. He turned to Mrs. Ali and said, "Looks as if our son is famous."

"Don't joke, please. What kind of future will he have if he is convicted and branded a criminal? I am sick with tension that our son could be jailed and you pick this time to exercise your humor," snapped Mrs. Ali.

Mr. Ali met Azhar's eyes. Azhar made a small signal with his hand, asking him to be silent. Mr. Ali looked away, turning his attention to the advocates and their clients. Rehman's team of lawyers were standing under the next tree. Mr. Ali walked over and the younger lawyer, carrying a briefcase, stopped him. Mr. Ali introduced himself and asked the senior lawyer what he thought was going to happen. Before he got a reply, a mobile phone rang. The younger lawyer took it out of his pocket, answered it, and handed it to his colleague.

The senior lawyer turned away to speak on the phone. When Mr. Ali asked the younger man, he just pointed to the senior lawyer and said, "Sir is very good. Don't worry. But he is very busy right now and cannot talk. He left an important case at a critical point in Hyderabad."

Mr. Ali rejoined his wife and Azhar with a sinking feeling about the whole situation. He wondered if it would have been better to hire a good local lawyer rather than this distracted advocate and his bag-carrier.

Suddenly there was a flurry of activity at the entrance to the court and the police started looking more alert. A police van drove through the gates and into the yard. They all moved toward the door to the courtroom, but were stopped several yards away by the police. The van was driven around to the rear entrance. They all waited in the sun, wondering what was happening. Rehman's lawyers went through the police cordon into the courtroom. About ten minutes later, a court attendant in a long white coat, with a red sash over his shoulder and around his waist, came out of the courtroom.

"The judge has declared that the proceedings will be held *in camera*," he announced, and went back inside, closing the doors to the courtroom behind him.

"What does that mean?" asked Mrs. Ali.

"It means we cannot go in," said Mr. Ali.

"How can they do that?"

"The judge can do whatever he wants," said Mr. Ali.

"It must be because of all the publicity this case has received," said Azhar.

They stood in the hot sun for a while, before finding the shade of a nearby tree. They stood for a long time, getting more and more uncomfortable. A small boy came around carrying bottles of cool water and made brisk sales until a police constable chased him out. Mrs. Ali chewed her nails. None of them spoke very much.

Finally, at about half past noon, the doors of the courtroom opened. Rehman's lawyer and his sidekick came out and briskly walked away. Mr. Ali and a couple of others tried to waylay them, but they were unsuccessful. Behind them, Rehman and his friends came out of the courtroom, smiling widely, their arms raised, pumping the air. Mr. Ali and the others left the lawyers and went to greet the young men.

Mrs. Ali hugged Rehman. Mr. Ali and Azhar hung around awkwardly patting him. His bruises were almost faded and the angry welt on his forehead had subsided somewhat.

"What happened?" Mrs. Ali asked.

"We've been acquitted. The judge agreed with our lawyer that the arresting officer had made a mistake by not serving us with a notice."

"So you've been let off on a technicality," said Mr. Ali.

"What do we care why?" said Mrs. Ali. "He's been released and that's the important thing."

"The lawyer has earned his fee, then," said Azhar.

They started moving toward the gate. Two of Rehman's friends came and shook his hand. One of his friends had to use his left hand because his right arm was in a white plaster cast. He gave a whoop and the three friends ended up in a big embrace.

Rehman asked, "Where are the others?"

"Most of them have gone," said the young man with his arm in the cast.

Rehman nodded. "What about you two? Are you still willing?"

"We are with you," said one friend, and the other nodded. "Some of the others said they'll come back later."

Mr. Ali realized with a jolt that Rehman was actually the leader of the group—not just a participant. They crossed the gates of the court compound and came up to where the TV crew was standing. The journalist waylaid them. Mr. Ali was not surprised that she addressed his son and seemed to know him by name. She was an attractive woman in her twenties and was carrying a microphone. She smiled at Rehman and asked him to stand on one side so the two of them were the only ones in the frame.

"Mr. Rehman, what do you say about your release?" asked the young lady.

Rehman said, "I've always had belief in our justice system. We were part of a legitimate protest to protect the rights of the villagers of Royyapalem."

"What are your plans now?" asked the journalist.

"My friends and I are going straight back to Royyapalem."

His friends nodded.

"No!" cried Mrs. Ali.

The TV camera swung toward Mrs. Ali. The journalist left Rehman and strode over to her.

"Who are you, madam?" she asked.

"I am Rehman's mother," said Mrs. Ali.

"Do you agree with your son's decision to go back to Royyapalem and rejoin the protest?" asked the journalist.

"Of course I don't agree. How can I, as a mother, be happy about my son going back to the place where he was beaten and arrested? Especially after the firing and deaths yesterday," said Mrs. Ali.

"What would you advise your son?" asked the journalist.

"I advise him to listen to his parents and stay here. He has done his bit. Let others now carry on the fight," said Mrs. Ali, in tears.

Rehman came over and hugged his mother.

"What do you say to your mother?" the interviewer asked Rehman.

"My mother is understandably emotional," said Rehman. "But sometimes we have to look beyond our own house and family. I don't expect our parents to be happy with our decision to go back to Royyapalem. But my friends and I are doing this for our country. We all want our country to develop, but not by trampling over its weakest citizens. There is no point in getting rich if we lose our soul along the way."

• • •

At dinner that day, Aruna's mother asked her, "How was your day today? You look tired."

"Yes, amma. Sir and madam were out the whole morning. Even after they came back, they were so upset that I had to look after the office myself," said Aruna.

"Poor people," said her mother. "Children can cause such trouble when they don't listen to parents. Thank God you two are so well behaved."

"Can we still go on the picnic to Simhachalam on Monday?" asked her sister, Vani.

"You are going to visit the temple, Vani, not on a picnic," said her father severely.

"Same difference, dad. Just chill out," she said.

They all finished their meal and Aruna's father switched on their television. After the usual political news, the newsreader said, "And now let's go to Vizag to see a mother's anguish."

The camera cut to the court, and Mrs. Ali's weeping face came on the screen.

"That's madam," said Aruna, aghast.

They all watched avidly as the young journalist on the screen talked to Mrs. Ali. The fact that Rehman and his friends were released was mentioned only in passing. Mrs. Ali's emotions were given much greater prominence.

Aruna's father switched off the television after the weather forecast. They were all silent for a few moments. Then her father said, "How shameful it must be for the parents to witness their son's arrest. And what a brute he is . . . even his mother's tears are not able to dissolve his will."

Vani said, "But what Mr. Rehman said is true, naanna. Sometimes you have to think beyond your own family. Everybody says that our freedom fighters were great people. Do you think their parents were happy that their children were fighting against the British instead of becoming lawyers or clerks in government service?"

Aruna's father said, "Don't argue. You are young and don't understand these things."

Vani made a face but before she could reply, Aruna said, "Vani is correct, naanna. But madam is not wrong to cry and tell her son not to go. Her son is also right to say that we should sometimes look beyond our own needs and help others. It's a sad business all around."

Vani said, "Tomorrow, I'll ask my fellow students what we are doing to support the farmers at Royyapalem."

Aruna's father said, "Now, don't you go getting involved in dangerous activities. We are poor people and cannot afford to get into trouble."

"The farmers are poor too, naanna," said Vani. "But no worries. I am not planning to go to Royyapalem myself. Don't you always quote what Lord Krishna told the warrior Arjuna on the eve of the great battle in the Gita? We all live in a society, and if we don't help others in their time of need, then we are not contributing to the community. We are no better than exploiters and thieves."

THIRTEEN

On Sunday, Mr. Ali started working again. He was finally able to put thoughts of his son behind him. Mrs. Ali was still in bed, unable to face the world.

Mr. Ali started preparing advertisements. Normally, this was a task that he relished, but today, his creative juices weren't flowing well and he found himself staring at a blank piece of paper for a long time. Aruna went through the enrollment forms to type out details of newly joined members into a list. This task had been neglected all week. Ten quiet minutes later, she waved an enrollment form at Mr. Ali and said, "This lady, Sridevi. She joined on Monday when I was not here."

"Yes?" said Mr. Ali, looking up.

"Did you show her the details of Venu, the computer service engineer?" asked Aruna.

"Who?" asked Mr. Ali, puzzled.

"Do you remember the computer service engineer——the divorcé

from the small town? He had an unmarried sister, too," answered Aruna.

Mr. Ali thought for a moment before he remembered. "No, I didn't show that match to Sridevi. She only wanted to see matches from her own community, and his name wasn't on that list."

"But they are from the same caste, sir," said Aruna, going to the cupboard and taking out the list.

"How do you remember that? You have an extraordinary memory," said Mr. Ali, impressed.

Aruna blushed and admitted, "Not really, sir. I came across his details the other day when we were going through the lists to identify nonmembers."

Aruna found the list and gave it to Mr. Ali. He read through the details and said, "No wonder I missed it. These details are in the 'Caste no bar' list. But you are right, they are from the same caste. Give me Sridevi's form." He stretched out his hand and took the form from Aruna.

He picked up the phone and dialed the number on the form.

"Hello! Sridevi, here. How can I help you?" answered a feminine voice.

"This is Mr. Ali from the marriage bureau here."

"Hello, sir. I thought I saw you on TV the other day. Was it really you and your wife?" asked Sridevi.

Mr. Ali sighed. By now the news of his son's public defiance must be known all over town. "Yes, that was me and my wife."

"Your son is a very brave man, sir," she said. "I really felt for your wife, too."

Mr. Ali grunted, not sure whether he was pleased or not at her praise. "Are you still looking for a match?" he asked.

"Yes, sir. I am still looking," she said.

"His name is Venu—just twenty-six, so quite close to your age. He is a computer service engineer in the city itself. He doesn't mind matches from any caste, but he is also a Kamma—your community," said Mr. Ali.

"That sounds good, sir. I cannot come today, but I'll pop in tomorrow around ten," she said.

"You don't need to come in. I can post the details to you. I have your address, and within the city, you'll get the letter within a couple of days," said Mr. Ali.

"Would you do that? Thanks very much, sir. My babayi, younger uncle, is coming to visit me tomorrow and it would have been a bit inconvenient for me to come in, so it will help if you just post me the details," Sridevi said.

"Your paternal uncle? That's good news, isn't it? You told me that your family was boycotting you," Mr. Ali said.

"The rest of my family is still boycotting me. My babayi has just come back from the Gulf and he called me up yesterday and said he wants to meet me. I am making dinner for him."

"That's great. Hopefully, he can bring the other members of the family around," said Mr. Ali.

"I hope so, sir. He doesn't have any daughters of his own and I've always been his favorite niece. Let's see what happens," Sridevi said.

"Good luck—both with your uncle and this match. We'll put it in the post tomorrow morning, so you should get it by Tuesday or Wednesday."

Mr. Ali put the phone down and said to Aruna, "Let us send her the list. Circle Venu's details with a red pen."

Aruna nodded and took out an envelope to write Sridevi's address. "What about Venu? Shall we send him Sridevi's details, too?"

Mr. Ali thought for a moment and shook his head. "No," he said. "I know we normally do that, but let us leave it to Sridevi. I don't want to impose on her. Let her make the first move, if she wants. She can always contact us if she doesn't want to talk to him directly. But write that at the bottom of the list. Say that we aren't sending her details to Venu and it is up to her to initiate contact if she wants."

On Monday morning, Aruna and her mother got up early as usual and made pulihora—yellow tamarind rice spiced with ginger and red chilies.

Vani came into the kitchen just as Aruna was mixing the spicy paste into the rice. She watched Aruna working for a moment and then asked, "Why do we always make pulihora for picnics?"

"The sour tamarind helps keep the rice from getting spoiled in the heat," said their mother, looking back from the stove where she was frying some boorulu—round lentil sweets with a sweet jaggery center. "Vani," she added, "pack a bunch of bananas and bottles of water. Remember, not all the bananas are for you to eat. Some of them are a gift to the deity at the temple."

"Okay, amma," said Vani.

They were ready by eight-thirty, but did not leave until after nine because they wanted the morning rush hour to reduce. They took a local bus to the main bus stand, where they changed to the bus going to Simhachalam. The conductor came up to them and Aruna bought a ticket. Vani showed her student pass.

The bus made its way out of the terminus and into the busy traffic outside. It took several minutes to negotiate the first junction, but after that the journey was relatively smooth. It made its way around Diamond Park, then past Sankara Matham—a temple devoted to Shiva—and finally reached the highway that ran along the foot of the mountain range. By this time, the bus was quite full, and so many people were standing that Aruna couldn't see across the aisle to the other side.

"We are lucky that we boarded the bus at its starting point. Otherwise, we would have to stand up," said Aruna.

Vani nodded.

The bus turned south on the highway and sped toward the temple town, keeping the mountain range on the right-hand side and the city on the left. Half an hour later, the stops became much less frequent as they left the city. Aruna was wearing her new sari and sitting by the window. She held up the dark green border of the sari across her face to shade herself from the sun, which was already very fierce. The open windows kept the bus cool, if dusty, when it was moving; the interior became stifling hot when it stopped. Aruna and Vani chatted about some of Mr. Ali's customers and their demands, and about some of Vani's classmates.

Vani said, "You know, we never finished stitching the zigzag pattern on the blue sari that I was going to wear for your wedding. It's still lying on the top shelf of the wardrobe."

Aruna grimaced and Vani apologized.

Aruna said, "No, don't be sorry. Those flowers are faded and on the rubbish heap now. There's no point in remembering their fragrance."

Vani looked at her with big eyes and hugged her hand tightly for a moment. The girls exchanged sad smiles and felt really close to each other as only two sisters can.

The bus stopped. Initially, Aruna did not pay any attention and continued talking to Vani. After a while, they stopped talking and realized that all conversation had slowly died out. People started craning their necks, trying to figure out what had happened.

After a few minutes, those who were standing started getting down. Once the bus was clear of standing passengers, a man came walking down the aisle asking everybody for their tickets. Through the windows, Aruna saw two more inspectors checking the tickets of all the standing passengers who were now milling about the roadside by the bus.

When the inspector came to their seats, Aruna showed her ticket and Vani her student pass. The man returned Aruna's ticket, but instead of returning Vani's pass, he called out to somebody. Another inspector came over and the first inspector showed him the pass. Aruna and Vani looked at each other quizzically. Vani shrugged her shoulders.

"Any problem?" Vani asked the men.

The first inspector turned back to her and said, "Yes, you are traveling without a ticket."

"What do you mean? I have my pass."

"The student pass is not valid for travel outside the city limits," said the inspector.

"Oh! I didn't know that. How much is the ticket? I'll buy one," Vani said.

"Too late now," said the man curtly. "You have to pay a fine."

"Fine? I told you I didn't know that the pass was not valid outside the city limits," said Vani.

"That doesn't matter. You have to pay the fine."

Vani looked as if she was going to protest. Aruna put a hand over her sister's hand and silenced her. "How much is the fine?" she asked.

"I don't know. That will have to be decided by the magistrate," said the man. He seemed to be enjoying discomfiting the girls.

"What?" said Vani, her eyes widening. "Magistrate?"

"We have a traveling magistrate with us. Come on, girls, get down."

"But—"

"Nothing doing. Will you get down by yourself, or should I call the police? We have some lady police as well."

Aruna and Vani looked at each other and got up slowly. Vani held the bag of food in one hand and clutched her purse in the other. Aruna held her handbag across her chest. They were marched down and held separately from the others. The hot sun beat down on them. Aruna covered her head with the edge of her sari. Vani was wearing her churidar—a long top in soft chiffon down to her knees and matching tight trousers with a dupatta, a long, thin piece of cloth over her chest, with the ends trailing over her shoulders. Aruna pointed at it and Vani used one end to cover her head. Aruna was conscious of the men and women from the bus staring at them.

Suddenly, a young man broke into a run. The inspectors shouted and the two constables with the inspectors raised their lathis, but the man dodged them and escaped. Soon, everybody's tickets were checked and the people on the ground got back into the bus.

We've lost our seats, thought Aruna.

The bus's engine growled to life and it suddenly moved forward.

"Hey!" shouted Vani, raising her hand as if to physically stop the bus, but it was too late. The bus picked up speed and went off in a cloud of diesel smoke and dust. The girls turned to the inspectors—they were the only passengers left. There was another bus waiting a hundred yards away and they were asked to walk to it. When they entered the bus, Aruna gasped in surprise. Most of the seats at the back had been taken away and the interior converted into a mobile courtroom. There was a comfortable seat where a man in black robes—the magistrate, presumably—was sitting, and in front of him was a prisoner's dock. There were some police constables sitting in the bus, including a couple of women constables.

Aruna and Vani walked toward the magistrate and Vani was asked to stand in the defendant's dock. She had been quite strong until then, but her lower lip trembled as she moved to the dock. Aruna's heart went out to her little sister.

The inspector who had checked their tickets came forward and said, "This girl was traveling without a ticket, sir."

The magistrate looked bored. "What's your name, girl?" he asked.

"Vani, sir."

"Your father's name?"

"Mr. Somayajulu, sir. Retired schoolteacher."

The magistrate wrote the details down in front of him. "Is the ticket inspector correct? Did you not have a ticket?" he asked her.

"No, sir. I have a pass—," Vani began.

The ticket inspector interrupted. "Sir, her pass is not valid outside the city limits. She was traveling without a valid ticket."

The magistrate raised his eyebrows at Vani. "Is that true?"

"I didn't—," began Vani.

The magistrate banged his gavel and Vani fell silent. "Guilty," he said. "The fine is one hundred and fifty rupees."

"But sir—," protested Vani.

The magistrate raised his hand. "The fine can go up to three hundred. You are a young girl who made a mistake and your father was a schoolteacher, and that's why I have given you such a low fine. Please pay the cashier on the way out."

He turned to the police officer next to him and said, "This place is no good. Let's try Gajuwaka—we'll catch more people there."

Aruna looked through her purse for the money. She discovered to her horror that she didn't have much cash. She remembered that she had paid for the rice earlier in the week and had not topped her purse up. She took out all the money and counted it. She had one hundred and thirty rupees. She looked through the purse again and found a five-rupee coin.

She asked Vani in a low voice, "Do you have any cash?"

Vani opened her eyes wide and went through her purse. "Twenty-five rupees," she said, giving the money to her sister.

"Good. At least we can pay off the fine."

Vani and Aruna went to the cashier. He was sitting near the door with a cashbox in front of him. Aruna paid the money, and the cashier put it away. Aruna continued standing there.

"Yes?" snapped the cashier, irritated.

"I am waiting for a receipt," said Aruna.

"Receipt?" he asked blankly.

"Yes," Aruna said calmly. Her father had told her to always ask for a receipt when she paid any money to a government official.

The man sighed and took out the receipt book, put a carbon paper underneath the first slip and filled it out. He tore the original out of the book and gave it to Aruna with ill grace.

Vani turned to the inspector next to the door and said, "This place is in the middle of nowhere. Can you give us a lift to the nearest bus stop?"

"No. We don't carry passengers," the man said curtly, and shooed them out of the bus. As they were getting down, Aruna heard him muttering, "Wants a receipt *and* a lift."

The sisters stood in the hot sun and watched forlornly as the mobile court revved its engine and vanished.

"What shall we do now?" asked Vani.

Aruna had been wondering the same thing. The checkpoint had been established halfway between two stops. They were miles from both the city and the temple.

In the city, Mr. Ali finally convinced his wife to leave the bedroom. They both sat at the dining table and Mr. Ali said, "Let's go to Azhar's house."

"I don't want to go anywhere," said Mrs. Ali.

"You can't just stay cooped up here. You have hardly come out of the bedroom for three days. It will do you good to get out," said Mr. Ali.

"No, just leave me alone. I don't want to meet anybody," said Mrs. Ali.

"You have to let go of these things," said Mr. Ali.

"I thought today was Monday," said Mrs. Ali.

"Yes, today is Monday. So?" asked Mr. Ali.

"So it means that Aruna is not in today. Don't you have to mind the office?" said Mrs. Ali.

"That's okay. It'll do us both good to get out of the house. Let's go," said Mr. Ali.

Mrs. Ali sighed. "I know where our son gets his bloody-mindedness from. Once either of you gets a thought in your head, there's no talking you out of it."

"Don't talk to me about Rehman. He's a foolish boy who won't listen to his parents and that's just a burden that we have to bear," said Mr. Ali.

Mrs. Ali got up and said, "All right, let me get ready."

In the fertile coastal plains of South India, nowhere is really far from some habitation or other. Aruna pointed to a hamlet a little way away. The sisters walked toward the palm-leaf–thatched huts. They picked their way along the side of the road, through the dust mixed with dried-up stalks of rice plants and crushed sugar cane. The sun was a white ball of heat in the cloudless sky. The trees on the edge of the road all had white circular bands painted on them, showing that they belonged to the roads department. Aruna and Vani walked in the shadows of these trees toward the little collection of huts. Vani pointed out a palm tree—its thin straight trunk was notched at intervals to make it easy to climb, and a clay pot was tied at the top of the tree.

Aruna looked at the pot and said, "Toddy."

Vani nodded.

Tappers cut the flower of the palm tree and tie a pot to the stump. Sweet, cooling sap called "neeru" oozes from the cut and collects in the pot. Aruna knew that while fresh neeru was delicious and nutritious, it was almost always fermented and turned into a strong country liquor called "arrack" that many villagers and poor people drank.

They reached the hamlet. One of the huts was a café selling tea and snacks. It had a long wooden bench along its side and the girls made their way to it. It was a relief to get out of the sun—the palm-leaf thatch and the cow-dung–polished floor kept the heat out and a cool breeze blew in through the open sides of the hut. An old woman could be seen in the darkest part of the hut. Aruna called out to her, "Baamma, can we sit here for a while?"

The old woman waved her hand, giving them permission. The girls sat down on the bench and the old woman came out of the interior. Her skin was wrinkled and dark and she wore a faded cotton sari of indeterminate color; a tattoo that had faded green looked like an armband on her right arm. She wore the sari in the fashion of poor, lower-caste women in villages—without a blouse. The leading edge of the sari draped over her sagging breasts. Aruna could see that she was a widow—she wore no jewelry and there was no sindoor on her forehead.

"Hello, ladies. Would you like some tea?" she asked, taking a home-made cigar out of her mouth to speak. One of her eyes was cloudy and she cocked her head at an angle to keep them in view of the other eye.

"No, baamma. The inspectors claimed we were traveling without tickets and took most of our money as a fine. We only have ten rupees and we will need the money to get back home," said Aruna.

"These gourmet people, they put on a uniform and the power goes to their heads. How can they leave two young ladies like you stranded? Don't they have sisters or mothers?" said the old woman. "Don't worry about the money. A couple of glasses of tea won't beggar me."

She went to the stove and poured them two glasses of tea from the constantly boiling pot.

Vani looked very doubtful about drinking from the none-too-clean glasses, but Aruna flashed her eyes at her sister and took a sip. Vani reluctantly lifted her glass.

"If you want to call anybody, Seenu over there runs a phone," the old lady said, pointing with her hand.

"That's a good idea, baamma," said Aruna. She turned to Vani and asked, "Whom shall we call? Do you know any numbers?"

"One of my classmates would definitely come if we called him. He also carries a cell phone with him all the time, but I don't know the number," said Vani.

"Let me try Mr. Ali. Sir will definitely find a way to rescue us," said Aruna.

She put the glass of tea down on the bench next to her and got up. Two huts away in the direction pointed by the old woman, there was a large yellow Public Telegraph and Telephone sign. Aruna walked up to it and told the young man sitting on a plastic chair, "I want to make a call."

The young man twisted in his chair, picked up the handset, and gave it to her. "Go ahead, madam. Local or long distance?"

"Vizag," she said, noticing that the young man was crippled, one of his legs shriveled by polio.

"That is local, madam."

Aruna dialed Mr. Ali's number, which she knew by heart. The phone rang and rang but nobody picked it up. She put the handset down and tried again. There was still no answer. Aruna put the phone back in its cradle and stood pensively, biting her lower lip. She didn't know what to do. After a few seconds, she sighed and opened her bag to take out her purse. "How much is it?" she asked.

"Nothing, madam. Nobody answered, so you don't have to pay," said Seenu.

As she was closing her bag, Aruna noticed a white card and took it out. Aruna's heart beat rapidly as she looked at Ramanujam's business card. It had his cell phone number. Did she dare call him? She looked furtively to where Vani was sitting—but her sister was out of her direct line of sight. She closed her eyes and took a deep breath. She opened her eyes and Ramanujam's name seemed to be in a larger font, standing out from the card. She turned to Seenu and said in a low voice, "Let me try one more number."

She dialed Ramanujam's cell phone. As the phone rang, she wasn't sure what she wanted—did she want him to pick up the phone or not? After the fourth ring, she cut the connection. She knew that cell phones automatically went to voice mail if the owner did not answer. She did not want to waste money on a call if she couldn't speak to Ramanujam directly.

She shrugged at Seenu and said, "I will try again in a little while."

Seenu grinned at her, showing his white teeth. "No problem, madam. I am not going anywhere."

Aruna turned away, her disappointment temporarily forgotten. She wondered how a young man who could not walk, stuck in this small place, remained cheerful. She ducked out of the sun into the old woman's hut and went back to sit next to Vani. Her sister looked at her expectantly and Aruna shook her head. Vani's face fell.

Aruna said, "Sir and madam must have gone out somewhere."

Vani said, "I wonder how long we will be stranded here."

FOURTEEN

Aruna picked up her by now cold tea and took a sip. The old woman started telling them her story. Aruna discovered that she was not that old—in fact, she was younger than her own mother. She and her husband had owned a small piece of land near the Sarada River. The land was fertile, she had given birth to a son, and life was good. She had become pregnant again and was expecting her second baby in a couple of months when tragedy struck. The Sarada River, which had given them their prosperity, turned on them with a fury, and a raging flood suddenly hit their house one night. Her husband helped her and their son climb on their big wooden trunk and hold on to the rafters of their house. He then went out to untie their cow. For two days she was stuck there until the waters receded; she was barely alive, her son had died at some point during the two days, and her husband had disappeared. The cow was gone and the crop had washed away. The government and various charities provided relief for a few weeks, and then hunger set in. She was heavily pregnant and needed to eat for two, but she had not enough food even to sustain herself.

"I didn't dare leave the place, because I didn't know when my husband would come back," said the old lady.

"Didn't anybody help you?" asked Vani.

"The whole village was in ruins. Everybody had troubles. Who had the time to help a woman on her own?" said the old lady.

"What happened then?" asked Aruna.

"About a month later, I went into labor and gave birth to a baby girl. But my breasts were dry and the baby died."

"How awful," said Vani.

"Did your husband ever come back?" asked Aruna.

"He must have died, though his body was never found. No, he didn't come back," she replied.

After a pause, the old lady continued, "But my husband's brothers came. They said I was a widow and shaved my head and kicked me out of the house." She paused, and must have been remembering the pain of those days because her eyes went blank. She looked at them with her good eye and said, "Things were difficult, but somehow I survived. Years later, I started working as a servant in a political leader's house, and he eventually got me this place on a government scheme to help poor widows. Things are not bad now—everything has become expensive but my needs are small."

The old lady finished her story and they all fell silent. Seenu came to their hut.

"Lady," he said to Aruna, "there is a phone call for you."

"For me? Who will call me here?" said Aruna.

"The same person you called, madam. He said he had a missed call from you," Seenu said. "Come quickly, he will call again in two minutes."

He turned back, moving quite fast with a shuffling gait, one shoulder hunched with strain as his hand supported his crippled leg every alternate step. Aruna followed behind him. The phone was ringing as Aruna reached Seenu's stall. He picked up the phone, answered, and handed it to Aruna. "Yours, madam."

Aruna said cautiously into the phone, "Hello, this is Aruna."

"Aruna, what happened?" said a male voice. It was Ramanujam. "I saw a missed call from this number after my ward rounds."

"Thanks for calling!" said Aruna with relief. "We are stuck here and I didn't know who else to call."

She explained what had happened and how she and her sister didn't have any cash with them. "I was wondering if you could, maybe, send your driver," she finished, a bit awkwardly.

Ramanujam thought for a moment and said, "No problem. I can do that. Where exactly are you?"

Aruna couldn't describe where she was, so she handed the phone to Seenu, who gave their location to Ramanujam.

She thanked Seenu and went back to the old lady's café.

"Who was it?" asked Vani, excited.

"Oh! A client of ours—I happened to have his card in my handbag, so I called him but there was no reply. He saw a missed call on his cell phone and called back," Aruna replied.

"So, what's happening?" said Vani.

Aruna replied, "He is sending his driver. Should be here in half an hour or so."

Vani said, "Driver? Excellent! What does your client do?"

"He is a doctor—a surgeon at King George Hospital."

They came out of the hut when they saw a car pull in. Aruna was surprised when she saw Ramanujam get out of the car. She couldn't stop smiling, though.

"I thought you were sending the driver," she said to Ramanujam.

"I am free until the evening clinic, so I decided to come myself," he said, grinning at the girls. "I feel like I'm playing hooky from school."

Aruna laughed and introduced Vani. Aruna could see that Vani was very curious about Ramanujam. She tried to look at him through her sister's eyes. He was a good-looking man, tall and broad-shouldered. He wore good clothes and came driving an expensive car; he talked very comfortably with both of them.

They now had transportation to the city. The old lady had come out of the hut to see them off, and Aruna turned to her and said, "Baamma, thanks for helping us. We don't have a problem going back to the city now, so let me pay you for the tea."

The old woman protested but accepted the five-rupee coin that Aruna gave her. As she was turning away, Ramanujam said, "Stop, granny. Let me have a look at your eyes." He held the old woman's chin and looked at one eye and then the other. He then closed the good eye and opened two fingers of his other hand.

"How many fingers can you see?" he asked. The old woman frowned with concentration, and said, "One?"

He then closed the other eye and asked again. This time she answered correctly. He repeated the tests by moving his hand to different areas in front of her eyes. Ramanujam finally said, "You have cataracts in both eyes. Your left eye is completely covered and your right eye is partially clouded. It is very important to get this operated upon. Otherwise you will soon go completely blind."

The old lady was clearly scared. "What can I do, sir? How much will it cost?"

Ramanujam reassured her. "Don't worry. It is a very simple operation. I am sure the government eye hospital runs free clinics."

She didn't look convinced. Ramanujam took out his mobile phone and called somebody. After the usual pleasantries, he said, "Ravi, when do you run eye clinics? I have a poor widow who's presenting opacity of the lens in both eyes. Totally covered in the left eye and about seventy percent in the other eye."

He listened for a while and asked a few questions. He said, "Thanks, I'll give her a letter, so you will know I sent her."

He asked the old woman, "What is your name?"

"Gauramma," she said.

"How old are you?" he asked.

"Fifty," she said.

His pen scratched out a letter and he handed it to the old lady. "Go to the eye clinic in King George Hospital on Thursday. When you get there, give this letter to the attendant and tell him to give it to Dr. Ravi. He will sort everything out."

"Thank you, sir. It must have been some good deed I performed in a previous birth that directed these lovely ladies to my door today and brought you here. Thank you," she said, tears running down her lined face.

They went to Seenu's stall, where Ramanujam gave him a small amount of money before taking their leave.

"It was good of you to help the poor woman," said Aruna. "She has had a difficult life."

Simhachalam is an old temple, built in the thirteenth century, dedicated to Lord Vishnu in the avatar of Narasimha—half man, half lion. According to legend, a demon king obtained a guarantee that he could not be killed by man or beast, neither during the day nor at night, neither in his house nor outside and neither on the ground nor in the sky. Confident that he was invincible, his depredations knew no bounds.

Finally, to stamp out the evil demon, the Lord burst out of a pillar in the form of a raging Narasimha and caught the demon king in his claws. The sun was setting as the half man, half beast brought his prey to the entrance to the evil demon's palace. There, in the doorway to the palace, neither inside the house nor outside, at twilight when it was neither day nor night, Narasimha, neither man nor beast, sat down and lay the demon king on his lap, neither on the ground nor in the sky, and killed him. Even today, Hindus do not stand in the doorway of a building.

Aruna, Vani, and Ramanujam entered a big courtyard crisscrossed with a maze of iron railings so people could form a queue for viewing the deity. It was not too crowded—just a few hundred people in front of them. They left their footwear with a temple employee and joined the line. Quite a lot of the people—both men and women—had shaven heads, as they had offered their hair to the Lord as a gift, and their bright heads glistened in the sun like so many lightbulbs.

Ramanujam turned to Vani and said, "Since we are here to thank the Lord because you passed in first class, why don't you shave your head and offer the hair?"

"No, thank you," she said, making a face. "Actually, we are also visiting the temple because my sister got the job at Mr. Ali's. Why don't you ask her to shave her head?"

Aruna saw Ramanujam looking at her long hair for a long moment, but he didn't say anything; she pretended that she hadn't heard Vani's comment.

The line moved quickly, and within forty-five minutes, they were near the sanctum sanctorum. They handed their gifts of flowers and fruits to a priest and went inside, facing the idol. Ramanujam and Aruna folded their hands and bent their heads. Vani rang a bell that was hanging there and knelt in front of the idol, making a deep obeisance. They could not make out the true shape of the idol—it was fully covered in sandalwood paste. Narasimha is an angry avatar and the sandalwood paste is to cool him down and control his rage. The idol is revealed in its true glory for only twelve hours every year, and the throng of devotees at the temple then is truly enormous. One of the priests standing there made sure they moved on in less than a minute, and they were soon out in the sun again.

They collected their shoes and sandals, and Ramanujam said, "Let's go and collect the prasaadam."

Aruna said, "We don't have the money to buy it, remember."

Ramanujam said, "Come to Simhachalam temple and miss out on the blessed sweet? There is almost no point in coming to the temple."

Vani laughed and Aruna said, "Don't talk irreverently about God's offering."

Ramanujam held his ears in his hands and said, "Sorry, mummy. I won't be naughty again."

Aruna laughed along with Vani.

He handed Aruna a hundred-rupee note. When he saw her hesitating, he said, "I am just lending it. Return it later."

Aruna thanked him and took the money. She did feel more comfortable with a bit of cash on her. There was an even longer line for the prasaadam than there was for the deity. They finally got to the front of the line and Ramanujam bought two half-kilo packets of the tasty sweet, made in the name of the deity.

"Now for the picnic," said Vani.

"That's a good idea. I know just the place. Let's go," he said.

They got into the car and Ramanujam drove them down the hill. At the bottom, instead of turning toward the city, he turned the other way and took them into the interior. The road had been recently laid and they had a smooth ride. Inside the air-conditioned car, it was cool and India looked its most beautiful through the tinted windows as they drove past green trees and looked at the rural life outside—farmers preparing their land for the coming rains, boys and wiry old men herding goats and buffalo, women carrying pots of water or firewood on their heads. They passed a pond and Ramanujam pointed out, "Look, a crane."

Soon, too soon for Aruna, the car turned off the main road and took a narrow, twisting lane. Within minutes they passed a small village and entered a large, gated orchard of mango and cashew nut trees. Crossing the cattle grid, Ramanujam drove the car into a sweeping gravel driveway and parked the car under the shade of a tree. They got out of the car and the girls looked around with interest—the driveway was flanked on both sides by painted bricks, half dug at an angle into the ground. There were bougainvillea, jasmine, marigold, and golden kanakambaram plants flowering all around. There was a large porch in front of the house, and a group of villagers were sitting on it, some on the ground, some on benches in front of a powerful-looking man in his forties.

The man stood up to greet them—he was tall and well built, with a broad chest and strong arms. His long black hair was swept back and he sported a thin handlebar mustache. His teeth were stained red with paan.

"Good morning, doctor. What brings you here?" he said in a deep voice.

"Morning, Mr. Raju. The ladies wanted to go for a picnic after visiting the Simhachalam temple, and I brought them here," replied Ramanujam.

"You should have called me. I would have had lunch prepared for you," said Mr. Raju.

"No, we already have food. I wasn't expecting you here—heard you were busy building the shopping mall in town."

"That's right. But today I had some property matters to settle, so I had to come around and talk to these people," he said, waving his hand at the villagers waiting patiently for the gentlemen to finish their conversation.

A young man brought three plastic chairs from the house and set them down near Mr. Raju's chair.

Mr. Raju asked them to sit down and took a seat himself. It was easy to believe that this man belonged to the Kshatriya caste, whose forefathers were soldiers and kings.

"Your sister and brother-in-law were here last weekend," he said.

"I know. They told me. They got us some mangoes," said Ramanujam.

"They took away a *lot* of mangoes," Mr. Raju laughed.

Ramanujam introduced the girls. "The ladies are sisters—Aruna and Vani. Their uncle is a priest at the Annavaram temple."

Mr. Raju and the villagers looked impressed.

Aruna and Vani joined their hands and said, "Namaste."

Aruna took out a sweet and gave it to Mr. Raju. "Prasaadam from the temple," she said.

Mr. Raju leaned forward and took it in his right hand, touched it to his forehead reverently, and ate it in one gulp.

"Where do you want to go for the picnic? The second guesthouse is free. Nobody is using it today," said Mr. Raju.

"No, we'll just go to our plot. It will be nice in the shade of the trees," said Ramanujam.

"Basava-a-a . . . ," said Mr. Raju loudly, turning toward the house. A young man came out. "Basava, cook these people lunch," said Mr. Raju.

"There is no need for the trouble. We have a packed lunch, and there are a lot of fruits out there," said Ramanujam.

"No trouble," Mr. Raju laughed. "We don't need to kill a chicken or a goat for you Brahmins, do we?"

Mr. Raju turned to Basava and said, "Use the vegetarian kitchen."

Ramanujam said to Basava, "Something simple—just rice and one curry."

Basava nodded and went back inside.

Ramanujam, Aruna, and Vani walked down a straight road through the orchard. Aruna was carrying their bag of food, and Ramanujam was carrying a mat that he had taken out of his car. On both sides of the path were mature mango trees. The trees were hanging heavy with yellow fruit. Parrots and mynah birds chirped and flew among the trees.

"Mr. Raju bought this orchard several years ago from farmers, laid these roads, and built the guesthouses. He then divided the area into plots and sold them. We bought a couple of plots at that time. We gave one of the plots to my sister when she got married," Ramanujam explained.

"It's lovely—so peaceful, you cannot hear anything except the birds," said Aruna.

Vani was skipping in front of them like a little girl.

"Yes, I know. We come here three or four times a year for picnics."

Ramanujam stopped after they had walked for a few minutes and said, "Here we are."

It looked no different from the rest of the area around them. "How do you know this is yours?" asked Vani.

"Do you see this stone?" asked Ramanujam, pointing to a stone post dug into the ground by the side of the road. Vani and Aruna nodded. It had the number 21 written on it in black paint. "Plot twenty-one is ours. All the way from this post to that one there," he said, pointing to another post a couple of hundred feet away. He then pointed through the trees. "There are another two posts marking the other side of the plot."

They got off the road and walked into the trees. The trees were regularly spaced, every ten or fifteen feet away from each other. It was cool under their canopy of glossy, dark green leaves. Ramanujam spread the mat under one of the mango trees. Aruna took out a bed-sheet from her bag and covered the mat. They all kicked off their shoes and sat down on the sheet.

Ramanujam said, "We'll be getting some hot food soon. Shall we wait for that?"

"I'm starving," replied Vani.

"I'm hungry too," said Ramanujam. "Let's start with some mangoes. Come on."

Vani immediately jumped up. He held his hand out to Aruna. Aruna hesitated for a second and stretched out her hand. Ramanujam pulled her up. A thrill went through Aruna as he held her hand. It was the first time that they had touched. Aruna blushed and stood, looking a bit confused. Vani had already gone ahead and Ramanujam turned away as well, to put on his shoes.

Aruna composed herself and thought to herself angrily, *It's no big deal. Doesn't mean anything. Relax.*

She couldn't relax, however, and was still standing there when Vani turned back and shouted at her, "Come on, akka."

Aruna joined them. "They look like Banginpalli mangoes," she said to Ramanujam.

"That's right," he said, "the best mangoes in the world. My father always says that if mangoes are the king of fruit, the Banginpalli variety is the king of mangoes. When Mr. Raju told my dad that the land held mature Banginpalli trees, he didn't stop to think about whether it made economic sense. He just put his name down for two plots without asking any more questions."

They each plucked a ripe fruit and Ramanujam said, "There is a waterpipe on the other side. Come on."

"How will we cut them?" asked Vani. "These mangoes are meant to be cut and eaten, not sucked like a Rasaalu mango."

"Every obstacle has a solution. Don't worry," said Ramanujam, laughing.

They walked over to the tap and washed their mangoes. Red dust splattered on their clothes even though they were careful to stand away from the water. Ramanujam went to an old mango tree with a large hollow. He took a stick and pulled a plastic packet from inside the hollow. He opened it and said, "*Voilà!* A knife for madam."

Aruna took the knife and expertly cut the mango into strips, leaving the large, hard seed in the middle with a thin covering of yellow flesh. The rich fragrance of the mango made her mouth water.

They wandered around the plot, eating the mango that Aruna had cut. They plucked some more ripe mangoes that were within their reach. Vani turned her dupatta into a sack to hold the mangoes. In one corner of the plot, there was a stand of cashew nut trees. They were smaller than the mango trees but the leaves were bigger. Ramanujam had a look and asked, "Have you eaten a cashew mango?"

Aruna looked at the green fruit that had a brown nut stuck to its bottom. It looked odd—somehow upside down. The girls shook their heads. Aruna replied, "No, I've never eaten the cashew fruit. We haven't eaten that many cashew *nuts*, either. They are quite expensive."

Ramanujam nodded and said, "It's a pity they are not ripe yet. Another month and we would have been able to eat the fruit and roast the nuts."

They made their way back to the picnic and sat down. Aruna cut one more mango and they ate it. Ramanujam stretched out on the sheet and put his hand under his head like a pillow. They fell silent, listening to birdsong and the hum of bees. "This is so peaceful," he said after a while. "I don't know what it is, but villages just sound different from towns. It must be the lack of people or something."

The girls just nodded. They were all feeling lazy in the warm weather after the sugar rush the mangoes had given them. Aruna sat next to Vani with her back to a tree and watched a troop of big black ants scurrying around, looking for food. In the distance a cricket could be heard, but she couldn't make out where it was. Its chirping seemed to be coming from all around. Slowly, the peaceful atmosphere seeped into Aruna and the morning's troubles seemed far away. She gazed at Ramanujam's lean and long frame stretched out in front of her for a long time. He turned his face and their eyes met. A slow smile stole onto his face; she blushed in embarrassment and looked away.

After some time, Basava came down the road carrying a cloth bag. Seeing him, Ramanujam and the girls got up. Aruna took the bag from him with a smile, and Ramanujam took out ten rupees from his wallet and gave it to Basava.

"There is no need for the money, sir," he said, pocketing the note, and left.

There was a lunch bucket, three stainless-steel plates, glasses, and some serving spoons in the bag. Aruna took them all out. Vani laid the plates and glasses in front of them. Aruna opened the lunch bucket. It had three containers stacked one on top of the other. Aruna separated them and put them next to each other. The top, and smallest, container had a potato and cauliflower fry, the middle one had lentil sambhar, and the bottom container was packed with steamed rice. They were all piping hot. Vani took out the food they had packed and laid it out in the middle.

"This is fantastic, isn't it?" said Ramanujam, looking at the spread. "Now I wish I hadn't eaten the second mango."

But they were still hungry and silence fell as they started eating.

After a while, Ramanujam asked Vani, "So you got first class?"

Vani had her mouth full and just nodded.

"Which college do you attend?" he asked.

"Gayatri," she answered.

They all started talking about their colleges. The girls were fascinated by Ramanujam's descriptions of hostel life and of life in Delhi. Neither of them had ever lived away from their family or left the state. They discussed the relative value of "science" versus "arts" education. Ramanujam, like most science graduates in India, held a low opinion of an arts degree. The girls disagreed. They said that an education is not just about getting a job. Ramanujam said he preferred Hindi movies to Telugu movies; the girls called him a snob.

They soon finished lunch. "Ahh!" groaned Ramanujam, rubbing his stomach. "I can't eat another morsel."

Aruna agreed.

Ramanujam stretched out again on the mat.

"Have you actually succeeded in finding any matches for your clients?" asked Ramanujam, staring up at the sky.

Vani had taken the plates and cutlery to the waterpipe to wash them.

"Absolutely. I know of a few definite cases, though I am sure there are a lot more. People come to us saying that one of their friends was successful because of us, but only a few of the actual people have ever come and told us. It's as if they are ashamed of having used our services, once the wedding is fixed. Not always, of course. A salesman recently found his bride through us, and he invited us to his wedding, this coming Sunday," said Aruna.

"Are you going?" asked Ramanujam.

"No," replied Aruna. "I would have liked to go. I've never been to a Muslim wedding before. But it's out of town, so I said I couldn't. Also, Sunday is our busiest day, and I need to look after the office because sir and madam are going."

After a pause, she continued, "What about you? Will you tell us if you find a match through us and invite me to your wedding?"

"Definitely," said Ramanujam. "I will invite you to my wedding."

"I don't believe you," Aruna laughed. After a pause, Aruna asked, "How is the search going, anyway?"

"So-so. Lot of leads, but nothing definite."

Vani came back with the clean dishes and sat down next to Aruna. She said, "I think we have to finish embroidering that blue sari soon."

Aruna frowned at her sister.

FIFTEEN

Around nine in the morning on Sunday, Mr. and Mrs. Ali arrived at the small town where Irshad's wedding was going to take place and were taken to a house crowded with people. They were expected, and a teenaged boy with a straggly mustache took them inside the house, telling them that Irshad was getting ready.

Irshad came out of the room and greeted them both warmly and said, "We are running a bit late but we should be able to leave in the next hour or so."

One of Irshad's friends said, "You'll be waiting on her for the rest of your days. I'm sure the bride can wait for you this one day."

Everybody laughed. Irshad's mother hugged Mrs. Ali and took her to another room where the ladies were gathered. Mr. Ali went with the men into the bridegroom's room.

Irshad told Mr. Ali that the bride's house was two blocks away. This house had been rented for the week by the bride's parents and given to the groom's family to use as a base for the wedding. A couple of young boys came in and announced, "The band is here."

There was a lot of confusion as the one bathroom in the house was overwhelmed by the rush. Some people got angry and muttered mutinously that the bride's family was being close-fisted and inconveniencing them by cramming them all into a too-small house. Children dodged in and out among the adults, playing hide-and-seek or tag. A bevy of teenaged girls, all dressed and made up, were standing around giggling, ostentatiously ignoring a group of boys trying to catch their eyes.

Mr. and Mrs. Ali came out and stood on the road. The house was stifling with so many people in it, and it was better to stand outside. Slowly, the confusion resolved itself, and more and more people made their way out onto the road. Mr. Ali pointed out to Mrs. Ali a white mare on the other side of the road. A once rich, now faded blanket covered its back under the saddle. A studded leather flap covered the front of the mare's face. Its groom was holding the bridle tight, so it wouldn't fidget.

Mrs. Ali said, "It's been such a long time since I've been to a wedding where the bridegroom used a mare. It is so much more romantic than a car."

A man came riding a Bajaj scooter down the road. He looked at the crowd in their wedding finery and at the horse, and slowed down. He tried to weave his way slowly through the people, but an old man in a dark sherwani and a maroon fez stopped him and said, "Can't you see the road is full of people? Find another way." The man on the scooter looked about him and must have seen it as a lost cause because he turned around. Just as the people standing on the road were getting restive in the hot sun, a little boy came running and shouted, "The bridegroom is coming out!"

Irshad came out of the house slowly. He walked haltingly, guided by

a young man. His face couldn't be seen because it was hidden behind
a thick veil of white jasmine flowers hanging from his turban. He was
brought in front of the horse and just stood there. Mr. Ali realized after a
few moments that Irshad had probably never ridden a horse before and so
did not know how to mount one. The fact that he could only see his feet
behind the heavy veil probably did not help, either. The mare suddenly
turned back and tugged at Irshad's veil. Before Irshad could react, half a
string of flowers were in the horse's mouth and the other half trailed on
the ground. The groom pulled sharply on the reins and tried to tug the
flowers out of the mare's mouth, but the animal just put its head down
and snorted loudly. Irshad hastily stepped back and stumbled against a
stone on the road. He clutched at the horse's mane and the animal moved
skittishly forward and back, stepping on one of Irshad's fancy shoes.

"Ow!" he cried, hopping on one foot. A black mark disfigured
his shoe.

The stableman hit the horse on its neck to stop it moving, which
made the horse even more unsettled. One of the guests who seemed to
know a bit about horses stepped forward to help. It was several minutes
before the beast calmed down.

Finally, Irshad partially lifted his veil and looked dubiously at the
stirrup and was guided onto the mare by the guest. Slowly the mare
was led out, and all the people fell behind the bridegroom on his mare.
The baraat—the wedding procession—was on its way!

The band struck up a popular tune from a Hindi film:

Color your hands with mehndi,
And keep the palanquin ready.
Your love is on his way,
To take you away,
My fair lady.

The bridegroom was followed by the men and women of his party in their finest clothes, and the garishly dressed band playing music. The procession wound its way slowly, taking the long way around to reach the bride's house. Along the way, people looked out of their shops and houses at the loud baraat going slowly past. A few beggars and a couple of intelligent stray dogs who could predict a feast attached themselves to the back of the procession.

Finally, they reached their destination. As Mr. Ali turned into the street, he could hear the shout, "The baraat is here. The bridegroom has come!"

The road was covered with a thick tarpaulin, a stage erected at the far end and rows of chairs placed in front of it. The horse balked at the edge of the tarpaulin and stopped suddenly with its head down. Irshad tottered precariously in the saddle and clutched the reins tight—his knuckles white. The groom quieted the horse. He had to tell Irshad three times to loosen his hold on the reins before Irshad let go. There was more confusion because Irshad did not know how to get down from the mare. He finally managed it with his dignity more or less intact. The bride's family welcomed Irshad.

When they reached the tent that had been erected across the road in front of the bride's house, a lot of the bride's relatives and friends were waiting for them. Jehangir, Aisha's brother, greeted Mr. Ali with a hug. A pretty ten-year-old girl took Irshad's hand and said, "This way, elder brother."

She led him through the rows of chairs to the stage. Young girls and boys from Aisha's family sprinkled rose-perfumed water from silver sprinklers over the bridegroom and his party. Irshad took off his shoes and turned to the little boy who had announced that Irshad was coming out of the house and said, "Remember what I said. I will give you a chocolate later."

The boy nodded and sat by the shoes. Irshad climbed onto the stage and sat down cross-legged. Mr. Ali was one of the two official witnesses to the wedding, and he joined the bridegroom as well. The groom's party followed behind them and occupied the seats in front of the stage. The bride's party then filled the gaps until all the chairs were full and other people were left standing.

A dignified-looking old man with a neatly trimmed white beard came to the stage and sat down next to Irshad. He introduced himself to Mr. Ali and Irshad. The man was the imam of the local mosque and had known the bride's family for years.

"I was the imam at the wedding of the bride's parents, too," he said, smiling.

The other official witness was Aisha's oldest uncle. Mr. Ali took out a lace skullcap from his pocket and put it on. So did Aisha's uncle. A roughly dressed young man, obviously the sound man, came crawling over the stage, gave the imam a microphone, and went crawling back. The imam tapped on the microphone and the loud noise from the speakers silenced the crowd. The sound of a little boy crying and his mother remonstrating him became audible in the sudden silence. Everybody turned toward the sound, and the boy and his mother went quiet.

The imam waited a few more seconds and then said into the microphone, "Assalamu 'alaikum"—Peace be upon you.

The crowd muttered, "Wa 'laikum assalam"—And upon you, too, be peace.

The traditional greetings exchanged, the imam said, "Bismillah . . ."—In the name of Allah, the most beneficent, the most merciful . . .

"We are gathered here in this assembly of Muslims and non-Muslims to celebrate the marriage of Mohammed Irshad, son of the late Mohammed Ilyas of Vizag, and Aisha, unmarried daughter of Janab Syed Jalaluddin of this town. Marriage is a most sacred relation. The bride and groom accept each other as husband and wife of their own free will, without coercion. Remember the verse in the Quran: Your wives are a garment to you as you are a garment for them. The garment is worn next to our bodies; so should a husband and wife be. Just as a garment hides our nakedness and defects, so should the husband and wife keep each other's secrets from the rest of the world. Just as clothes provide comfort in inclement weather, a wife and husband should comfort each other against the trials of the world. Just as clothes add beauty and grace to our looks, so does a wife to her husband and a husband to his wife."

The imam looked around at the crowd and then turned to Irshad. He said, "Many men oppress their wives, but remember this is not Islamic. The Quran says that if you have certain rights over your wife, your wife too has certain rights over you in all fairness. Remember that Islam allows a woman to keep her own money and conduct her own business. Who does not know the example of the first and most beloved wife of our Prophet, Khadijah, who had her own business and even hired Mohammed, peace be upon him, as her agent to trade on her behalf? Fear God in your treatment of your wife, for you have taken her on the security of God. Your wife is your noble helper, not your slave."

The imam continued, "Of course, it is not all one way. Wives too have responsibilities to their husbands. A woman should protect her honor and her husband's property. A virtuous wife is indeed a man's best treasure. Insha'allah, God willing, this union will produce children; it is the woman's responsibility to raise them to be good people and good Muslims."

The imam opened the marriage register and got up. Mr. Ali and Aisha's uncle got up as well and followed him into the house where

Aisha and the other ladies were listening to the imam's words through a speaker. Aisha was sitting on a bed, wearing a red sari with a golden border. A bright red veil covered her head and shoulders. Her hands were colored with intricate henna patterns. She was surrounded by her mother and various female friends and cousins.

The imam asked Mr. Ali and Aisha's uncle to stand next to him. In front of the official witnesses, he asked her loudly, "Do you, Aisha, accept of your own free will Mohammed Irshad as your husband, with dower ten thousand rupees payable to you on your demand?"

"Yes," replied Aisha softly, from under her red veil.

The question was repeated twice more and was answered yes each time. The imam gave the register to Aisha and asked her to sign it. The three men left the room and came outside to where the bridegroom was sitting.

The imam asked, "Do you, Mohammed Irshad, accept of your own free will Aisha as your wife with dower ten thousand rupees payable to her on demand, which dower shall be her own personal property to spend or dispose of as she sees fit?"

"Yes," replied Irshad.

The question was repeated twice more and answered each time. The imam gave the register to Irshad and asked him to sign it. The two witnesses and finally the imam then added their signatures.

The imam closed the register and said, "I declare you, Mohammed Irshad and Aisha, as married in the presence of this assembly as witnesses to your marriage. God bless you and grant you a long and happy married life. Let us say a prayer to Allah for He has given us this boon of marriage to support us, to comfort us, and to make us whole."

The imam was the first to congratulate Irshad. Mr. Ali, sitting on the stage as a witness, was next. Aisha's father, uncles, and brother all shook hands with Irshad and hugged him three times, once on the right shoulder, then on the left shoulder and finally on the right shoulder again.

All the people got off the stage. Everybody wore shoes except Irshad, whose shoes were nowhere to be found. "Where are my shoes?" he asked.

All the people looked back at him blankly.

"Where is Pervez?" he asked.

They saw the young boy sitting a little distance away in a chair, eating an ice cream in a cone. Irshad had arranged for the young boy to look after his shoes, but it looked as if he had been outsmarted.

"Okay," he said. "Who has taken my shoes?"

"Your shoes, uncle?" asked the ten-year-old girl who had led him onto the stage, looking innocent.

He had gone from "elder brother" to "uncle" during the ceremony. Mr. Ali smiled. The girl was definitely not as innocent as she looked.

"Yes, dear. My shoes," Irshad said patiently.

"Are they lost, uncle?" she asked brightly.

"Yes, my girl. Where are they?" he asked.

"I can find them for you if you give me a fee," she replied.

"All right," Irshad said, taking a hundred-rupee note from his pocket and giving it to her.

The girl waved the hundred-rupee note in derision. "Nah!" she said. "That's not worth my time."

Irshad added another hundred-rupee note. She looked at him with the best sneer she could manage on her young face. Irshad sighed and added a five-hundred-rupee note.

"Shall I tell my aunt that she married a stingy man?" she asked, playing her trump card.

Irshad looked around. Everybody was laughing and he was embarrassed. He was definitely coming out second best in these negotiations.

He added three hundred rupees more, bringing the total to a thousand rupees. The girl looked thoughtfully at the money and glanced around at one of her older cousins standing a little bit away. The older cousin nodded discreetly and the girl turned to Irshad, took the money, and disappeared. She reappeared in a couple of minutes with the shoes.

"They were just around the corner, uncle. I don't know how they landed there," she said.

"I'm sure you don't." Irshad laughed, putting on his shoes.

Irshad was led into a room in the house. Mr. Ali decided to stay outside while people started stacking the chairs and unfolding tables for the wedding feast in the tent.

Mr. Ali started chatting to the other official witness, Aisha's oldest uncle. The gentleman's name was Mr. Iqbal and he had worked for the state government before retiring, in the irrigation department.

"Let's go and have a look at the food being prepared. It must be almost ready by now," he said, taking Mr. Ali's arm by the elbow.

The two men went through the crowded house to the open area at the back. There, the scene was one of organized chaos. Men and women rushed around carrying spices and utensils. Three large stones were placed in a triangle and a big cauldron, taller than a big boy, was on the stones. Stacks of firewood were burning under the cauldron. Steam enveloped a man stirring the spicy brinjal and bottle-gourd khatta with a five-foot-long iron spatula. A fat, bare-chested man with a towel tied around his forehead, to keep the sweat from pouring into his eyes, was standing next to an even larger cauldron. The large cauldron was sealed tight with a ring of cotton cloth covered with dough between the lid and the pot, and the fire underneath was banked. White-hot embers from the fire were spread on the lid, so the food inside was steaming as if in an oven. This was the famous dum biryani, without which any South Indian Muslim wedding is incomplete.

The menu at a South Indian Muslim wedding feast is always the same—mutton biryani, brinjal, and bottle-gourd side dish as a sauce, and a coconut and onion raita. Long after everything else is forgotten and the bride has become a matron with grown-up children, the biryani will still be remembered and used to grade the quality of the wedding celebration. The best meat is mutton from full-grown ram. There must be at least as much meat by weight as the rice—preferably one and a half times or even twice as much, if the family can afford it. Ideally, the rice should be basmati, but few families can afford that, and so a local long and thin-grained variety is acceptable. The meat and rice alone are not enough, however. There is the skill of the chef and the right combination of onion, chilies, ghee, salt, spices—cloves, cardamom, cinnamon, poppy seed, ginger, garlic, and a vast number of others—cooked for the right amount of time at the correct temperature. Cooking for a thousand people in one batch is not a job for the fainthearted, especially when all the guests have eaten the dish scores of times before and fancy themselves as critics.

Mr. Ali looked at the fat man and knew that he was the biryani chef. He was walking around the cauldron, checking the seal around the lid. The bride's uncle saw Mr. Ali looking at the chef. He said, "His name is Musa. He is a good cook, but not as good as his father. His father cooked the biryani at all our weddings, and people still talk about those feasts."

Musa gave a shout and several men ran to him, including the man stirring the khatta, or wet curry. The moment of truth had come. Mr. Ali and the bride's uncle moved to one side to give the men a clear space. The embers on the lid were swept away carefully. Two long wooden poles were brought and placed under the overhanging lip of the cauldron. The poles were tied together with old cotton saris. All the men took up position, holding the poles.

The chef counted, "One, two, three!"

On the count of three, the men's arms bulged and their faces tightened with strain as they lifted the hot and heavy cauldron off the stones and placed it on a sandpit previously prepared next to the stones, so it was away from the fire. The dough around the lid was dried up and it was hastily chipped away and the lid taken off. A vast amount of steam arose from the cauldron, bringing with it an aroma of cooked rice, meat, ghee, and spices. Everybody stopped, and all eyes were on the chef as he dug a big spatula into the food and took out a sample of the biryani. He tasted the rice, felt the texture of the mutton between his thumb and index finger, and popped it into his mouth. He chewed for a few seconds, and nodded and smiled. Mr. Ali had been unconsciously holding his breath and he let it out with big relief. The frowns of concentration around him were replaced by smiles. Musa turned around and called the bride's father. The bride's uncle joined her father in going to the chef, and pulled Mr. Ali along with him. They all tasted the biryani and gave it their approval. Musa nodded in satisfaction and shouted at his men to put the lid back on the cauldron, leaving a little gap for the steam to escape, and retired. His job was done.

After lunch, there was a lull while everybody rested, the bride and the groom separately. In the late afternoon, Mr. Ali knew, other ceremonies start, like jalwa—the show. In this ceremony, the bride and the bridegroom are shown to each other, traditionally, for the first time ever. There is much ribaldry and teasing of both the partners. Then comes the bidaai, the good-bye, when the bride takes leave of her father's house and her childhood, and accompanies her new husband to her new house to start her new life. There are always lots of tears at every bidaai, and there would be at this wedding as well.

Mr. Ali did not want to stay for all this, however. He looked around until he saw his wife talking to some ladies of the bride's family. He finally caught her eye and she came over.

Mr. Ali said, "That was a good wedding, wasn't it?"

Mrs. Ali sighed. She said, "You know how young women become broody when they see their friends' babies? I feel like that now."

Mr. Ali looked at his wife, alarmed. "What?" he asked. "Broody?"

"No, silly!" She laughed. "I long to see our son's wedding. I wish to see him on a horse with a floral veil covering his face going for his bride."

"I know what you mean. I feel like that too, but I don't see when our silly son will give us that pleasure," he said. "Anyway, let's go. I don't want to see all the crying and wailing at the bidaai."

Mrs. Ali agreed. They said their good-byes and left.

SIXTEEN

Aruna was in the office and getting bored. She wondered how Irshad's wedding was going. She had never attended a Muslim wedding before, so she didn't know the sequence of ceremonies. Mr. Ali had missed the deadline for placing the ads in the Sunday papers and it was very quiet. No clients had come in all morning and there were hardly any phone calls.

Mr. Ali had told her to contact a Kapu girl's father and give him the details of a potential match. The bridegroom was working in a multi-national company in Delhi, though the boy's parents lived locally. She called the father, but he was not at home. She left a message and hung up. She decided to write the postcards they used to reply to people who responded to their advertisements.

Half an hour later, Aruna had written a pile of cards and her fingers were cramped. She dropped the pen on the table and massaged the fingers on her right hand. She was thinking of shutting shop and going home early when the doorbell rang and in walked Ramanujam.

"Hello," she said in surprise.

"Hi, Aruna," he replied.

"Did Mr. Ali call you and say that you had more matches?" she asked. "I don't remember any coming in."

Ramanujam did not say anything. She got up and pulled out his file from the cupboard. There was no note in it and she checked the new joiners file. A Brahmin girl had joined the day before, after she had gone home.

"Must be this one," she said, and took the form from the file.

She read out the details of the girl, "Twenty-four years old, five feet, seven inches." She looked up at him. "She's quite tall, isn't she?"

Ramanujam nodded.

She went back to reading the form, "Graduate in home science, doesn't want to work after marriage, fair. The family's wealthy, too. They own several houses in town and are willing to give a large dowry. They haven't said how much, though. She has one brother and he is a doctor in America."

She looked up at him and said, "Sounds ideal to me. What do you think?"

Ramanujam said, "I——"

"Oh! Look," interrupted Aruna. "We've got a photograph of her."

She jumped up and went to the cupboard and took out a photograph. She looked at the photograph and handed it to Ramanujam. She said, "She looks beautiful. I wish I had a complexion like that." She laughed ruefully.

Ramanujam looked briefly at the photograph and set it aside. "Aruna . . ." he said.

Something in his tone caught Aruna's attention. She slowly sat down in her chair.

"Relax," he said. "I didn't come for any matches."

"Oh," she replied, puzzled. "But it doesn't matter what you came for. This girl is still very suitable. I am sure your family will find her perfect."

"I was in the area, so I thought I'd drop by," he said.

"That's good of you. Sir and madam are out and it has been very quiet. It's lucky that you came when you did. I was actually thinking of shutting the office and going home early," Aruna said. "By the way, thanks very much for taking us to your orchard. We had a wonderful time. Vani also asked me to thank you."

"I enjoyed the day very much. I should thank you. Or maybe I should thank the ticket inspector who was so officious." Ramanujam laughed.

Aruna shuddered. "Thank God you called back after I missed you. I was getting worried—stuck out there with no cash. That reminds me, let me return your money," she said, taking out a hundred-rupee note from her purse.

He waved it away. "Don't be silly!" he said. "If you hadn't called, I would have missed a lovely day out."

"No, no," said Aruna. "You said it was a loan."

"All right," Ramanujam said, and took the money from her. "How is Vani? Tell her that I haven't forgotten about the cashew mangoes. When they are ripe, I'll get some."

"Thank you," said Aruna. "She really loved the orchard."

"What about you? Did you like it too?" asked Ramanujam.

"Of course," said Aruna. "It was absolutely wonderful. We lived in several villages when I was growing up and it reminded me of them. But it wasn't just the place. I thought the company was good too."

Ramanujam looked at her intensely. "Really?" he said.

Aruna blushed. "Yes," she said, lifting her chin. "I enjoyed your company."

"That's what I like about you, Aruna," said Ramanujam. "You are so artless."

"Is that a compliment?" asked Aruna.

"Yes, it is. Most girls think it is cool to be coy," said Ramanujam.

"I know, but I've grown out of it," said Aruna, laughing.

"How is your dad?" asked Ramanujam. "Is he still opposed to you getting married?"

Aruna's eyes flashed. "It's not that he doesn't want me to be married. We don't have the savings for a wedding without going into debt. Also, he cannot see how the family can manage once we are in debt and I am not earning."

Ramanujam said, "Sorry. I didn't mean it like that. So the problem is not going away?"

Aruna sighed. "No," she said softly.

"Shall we go out for lunch?" asked Ramanujam.

"No," said Aruna, shocked. "My parents are expecting me at home."

"Some other time?" asked Ramanujam.

"Maybe," said Aruna doubtfully. She had never gone out with a man except for the picnic, and even then, Vani had been there. She supposed that rich people did that sort of thing regularly and going out for lunch didn't mean anything. Among her own family and friends, there would be a scandal and her reputation would be ruined if anybody saw her with a man.

They both fell silent and Aruna started fiddling with some papers on her desk.

After a little while Ramanujam said, "Aruna . . ."

Aruna looked up from her desk. "Yes?" she said.

Before Ramanujam could continue, the phone rang. "Sorry," she said to him, picking up the phone.

It was a client who had become a member a week before and had not yet received his lists. Aruna looked through the new joiners file and found his details. The lists had been sent out only a couple of days earlier, because of all the delays during the week.

"Your lists are in the mail, sir. Please call us back if you don't get them in the next couple of days," she said.

Aruna put the phone down and said to Ramanujam, "Sorry."

"That's all right," said Ramanujam.

"What did you want to talk about?" asked Aruna.

Ramanujam took a deep breath. "Aruna, will you marry me?" he asked.

Aruna was startled at the question and looked into his face.

"No, Ram," she said, using his name for the very first time. "I cannot marry you."

He looked shocked and Aruna knew she had wounded him. She was sure she was doing the right thing, but by God, why did it hurt so much?

Aruna closed her eyes, but she could still picture him smiling in her mind. She remembered her relief and how safe she had felt when he stepped out of the car outside the old lady's café the other day.

She opened her eyes to find him still looking at her intently. *He is absolutely perfect,* she thought, but the whole idea was impossible. His family was looking for a beautiful bride from a wealthy background. His mother and sister were so sophisticated and she would be too gauche in their midst. She couldn't imagine Ram being comfortable in her father's front room, sitting on the metal folding chairs with the paint faded from the seats after long use. And the scandal! What would her father say if she went home and announced that she had found her own husband? On top of all this, how would her family cope without her income? Vani might have to leave her education unfinished.

Ramanujam sat on the sofa, his head hanging down. Aruna wanted very much to sit next to him and hug him. Why did she have to refuse him? Wouldn't it be so wonderful if she could just say yes and not worry about the consequences? They got along quite well—they could talk about a dozen subjects, they made each other laugh. He was rich, with a good job, and was without doubt a great catch in the marriage market. She knew that, given her family circumstances, she was lucky to get any proposal, let alone from somebody as eligible as Ramanujam. *It's a dream, and poor people cannot afford dreams,* she told herself. *That way lies unhappiness.* She had to stick to her duty and let her karma unwind itself as it would.

Ramanujam got up after a minute. "Bye, Aruna," he said.

She stood up as well. "I am sorry. I hope we can still be friends. I'm still hoping to eat the cashew mangoes, you know," she said, smiling sadly.

"Are you sure?" he asked.

"Yes," replied Aruna, even though she knew this was dangerous. It would be best if she cut him off completely, but she couldn't bear to do it just yet. She thought he was one of the most handsome men she had met. He was the first man who had proposed to her for her own sake, not as the result of a match sought between two families. The thought of never meeting him again was unbearable, even though it was taking all her strength to keep her resolve.

Ramanujam nodded. "See you around, Aruna. I hope you have the best in life always," he said, and left quickly.

Aruna waited until she heard the door of his car slam shut and the car move away. She moved slowly to her desk and sat down. Suddenly, without any warning, she burst into tears. Why? Why? Why was life so difficult?

He would probably forget her soon and move on. She doubted if she could do the same.

• • •

Mr. and Mrs. Ali found their taxi. The driver was snoring in the front seat of the taxi with a door open. He was, no doubt, sleeping off the excellent biryani. Mr. Ali woke him up.

"Sorry, sir," said the driver, getting up. "Are we leaving now?"

"Yes," said Mr. Ali. "Let's go."

They got into the car and settled in the backseat. As the car was about to start, Mr. Ali leaned forward and asked, "Do you know the way to Royyapalem? How long will it take?"

"It is not far, sir. It will take less than an hour," said the driver.

Mr. Ali turned to his wife and asked, "Shall we go there?"

Her eyes were shining and she nodded eagerly.

Mr. Ali turned to the driver and said, "Let's go to Royyapalem first."

"The taxi has only been paid for a direct journey," said the driver. "It will cost two hundred rupees more to go there. Also, if we don't get back to the city by seven, there will be a waiting charge as well."

"That's all right," said Mr. Ali. "Let's go."

Royyapalem was a village by the side of the highway. The taxi left the highway and turned left into the village onto a narrow road that was heavily pitted with potholes. Mrs. Ali had heard so much about Royyapalem in the last few weeks that she was disappointed to find that it was just another small village, like many she had seen over the years. There was something strange about the village, though, that she couldn't quite figure out at first. As they jolted down the road, she saw a few brick houses and many thatched huts crowding the road. There were stray dogs panting in the shade of the houses, and the taxi slowed down almost to a stop to get past a black buffalo standing in the middle of the road defecating. They came to a small market. Mrs. Ali knew it was a market because there was an open place with little mounds on either side of the road. In the evening, each mound would become a stall selling a different vegetable. As they crossed the market, Mrs. Ali suddenly realized what was eerie about the village.

She turned to her husband and said, "There's nobody about. There are always people walking by or just sitting in front of their houses looking at the road in every village I've been to, but here, the place is empty. It looks abandoned."

Mr. Ali nodded. "I was thinking the same thing," he said.

The road turned and twisted until it came to an open square in front of a pukka building with a statue of Gandhi in front of it. There were a lot of people here. There were many police with lathis standing in little groups. Red and orange tents, not unlike the one used at Irshad and Aisha's wedding, had been erected down one side of the square. The tent in the middle was bigger than the others and it had a long banner in front of it, on two long bamboo poles, with the words, JUSTICE FOR FARMERS.

A police constable came up to them and the taxi stopped. He bent at the waist and put his head in at the taxi's window.

"Why have you come here?" he asked.

"We've come to see our son," said Mr. Ali.

"You are not allowed to come into the village," said the constable.

"Please," said Mrs. Ali, leaning forward and turning toward the constable.

The constable looked at her and said in surprise, "I know you, madam. You were the mother on TV."

Mrs. Ali said, "Yes, I was."

The constable said, "We were all watching TV in our house when we saw you. My mother was most affected. She said that she totally understood your feelings. We are Christians, madam, and she said a special prayer for you at Mass the next Sunday."

Mrs. Ali said, "Oh, that's very kind of your mother. Please give her my thanks."

The constable nodded and asked them to park the car to one side and walk over to the big tent in the center.

As they were walking down, another police constable tried to stop them, but the first one shouted out, "It's okay. I've given them permission."

"The power of celebrity," said Mr. Ali.

"Don't mock. It's letting us see our son," said Mrs. Ali.

At the entrance to the tent, a young man stopped them. Mrs. Ali recognized him as one of Rehman's friends from the city who had appeared for trial alongside her son. He seemed surprised to see them.

"Sir, madam . . . has anybody told you?" he said.

"Told us what?" said Mr. Ali.

"Rehman was perfectly fine until two days ago. He probably ate something that disagreed with him, because he was sick and fell suddenly ill."

Mrs. Ali was worried now. She went quickly into the tent, with her husband and the young man following her. There was nobody inside.

"Where is Rehman?" she asked.

"Over there, madam," said the young man, and took her to a corner that had been curtained off.

They went behind the curtain. Rehman was lying down on a charpoy, a rough cot strung with hemp rope. He appeared to be sweating. There were three other men standing around the cot.

"What's happened to my son?" cried Mrs. Ali, and rushed to the cot.

Rehman propped himself up on a pillow with difficulty. He grimaced and said, "I'm all right, amma."

She sat down on the cot next to Rehman and hugged him. "You are burning up," she cried.

Rehman patted her hand and turned to the men. "Leave," he said. "Section One Forty-four is still in force. Only five people are allowed here at a time. Let's not give the police an excuse to arrest us."

The men left quickly and Rehman turned to his parents. Mr. Ali was now sitting on the other side of the cot, and he put a hand on his forehead.

"You are really unwell, son," he said.

"It's all right, abba. Just a fever," said Rehman.

"What did the doctor say?" said Mrs. Ali.

Rehman didn't say anything. His friend who was standing at the foot of the cot said, "He hasn't seen a doctor yet."

"How come?" said Mrs. Ali, turning to the friend. "He's really unwell. Even if he doesn't want to, you should have forced him to see a doctor. What kind of friend are you?"

The friend appeared embarrassed. He hung his head and shuffled his feet. She turned to Rehman. "You are going to see a doctor now, and I won't hear a word from you."

Rehman dropped back on the cot. "Ammi," he said in a weak voice, "there is no doctor in this village."

"No doctor? What do you mean, no doctor?" said Mrs. Ali.

"You grew up in a village, ammi. You know better than me what villages are like," said Rehman. "There is no doctor here. Even if there was a doctor, there is no pharmacy."

She fell silent.

A young man came in and said to Rehman, "Sorry to disturb you, Rehman, but I've got a student union president from Vijayawada on the phone. He is asking how many men you want him to bring here. He says he can mobilize over five hundred college students."

Rehman thought for a moment and said, "There's no point in bringing them all here. They'll just be stopped outside the village by the police."

He closed his eyes and Mrs. Ali mopped his brow with her handkerchief. He opened his eyes and said, "I know. Tell him to organize a protest rally in Vijayawada supporting us. In fact, this is a great idea. Ask him to speak to student leaders in other towns. Let's do it as well. Let's take a few days to organize this properly and have simultaneous protests across the state. We'll rattle the government to its bones."

The young man who had come in was excited too. "That's a fantastic idea. I'll get to it right now."

Rehman tried to get up but failed.

Mrs. Ali said, "Rehman, you are so weak. Come back with us to the city. You can see a doctor and come back when you are better."

Rehman shook his head. "No, ammi. We are almost at the end here. We just have to be strong here for a little longer and we'll win. I cannot leave now."

Mr. Ali said, "Don't be stubborn, Rehman. You are not well. Who knows what disease you've got? You don't get a high temperature from eating something dodgy. This is definitely different. I can feel it. The sooner you see a doctor, the better."

Rehman's friend said, "You could be right, uncle. He said that there were traces of blood when he was sick."

Rehman glared at his friend and his friend quickly covered his mouth with his hand.

"Don't silence your friend," said Mrs. Ali. "It sounds really serious. Please come home with us."

They argued for several minutes until Rehman fell back to the bed in exhaustion, but he did not give in. Finally, Mr. and Mrs. Ali said their good-byes.

When they came out of the tent, Mrs. Ali gave their phone number to Rehman's friend and said, "Please call me every day and tell me how he is doing."

"I will, madam," said the friend.

They walked back to their taxi. A young woman hailed them as they were about to get in. It was the same journalist who had interviewed Rehman and Mrs. Ali at the courthouse.

"Sir, madam," she said, "my name is Usha. Can I have a quick chat with you on camera? The police won't let me go into the tent. I have been waiting since morning to speak to your son, but I don't see him at all."

Mrs. Ali declined initially, but the young woman persuaded her.

"Your son is really brave, madam. He's a hero and our viewers will love him," Usha said.

Soon, the camera was pointing at Mrs. Ali and Usha.

"You asked your son not to come back to Royyapalem. Now that you have seen him here, what is your opinion?" the journalist asked.

"As a mother, my fears have come true. My son is unwell in the tent but he will not give up the struggle. The protest is going strong and he says he cannot leave here now," said Mrs. Ali.

"I am sorry to hear that your son is unwell. What's wrong with him?" Usha looked concerned.

"He has a high fever. I don't know what's wrong with him," Mrs. Ali said, and tears flowed down her cheeks. "No doctor has seen him and he refuses to leave the village and come to the city. The government wants to build big industries here, but there isn't even a doctor in this village. The people in power should get their priorities straight."

The young woman signaled to the cameraman. "Wrap," she said.

· · ·

Mrs. Ali was very depressed after coming back from Royyapalem. She was also severely embarrassed over the next few days. The clip of her talking to the journalist, titled "A Mother's Further Anguish," was played again and again on TV.

A couple of days after they came back, she overheard Mr. Ali talking to Rehman on the phone.

"Your mother is feeling very down. She is not meeting anybody and is refusing to step out of the house. She is not even standing at the gate in the evenings to watch the world go by," said Mr. Ali.

He listened for a while and then said, "What do you mean, the protest is important? Do your mother's feelings have no importance? She and I are worried that you have contracted some serious illness. Just come for a day, get checked by a doctor, and go back."

The conversation went on for a while and Mr. Ali's voice took on a pleading note. Rehman obviously did not budge, because Mr. Ali put the phone back on its hook, and leaned back in the chair and closed his eyes. He looked tired, and Mrs. Ali's heart went out to her husband. She slipped away and expected Mr. Ali to mention the call later so they could discuss it, but he never did.

Each day in the evening, she got a call from Rehman's friend. A few days went by and the news was finally encouraging. Rehman's temperature came down and he was able to get out of bed for a couple of hours. He progressed well after that. One week after their visit, Mrs. Ali spoke to Rehman. He was now back to normal. He told Mrs. Ali that they had been able to contact student leaders across the state and were organizing protest marches on the following Tuesday. Mrs. Ali told Rehman to be careful.

Mr. Ali refused to speak to his son. Mrs. Ali was again torn between two powerful forces, neither of which would give way.

SEVENTEEN

Aruna had been depressed all week. The spark had gone out of her. She felt like a ryot, a tenant farmer, who sees locusts swarming on his ready-to-be-harvested field—watching his crop disappearing and knowing that his difficulties are just beginning. Aruna hadn't told anyone about Ramanujam's proposal—not even her sister. She went about her days like an automaton.

On Monday, Vani said to her, "Come to Jagadamba Junction at nine in the morning tomorrow."

Aruna said, "Why? I have to be in the office by then."

"Akka, you've been miserable all week. It will do you good to do something different," said Vani.

"I am not miserable," said Aruna.

"Yes, you are. Amma's noticed it too. We think you are working too hard. Just come there tomorrow. I will guarantee that once you tell him what you saw, your boss won't mind that you came late to the office," said Vani.

"What? How do you know what Mr. Ali will say, anyway? You haven't even met him," said Aruna.

"Don't argue, akka. Just do it for me, please . . ." said Vani.

Aruna sighed. "All right. I'll come, just to prove that I am not depressed."

"Good!" said Vani.

The next day, Aruna left home a bit earlier than normal to go to Jagadamba Junction. When she reached there, she was surprised to see police everywhere. She stood in the shade of a shop and watched. The eponymous Jagadamba cinema was opposite her. A large poster at the cinema showed a blond girl screaming in terror at some unseen horror. It was the only cinema in town that regularly showed Hollywood movies. All the others showed Hindi or Telugu movies.

Aruna waited for a while, looking at her watch in irritation. It was almost nine-twenty and nothing was happening. The place looked more crowded than normal, but Jagadamba Junction was always busy, so she couldn't really tell. Two roads led out of the northern end of the junction on either side of a small old Christian graveyard: one leading uphill to the University and the other to the newer part of town. The road to the south led to the old part of town, and the road to the east led to the collector office and to King George Hospital. Ramanujam came to her mind with KGH, and she couldn't stop thinking about him.

She must have looked miserable, because somebody said, "Why are you feeling so bad, lady? You are young and you look healthy. I am sure everything will turn out for the best."

Aruna snapped out of her reverie and looked at the old toothless woman in front of her. She had never seen the woman before in her life. Aruna shook her head and said, "It's nothing, baamma. I am all right."

The old woman nodded and walked away. Aruna looked around. It was definitely more crowded now. And the people were not walking. They were all standing there, as if waiting, like her, for something to happen. After five minutes or so, she heard a noise coming down the University road. It was getting louder and louder, and soon everybody craned their necks in the direction of the noise. The police were talking on their radios and had lined up along the road. Suddenly, there was no traffic.

A noisy procession of students came walking along the road. The procession went on and on; there must have been over a thousand students marching. Some of them had drums and trumpets. Many of them were carrying banners: JUSTICE FOR FARMERS; RESPECT ROYYAPALEM RYOTS RIGHTS; VILLAGERS REQUIRE DOCTORS, NOT MULTINATIONALS; LISTEN TO PEOPLE'S TEARS, NOT TO STOCKS AND SHARES; DOWN WITH WTO.

Aruna wondered how the World Trade Organization had gotten entangled in this protest. Was it a leftover banner from an earlier protest?

A student at the front was walking backward, facing the rest of the procession. He had a megaphone in his hand, and said in an amplified voice, "Justice for . . ."

"Farmers," the students thundered in reply.

The drums boomed and the trumpets blew.

The megaphone-wielding student shouted, "Doctors, not . . ."

"Multinationals," came the loud roar.

The procession walked slowly past Aruna. She tried to look for Vani, but her sister could not be seen in the crowd.

"Government," shouted the voice from the front.

"Down! Down!"

The drums went *boom! boom!*

The trumpets blew loud and clear.

It took more than five minutes for the procession to clear the junction. She heard someone say that the students were marching to the district collector's office, where they would present a letter with ten thousand signatures protesting against the Royyapalem land seizures. Aruna waited until the crowd dissipated and took a bus to Mr. Ali's house.

The next week, Aruna's fugue did not dissipate. She thought it must be the weather. After the first shower, the rains had been delayed and a hot spell had taken hold. It was over 104 degrees every day and was very humid as well.

Her mother asked Aruna to take some time off, but she refused. The day after that, just as Aruna was about to leave for the office, her father told her that he wanted to visit his brother at Annavaram and he needed her help.

"Did amma put you up to this?" asked Aruna.

Aruna's father gave her a severe glance and Aruna blushed. "Sorry," she said.

"You are looking run-down, Aruna. A few days' break will do you good. And I really need your help. I don't want to travel on my own," he said.

"No, naanna. I don't want to leave now. We are very busy in the office at the moment," she said, stepping out of the door.

At ten in the morning, Mr. Ali went to the bank to deposit a check that a client had given. Aruna was alone in the office. The postman had just left and she was dealing with the day's mail when the phone rang.

"Hello, Mr. Ali's Marriage Bureau here. How may I help you?" she said.

"Hello. Is Mr. Ali there?" asked a woman's voice, sounding vaguely familiar.

"No, madam. He is not here. Can I assist you?" she asked.

"Maybe you can," said the voice. "We are clients of yours—my brother is Ramanujam, the doctor."

Aruna's heart stopped for a moment and she gripped the phone tightly. She gulped and said, "I remember you, madam. You came with your brother and mother. What can I do for you?"

She was pleased that her voice sounded steady.

Ramanujam's sister answered, "We had a family conference yesterday and decided that we need to intensify the search. I think you should advertise again, and more widely."

Aruna said, "Okay, madam. I will tell sir what you said when he comes in."

"You do that. I am busy for the next couple of days, but I will drop in to your office after that."

Aruna put the phone down slowly and stared sightlessly across the verandah. Suddenly, her composure broke and she buried her face in her hands and started sobbing.

"Is everything okay, Aruna?"

Aruna looked up and found to her horror that Mrs. Ali was standing in front of her. She nodded and turned away quickly. Mrs. Ali was silent for a moment and Aruna hoped that Mrs. Ali hadn't noticed her crying.

"What happened, Aruna? Why the tears?" asked Mrs. Ali gently.

Aruna turned reluctantly back to Mrs. Ali and said, "I don't know what to do, madam. I'm so confused." Fresh tears flowed down her cheeks.

Mrs. Ali said, "Come, my dear. Let's go inside. Anybody can walk in on us here."

She led Aruna into the house and sat down next to her on the settee. "There, there, don't cry, my dear. Everything will be fine. Tell me, what's the problem?"

Aruna was silent for a moment, her natural reticence warring with her need to tell somebody. Mrs. Ali just sat quietly next to her.

Finally, Aruna said, "Do you know Ramanujam, madam? One of our clients."

Mrs. Ali thought for a moment and said, "Yes, I remember. He is a doctor, isn't he?"

"That's right, madam."

Aruna didn't say anything else, and after a couple of seconds, Mrs. Ali prompted her. "What about him?"

Aruna said, "He proposed to me, madam."

Mrs. Ali laughed and said, "What is there to cry about, my dear? You should take it as a compliment."

"I said no, madam. I refused." Aruna started to cry again.

"Have you talked to anybody about this?" Mrs. Ali asked.

Aruna shook her head through her tears. Mrs. Ali put her arm around the young woman's shoulders and said, "You shouldn't bottle these matters up. Talk to me. Tell me, do you like him?"

Aruna nodded. "God forgive me. Yes, I do. I like him. After I said no, I thought the pain was only temporary. I thought that I would be all right again in a few days. But, no! The pain has only gotten worse. It's just consuming me and I don't know what to do."

Mrs. Ali stayed silent and hugged her while Aruna cried herself out. After a little while, Aruna stopped crying, wiped her eyes on her dupatta, and looked up, embarrassed.

"Sorry, madam," she said.

"There's nothing to be sorry about. You needed a good cry. So, tell me, if you like him so much, why did you refuse him?"

"Think about it, madam. You know what kind of girl his family is looking for for him. I'm not suitable at all. They are looking for a beautiful girl from a big family. I'm not beautiful. We are a very ordinary family—not millionaires like them."

"Don't run yourself down, my dear. Money isn't everything. Knowledge and character are more important, and in these matters your family is no less than any other family in this land."

"But that's not all, madam. My family needs me right now. My sister is in college, and my father's pension has been cut. It will be difficult for them to manage just on that pension. I need to work and support them until my father's pension recovers and my sister finishes her education. Ramanujam's family doesn't want a working woman as a wife. And even if I worked, which husband would agree to let me give my earnings to my parents? I cannot think of marriage for another three or four years, at least," said Aruna.

Mrs. Ali said, "Aruna, sometimes in life you have to be selfish. Your family will manage somehow. Ramanujam is not going to wait three or four years to get married. His parents won't allow that. Think about yourself, too. It is well known that it is more difficult for girls to get married as they get older. In a few years' time, your sister will get married and go away. Your parents are old—who knows how long they will be around? You will become lonely and embittered. Your sister will start resenting you because human beings cannot remain grateful for long, you know. I have seen cases like this—and it always happens to the best girls, just like you. Ironically, girls who don't think so much about their family and are a little bit self-centered are not only happier themselves, but also maintain good relationships with their families."

Aruna said, "I know you are wiser than me, madam. But I'm not sure if I can do anything different. Also, he is a rich man and we are quite poor. As a son-in-law, he will come sometimes to my parents' house and expect to be treated properly. How can my parents afford that? And if he insulted my parents because of our small house or our poverty, then I couldn't bear it."

Mrs. Ali said, "If he was so boorish as to do that, then he is not the man for you. But Ramanujam doesn't look like a man who will act that way. Don't forget that you are both from this town. It's not as if he will ever need to stay overnight at your parents' place. He will come for short visits, and I'm sure he will give your family the courtesy they deserve."

Aruna said, "How do we know, madam? He has always been rich, so how does he know how to handle poor people? Anyway, this is all moot. I insulted him by refusing his hand in marriage and I doubt if he will look at me again. His sister called just now and asked to advertise once again for more matches. Men are proud, madam, and they cannot take a rejection sanguinely."

A few minutes later, Aruna got up from the settee and said, "Please don't tell sir about this. It is very embarrassing."

Mrs. Ali nodded and said, "You've done nothing wrong to be ashamed about, my dear. But if that's what you want, I'll keep it to myself."

Aruna smiled softly and said, "Thank you, madam."

That afternoon, after lunch, she went to her father and agreed to take a week's leave and accompany him to his brother's place in the temple town of Annavaram.

Aruna's absence was a shock to Mr. Ali's system. He realized just how much help it was to have an efficient assistant. He had to curtail his walks and, quite often, his afternoon naps. Luckily, it was so hot that few clients came until after five in the evening. *But all it takes to break a siesta is one client,* he thought sourly.

On Wednesday, all the clients had gone and he was just about to close up when in walked an old client—Sridevi, the florist divorcée.

"Namaste," she said, folding her hands.

Mr. Ali returned her greeting and said, "Did you get the details of Venu, the computer service engineer that we sent? Are you looking for more matches?"

"No." Sridevi laughed. "I am getting married again, and I was in the area, so I've dropped in to say thanks."

"Really . . . that's great news. So, did you manage to get in touch with Venu?" asked Mr. Ali.

"No. I am not marrying him or anybody you gave me the details of, but I would still like to thank you," she said.

"How come?" asked Mr. Ali, puzzled. "Please take a seat," he added, realizing that she was still standing.

She took a seat and said, "It's probably easier if I tell you the whole story."

Mr. Ali nodded and put his pen down, giving her his full attention.

"As you know, after I got divorced, my family boycotted me. They wouldn't speak to me or invite me to any family functions. It was as if I had never existed. That was hard to bear. Anyway, I kept busy with my business and that was some compensation. I finally decided to make a clean break and get married again. That's when I contacted you. Do you remember I said that my younger uncle was coming for dinner when you called about Venu?"

"Yes, I remember," said Mr. Ali.

"He is my father's youngest brother. He stayed with us while he was at University and I was a child. I'm his favorite niece. He had gone to Oman just before I got married, and he was really upset that he could not attend my wedding. Anyway, he's done well in the Gulf and has come back a very rich man. He brought lots of gifts for everyone, including me, and found out that the family had cut me off. He contacted me straightaway and came around to dinner."

Mr. Ali nodded.

"At dinner, I couldn't stop talking and finally started crying. He consoled me and left. I thought that was the end of it, but then, two days later, he came to my shop at the hotel and said he felt like eating Chinese food. I was surprised because it was three in the afternoon. He took me to the restaurant in the hotel itself. The restaurant was completely empty except for one man in a corner table. It was my ex-husband. I wanted to leave, but my uncle stopped me. As you can imagine, the atmosphere between my ex-husband and me was very stiff in the beginning, but slowly we relaxed. We had always gotten along together except for a few specific issues. My uncle got a phone call on his mobile phone after a while and he ducked out, leaving us alone. We started talking and I found out that he had not remarried, which surprised me because I would have expected his parents to get him married off to some poor girl as soon we were divorced. My ex-husband even knew that I owned the florist's in the hotel. After some time, my uncle came back. He saw how we were getting along and told us that he had booked and paid for a dinner for two at another restaurant that weekend, but his friend had dropped out. He wanted us to go in their place. I suspected a rat and said that he could not possibly expect me to go out with a man who was not my husband," said Sridevi, stopping and looking up at him.

Mr. Ali nodded and waved his hand, asking her to go on.

Sridevi continued, "My uncle laughed and said that Hinduism does not recognize divorce. So, even though the law might say that we were not husband and wife, in front of God we were still married. My ex tried to interrupt him, but my uncle had just got started. We are not Muslims, my uncle said, whose religion allows them to divorce, nor even Christians who vow till death do us part. You are Hindus and you were married with the sacred fire as witness. You went around the fire seven times as part of the wedding ceremony, and you are bound even beyond death—seven lifetimes together, in fact."

Mr. Ali nodded in understanding. "What happened then?" he asked.

Sridevi continued, "We went out a few times and found that we actually got along quite well, and I warmed up to the idea of getting back together with him again. However, my ex wasn't showing any signs of wanting to move forward until I mentioned to him and my uncle that I was considering the match you sent me. Once I said that, my ex was suddenly a man in a hurry. Apparently, he did not like the idea of me marrying anybody else! Suddenly, he was the one pushing for marriage and I was the one holding back. Anyway, because I was now in a position of strength, I negotiated what I wanted—we would move out of his parents' house and set up on our own. I will continue to run my business, and any money that I earn will be mine to keep and spend as I want. I told him I planned to hire a full-time maid with the money I was earning, so there would be no more complaints about the cooking or the housekeeping. So, all's well that ends well, and I'm getting married in a fortnight at the register office."

"That's fantastic news," said Mr. Ali. "Best news I've heard all week."

"Thank you, sir," she said.

Mr. Ali said, "I'm now talking as somebody elder to you, so don't take this amiss. Marriage is all about compromise. I always say that most people become my clients because they are not flexible enough. They want everything—a tall son-in-law in a good job who is the only son of a wealthy family, when their daughter is rather plain and they are not willing to pay a large dowry. Or they want a beautiful, well-educated daughter-in-law in an executive position when their own son is a tenth-class failed loafer. To find a partner, you need to compromise. But the need for compromise doesn't end there. Married life is the greatest pleasure—*if* you compromise; otherwise, it is hell on earth. You are a very lucky woman. Due to the grace of God and your uncle's efforts, you are being given a second chance. Don't throw it away. Certainly, the money you earn is yours—but don't flaunt it. Give your husband a share of your earnings every month so he can use it to run the household. Don't make him ask for the money. Ask his advice on how to invest your money. He has agreed to separate from his parents. Go with him to visit his parents regularly—once a week or fortnight. Keep them on your side—ignore any snide remarks they make, give them little gifts now and then. Sure, you will hire a full-time maid, but give the maid an occasional day off and cook dinner for your husband. I am not saying that you should be the only one to compromise, but you are the only person *you* have control over."

Sridevi nodded, and said, "Thanks for your advice, uncle. I'll definitely keep it in mind. You are right. I am a lucky woman who has been given a second chance."

As he was showing Sridevi out, Ramanujam's sister came in.

"Hello, please sit down," he said. "Aruna told me that you called."

She sat down on the sofa and said, "We are not getting any more matches. I think we should advertise again."

Mr. Ali nodded, and said, "That's probably not a bad idea. I've already prepared an ad. Let's concentrate on English newspapers this time. It will cost more, however. Our fees don't cover the cost of a second advertisement in the English papers. It will probably cost another two or three hundred rupees."

"That's no problem," Ramanujam's sister said, and took out three hundred rupees from her purse.

"Let me see if we've received any Brahmin matches recently," said

Mr. Ali. He went through the new joiners list and came across one almost at the end.

"This came in about ten days ago. I don't think we've sent it to you," he said. "The girl's name is Sita—ideal for somebody called Ram!"

Ramanujam's sister smiled, and Mr. Ali continued, "She is twenty four-years old and five feet, seven inches tall."

She looked up at him and said, "Perfect height."

Mr. Ali nodded and said, "Home science graduate, doesn't want to work after marriage, fair. They own several houses in town and are willing to give a large dowry. They haven't said how much, but they've told me that for the ideal match, money is not going to be a problem. She has a brother who is a doctor in America."

Ramanujam's sister said, "The match sounds very good. Do you have a photograph?"

He looked at the form again and said, "Yes, we do have a photograph."

He took out the photo from the wardrobe and gave it to her. She looked at the picture intently and said, "She looks beautiful—so fair and slim."

Mr. Ali copied the details out onto a piece of paper and gave it to her. She folded the paper and put it in her handbag. "Can I take the photograph as well?" she asked.

Mr. Ali hesitated. "Normally, we don't allow photos of girls to be taken away."

She replied, "I understand, but I promise to send it back. The match is so good that I don't want to waste any time."

Mr. Ali nodded and said, "All right, but please take care of the photo and make sure we have it back in a couple of days."

She nodded and stood up, ready to go. Mr. Ali got up as well and saw her to the door.

She asked, "Where is your assistant? Is it her day off?"

"No, she was not feeling well, so she's taken a week off," said Mr. Ali, and closed the gate behind her.

The next day, Mrs. Ali was making dosas, black-gram crepes, for breakfast while Mr. Ali was shaving. As usual, he had the radio on high volume and was listening to the news.

The newscaster said, "At an early-morning briefing today, the state government has announced that land acquisition will stop at Royya-palem. The chief minister said that his government was not against farmers and that they would consult more widely on the locations for Special Economic Zones. The government will also take another look at the compensation packages that are being offered and see if at least one member of each displaced family could be guaranteed a job in the Economic Zone. The announcement follows days of widening protests across the state that have shaken the government and brought its very survival into question."

Mrs. Ali screamed in joy and Mr. Ali jerked his head up and said, "Oww!"

He had nicked himself with the razor. Blood flowed from his chin and Mr. Ali dabbed at his wound with a towel. He washed the shaving cream off his face and came out. His chin stung.

"Did you hear that? Isn't it great news?" asked Mrs. Ali, and peered at him more closely. "Why is there blood on your chin?"

"Because you screamed," said Mr. Ali.

"The news is worth screaming about. I cannot help it if you cannot shave without cutting yourself even after practicing every day for the last fifty years," said Mrs. Ali.

"It is good news," said Mr. Ali. "But my views haven't changed. If he didn't come home when we asked him to, then he need not come here ever again."

Mrs. Ali's smile faltered. "Leave it be," she said. "It's not important now. Let the past go."

"I can't let it go," said Mr. Ali. "I didn't tell you this before, but I called him again after we came back to town. I told him that you were depressed and that you were not getting out of bed. He still refused to budge. I have no time for a son who does not care for his parents."

Mrs. Ali started to say something. Mr. Ali raised his hands. "I don't want to hear any more. My decision is final. Don't argue."

Mrs. Ali was not happy, but she knew her husband well. Once he made up his mind, it was difficult to change him. She sighed and went back to her cooking.

EIGHTEEN

On Monday, Mr. Ali was talking to a Christian man about a bride for his younger brother when Ramanujam came in. Mr. Ali greeted him. "Hello," he said. "Your sister came in the other day and took the details of a match."

"She told me," replied Ramanujam. "Please finish with this gentleman first. I will wait."

Once the other client left, Ramanujam took Sita's photo from an envelope and gave it to Mr. Ali. "Thanks for sending the photo with my sister," he said.

Mr. Ali put the photograph away and turned back to Ramanujam. "What did you think of the match?" he asked.

Ramanujam said, "I heard Aruna is not well. Is she all right?"

Mr. Ali was surprised by the change of topic, but replied, "She was very listless the last two weeks. So she's taken a week off and her father has taken her to Annavaram. I hope the change of scene will do her good and she will come back to her normal self."

"I have a confession to make," said Ramanujam. "I'm actually quite happy to hear that Aruna is feeling like that."

"Really? And why would that be?" asked Mr. Ali sharply. The smile slipped from his face. He looked on Aruna like a daughter, and Ramanujam's remark took him by surprise.

"It's not like that," said Ramanujam. "I like her a lot. You see, I've met Aruna a few times here and outside and I've had long chats with her and I don't know . . . I think of her all the time. I might be seeing a patient, and suddenly, I remember Aruna's smile or the way her eyes shine when she is looking at me. I can hear her voice mocking me gently or laughing at something I've said. I don't know if this is love. All I know is that I've never felt like this before."

Mr. Ali pursed his lips. Aruna was in his care while she worked in his house, and he was disturbed by what he heard. "So why are you happy that Aruna is not feeling well?" he asked.

"Since when did Aruna start feeling depressed?" asked Ramanujam in reply.

Mr. Ali thought back and said, "I think her depression started about the time we went to a wedding in Kottavalasa. I remember she was all right the day before, and I didn't see her on the Sunday because we left early and she wasn't here when we came back. I thought it was odd at that time, because I was expecting her to be around when we came back. Monday was her day off. It was after that. Yes, I am sure—it started then."

Mr. Ali was silent for a moment and looked at Ramanujam sharply. "Did you come here that day when we were away? Did you say anything to her to make her depressed?"

Looking at Ramanujam's face, Mr. Ali's fears were confirmed. "I'm right, aren't I? You did come here that Sunday. What did you say to her? If you've done anything to make her sad, I won't forgive you. Doctor?

Pah! You should be ashamed of yourself. I'll call your parents and tell them what kind of son they've raised. I should not have left her alone in the house to manage by herself. That was wrong of me."

Mr. Ali didn't realize when he had stood up from his chair and his voice was raised in anger. Mrs. Ali came out. "What's the matter?" she asked.

Mr. Ali pointed his finger at Ramanujam. "This man . . ." he said, spluttering. He was unable to carry on.

Ramanujam raised his hands. "Uncle, it wasn't anything like that. Please relax and let me say what happened. I proposed to her. I asked her to marry me."

"What?" said Mr. Ali. He glanced at his wife and was surprised to see her unmoved, almost as if she had known about it already.

"Yes, I asked Aruna to marry me and she refused. She says she cannot marry me."

"Good," snapped Mr. Ali, ungraciously. He was still angry.

Mrs. Ali took a seat and asked her husband to sit down as well. But Mr. Ali was too wound up to sit down. Finally, Mrs. Ali asked her husband to get three glasses of water. "Can't you see that our guest is thirsty?" she asked him.

Mr. Ali muttered something under his breath but his innate courtesy won out. By the time he came out with three glasses of water on a tray, he was less angry and more rational. Just then a man arrived. Mr. Ali went to the gate and the man asked, "Is this the marriage bureau? I've seen an advertisement in the newspaper."

Mr. Ali replied, "Yes, this is the marriage bureau. But it is closed for the day. Please come back tomorrow, a little bit earlier."

The man went away and Mr. Ali closed the gate. It was the first time he had ever turned away a potential client. He came back inside and sat next to Mrs. Ali, facing Ramanujam.

"Right," he said. "Please tell us again what happened."

"There isn't a lot more to add," said Ramanujam. "I like Aruna a lot and I thought she liked me as well. I asked her to marry me and she refused. I went away, wondering how I could have misread her so badly. However, when I heard from my sister that she had been feeling depressed and had taken time off, I felt a new hope. Maybe she does have feelings for me after all. So, I started thinking about our conversation and it struck me that she did not say that she *will not* marry me. Aruna said that she *cannot* marry me. That's why I am here—to ask for your help in talking to Aruna again, to convince her to marry me."

Mr. Ali thought for a moment. He had obviously misjudged the young man in front of him. "I'm sorry for what I said earlier. I shouldn't have spoken like that," he said.

Ramanujam waved his hand, brushing away the apology. "You were concerned for Aruna's welfare. That's not wrong," he said.

"Let us say that we can help convince Aruna to marry you . . ." began Mrs. Ali.

Ramanujam's face brightened with hope, and she quickly added, "Not that I am saying we can, but just say that we can. Have you really thought this through? The potential brides that your parents and sister are looking for for you are more beautiful than Aruna. They are taller, fairer, and more glamorous."

Ramanujam replied, "I've seen a lot of photos and some of the girls that my sister and parents have short-listed. Aruna is more beautiful than any of them. They all look artificial, made-up. Aruna is a natural beauty. She is so simple, unaffected. She looks so elegant even in old clothes, unlike those others who have to dress up in finery and wear expensive jewelry to look their best."

Mr. Ali said, "Ramanujam, it certainly looks as if you like Aruna very much. But have you thought about your family? How will they take it?

Here they are, going everywhere to find the perfect bride for you, and you come home and tell them that you've chosen one yourself."

Ramanujam said, "That's okay, uncle. The moment Aruna agrees, I will convince them. I'm sure they'll love Aruna just as I do. They've never denied me anything in the past, and I don't think they will frustrate me in something so important."

Mrs. Ali said, "You are being naive, young man. They may not deny you. They probably won't even behave any differently to you. But they'll probably make Aruna's life hell. I assume you are planning to stay with your parents even after you are married?"

"Yes, madam. Of course we will stay with my parents after getting married. Why would we go anywhere else?" said Ramanujam.

Mrs. Ali said, "As I said, they can make life difficult for Aruna. They can make her work like a servant or not talk to her at all or put her down in front of your relatives and insult her. They can do a hundred things to make her miserable, and Aruna, being the kind of girl she is, will probably not even complain to you, so you don't get upset."

"You don't know my family, madam," said Ramanujam stiffly. "They are not like that. And we have servants in our house who've been with us for years. Why would Aruna have to do any housework that she doesn't want to? It doesn't make sense."

Mr. Ali went behind his table to the filing cupboard and took out Ramanujam's application form. He read from it, "It says here that you are looking for a tall, fair, and educated girl from a rich family who will pay a large dowry. While I agree with you that Aruna is a handsome girl, she is not tall or very fair. And while she is an educated girl, she is most definitely not from a rich family. In fact, the reason she has not got married so far is because her family cannot afford a wedding or a decent dowry for her."

Ramanujam looked embarrassed. He said, "Uncle, you cannot hold this against me. All those conditions were laid down by my family—I never asked for a dowry."

Mr. Ali said, "You may not have, and that's a credit to you. But you went along with your family's demands. You never opposed them and said that you didn't want a dowry from the girl you married. What happens tomorrow when your family ill-treat Aruna because she didn't bring any dowry? Will you oppose them then, when you don't have the strength to oppose them now?"

Ramanujam said angrily, "Sir, you are insulting my family. We are respectable people and would never treat somebody badly just because they are poor."

Mrs. Ali said, "Calm down, Ramanujam. We have seen rather more of this world than you have. Such things should not happen in respectable families, but they do. We read about so many such cases in the newspapers. People have become materialistic these days and don't care that the wealth a daughter-in-law brings into a house is not to be measured in money or land. It is in her culture, her good nature, and the happiness she brings their son. It's sad, but that's the way it is. These things do happen, you know."

Ramanujam sighed and said, "Uncle, auntie, tell me how I can convince you that Aruna would be happy with me and my family if we got married. Don't ask me to leave my family and set up my own household—that would break my parents' hearts. Tell me anything short of that, and I'm willing to do it."

Mrs. Ali said, "Aruna is an intelligent girl, and I'm sure she's thought about all these things and that's why she said she could not marry you. To convince us, and more important, to convince Aruna, you first need to be aware that such bad things can happen, even in otherwise perfectly good families. You cannot deny it to yourself. Acknowledge clearly to yourself and to us that a daughter-in-law can be ill-treated in any family, however respectable or normal. And the risk of ill-treatment increases if you marry against their wishes and you continue to live with your parents."

Ramanujam was silent. Mrs. Ali waited for a few seconds and said, "You have to say it aloud—only then will it become true in your heart. Go on, it is not an insult to your family. I am not saying that it will definitely happen. But it *may* happen, and the power to prevent it is in your hands. But to unleash that power, first you need to acknowledge its necessity."

Ramanujam still remained silent. The anguish on his face was clear. He obviously idolized his parents and loved his sister.

Mr. Ali said, "Ramanujam, you are doing it for Aruna. We are not asking you to say it to the whole world—just to Aruna and the people who have her interests at heart, and, most important, to yourself."

Ramanujam took a deep breath and sighed. His head was bent low and he looked at the ground in front of him. "You are right. You are both more experienced and worldly-wise than me. I agree. If Aruna agrees to my proposal, I will be marrying a girl not chosen by my parents or sister. They might look down on her because she is not the image of my bride that they have in mind. I don't think that they will actively ill-treat her, but they can make her feel left out and miserable," he said.

Mr. Ali said, "Repeat it again. Make it true to yourself."

Ramanujam looked up at Mr. Ali in surprise. He opened his mouth to protest, but then stopped, and said, "Aruna may be treated badly by my family if I marry her."

Mr. Ali beamed at him.

"Congratulations, Ramanujam. You have just cleared the most difficult hurdle. Now that you've recognized what can happen, it is much easier to guard against it," Mr. Ali said. "Your bride—any bride—leaves her father's house and follows her new husband into his house. She is placing an enormous trust in her husband. You, as the husband, have to safeguard that trust. There will be conflicts between your parents, especially your mother, and your bride. After all, she has come into a settled household and is bound to disrupt it somewhat. Also, your parents might feel insecure. They might feel that they are losing a son to this strange woman. You must not be blind to these conflicts. You have to take a firm line on these matters—not always in favor of your wife, but not always supporting your parents, either. You can expect your wife to change in some things, and you must tell her that she is younger and should be more open to change than your parents. But you must equally tell your parents that some things will necessarily be different with a daughter-in-law in the house. Your wife must know when you tell your parents this—she must not feel lonely and lost, as if nobody in the world is taking her side. It is a difficult job—a man can feel torn between his role as a son and as a husband. But nobody ever said that being a man is easy. Can you do this?"

A look of resolve came on Ramanujam's face. "Yes," he said, "I think I can do it. As you say, it will not be easy. But for the sake of the love I feel for Aruna and for my parents, I will do it. I will be alive to any conflicts that may arise and attempt to resolve them. I will make sure that Aruna does not feel lonely in her new house."

Mr. Ali said, "You may still have to leave your house and set up on your own with Aruna. You will have to make it clear to your parents that while you love them, Aruna's happiness matters, too."

Ramanujam looked unhappy, and Mrs. Ali added, "The very fact that you are willing to say such a thing will make it less likely to happen. Aruna is a mature girl, and she will not try and break up your family. You know that."

Ramanujam nodded. "You are right," he said. "I have to have confidence in my parents and in Aruna, that they are all sensible people. I just have to make sure that any problems are nipped in the bud before they fester like an ill-bandaged wound."

"All that remains now is to convince Aruna," said Ramanujam, after a moment's silence. He stood up to go. "Thank you, uncle and auntie, for all your help. Aruna is a lucky girl that she has people like you looking out for her."

"Should we tell Aruna about this chat?" asked Mr. Ali, after Ramanujam was gone.

Mrs. Ali thought for a moment and replied, "I don't think so."

"Are we doing the right thing by encouraging Ramanujam? Shouldn't we respect her wishes?" said Mr. Ali.

"Normally I would have agreed with you. But she doesn't know her own mind. She has thought through some of the issues and refused him, but she is not happy about it. That's why she has been so distressed since then, poor girl. Ramanujam really seems to like her and if, as he says, he will look out for her, he is a fantastic match. We cannot ignore that—we have to try and push her to make the right decision. If they were from different castes, I would have been more wary. But they are both Brahmins, so a lot of problems won't even come up," said Mrs. Ali.

"Yes," said Mr. Ali, "they are both vegetarians, for a start."

"You and your obsession with food!" Mrs. Ali laughed. "I'm thinking about what you were saying to Ramanujam when I came out. You said you were wrong to leave her alone in the house to face him. You were right—would you leave your daughter and arrange for a man to come and talk to her? I don't think so. If and when he comes back to talk to her, she cannot be on her own."

"But what can we do? We can't stay here. They need some privacy to work this out," said Mr. Ali.

Mrs. Ali said, "We cannot ask her to be alone. That's wrong. Let me think about it."

They were both silent for a few moments. Then Mrs. Ali asked, "Do you really think it is so simple? That he will come in on Wednesday and propose and the two will be united?"

Mr. Ali thought for a second and shook his head. "I doubt it. He has to convince his family. Ramanujam is a nice guy, but his sister is one sharp woman—the kind who can count your intestines if you yawn in front of her. She is not going to agree to this match, and I am not sure that he has the strength to go against his whole family."

Mrs. Ali sighed. "I know what you mean. It's a pity—they would make such a good pair."

Aruna came back to work on Tuesday. She smiled more readily than before her holiday and the break seemed to have done wonders for her equanimity.

Mr. Ali had been tied to the desk all week and took the opportunity to leave Aruna in the office and go to the bank and the post office. It was midmorning before all the clients went away and Aruna was by herself. Mrs. Ali came out with cool lemonade for both of them and sat down. Aruna thanked Mrs. Ali, and they both slowly sipped from their glasses.

"How was your holiday?" asked Mrs. Ali.

"It was good, madam. We went to my uncle's house. It was quite lucky that we went, because my aunt had fallen ill, so I was able to take care of her and look after the household."

Mrs. Ali opened the Telugu newspaper and started reading it. "This is interesting," she said.

"What, madam?" asked Aruna, looking up from her work.

"Are you embarrassed about your English?" said Mrs. Ali.

"Me?" asked Aruna.

"No!" Mrs. Ali laughed. "That's what it says here in the paper. They are going to run a series of weekly articles to help their readers improve their English language skills."

They were both silent for a moment. Mrs. Ali pursed her lips in thought and then said, "I might do it. I know a little bit of English, but it will be good to be more conversant in it."

The phone rang and Aruna picked it up. As she listened, her eyes widened and her color paled. She slowly put the phone down and a tear trickled down her cheek.

Mrs. Ali quickly walked over to where Aruna was sitting. "What happened, Aruna?" she asked. "Is everything all right?"

Aruna slowly turned her head and looked at her. "Why shouldn't it be all right, madam? After all, what is it to me?" she said, laughing mirthlessly.

Mrs. Ali was really concerned now. "Stop it, Aruna!" she said sharply. "Who was it on the phone, and what did they say?"

Aruna said, "That was Ram's sister, madam. She says they are all going to see a potential bride this evening and meet her family."

Mrs. Ali took Aruna's hands in her own. "I'm sorry, dear. I'm really sorry."

That evening, Aruna ate her dinner mechanically. It was obvious that she was not enjoying it.

"What's wrong with you, Aruna?" asked her mother. "I made your favorite plantain fry and drumstick sambhar, and you are eating your food like it is so much coal."

"Nothing, amma. I'm all right."

"You were fine this morning and now you are all depressed. Is everything okay at work?" asked her mother.

"I've just got a headache. I think I'll go to bed straight after dinner," Aruna said.

Less than fifteen minutes later, she was in bed, the sheet completely covering her head to block out the light in the room. In the darkness, her pillow slowly became wet, despite her efforts to stop her tears. She wondered if Ram was talking to the girl. Was he telling her about his time in Delhi? Were they laughing about his efforts to meet girls at the hostel? She had made the choice of her own free will, hadn't she? So, why feel miserable? He could meet anyone he wanted to. She didn't care.

After a few minutes, she started reciting the three-thousand-year-old Gayatri Mantram under her breath in Sanskrit, as her father had taught her to do whenever she was unhappy or confused. *"Om bhoor bhuwah swaha* ... O God, Thou art the giver of life, the remover of pain and sorrow, the bestower of happiness; O Creator of the Universe, may we receive Thy supreme light; may Thou guide us in the right direction."

She had to recite the mantra several dozen times before sleep finally claimed her.

The next day, Mrs. Ali left early in the morning to visit her sister. She gave the front-gate keys to Aruna.

"I won't be back till late in the evening," said Mrs. Ali. "Sir said that he had to go out in the afternoon. Keep the keys with you and lock up after yourself in the evening if necessary."

Aruna put the keys in her purse.

Both Aruna and Mr. Ali were busy with clients before lunch. Just as they were about to close for lunch, they got a call from Venu, the divorced service engineer. Mr. Ali picked up the phone.

"I am sorry," said Mr. Ali. "We haven't got any matches for you. We sent your details to one divorced lady that we thought was suitable, but it didn't work out. She got married through family contacts. There isn't anybody else on the books right now."

Mr. Ali put the phone down and shrugged at Aruna. "Sometimes, there is nothing we can do," he said.

"Yes, sir," said Aruna.

Soon afterward, Aruna went home for lunch.

Aruna came back to the office after lunch just before three and let herself in with the keys that Mrs. Ali had given her. Mr. Ali was not at home. Aruna was surprised because he normally did not go out until it had cooled down. There were no clients to disturb her, and Aruna started catching up with her filing work. Leela came in and said to Aruna, "Lady, I will be in the backyard, washing dishes."

Aruna smiled at her and went back to her work. About twenty minutes later, the gate opened and in walked Ramanujam. Seeing his tall, handsome figure stride in, Aruna was struck dumb. He had to say hello a couple of times before she recovered and said, "Namaste," fairly formally.

She was flustered and started looking through the papers that she was filing, as if the answer was hidden somewhere in the papers. Ramanujam waited patiently without speaking, until Aruna was able to face him.

"What can I do for you?" asked Aruna.

"The biggest step in your life—you can marry me," he replied.

"No! Not that again. Please leave me alone," she cried.

"I don't think I was very clear last time, Aruna. That's why I've come here again. I love you, Aruna. I love you very much. Please marry me . . ." he said.

"I thought you went to see that rich girl last night," said Aruna.

"Yes, I did. My family dragged me there, and it made me realize that you are the only one for me. I love you, Aruna. Please say yes."

"No! How many times must I tell you? No. Please stop torturing me."

"On the contrary, Aruna. It is you who are torturing both yourself and me. Look in my eyes and tell me that you don't have any feelings for me, and I will leave you. I will go away and never talk to you again about marriage."

Hope flared through Aruna. "I . . ." she began strongly, and looked into his eyes.

She struggled to say the next few words that would free her, but she was swept into his deep brown eyes and the words choked in her throat. "I . . ." she repeated, brokenly.

Ramanujam waited and the silence dragged.

Finally, he broke in and said, "Aruna, my heart tells me that you love me. Why don't you admit it?"

Aruna cried fiercely, "Yes, I love you. There, I've said it. I'll say it again. I love you. I love you. I love you! Satisfied?"

"That's a start." Ramanujam beamed, a wide smile on his face. "I feel great. I feel strong—like Hanuman, the monkey god who could cross the oceans in a single bound."

"Then, like Hanuman, you can remain a bachelor. Because I still won't marry you," said Aruna grimly.

Ramanujam's smile faltered. "Why not, darling?" he asked softly.

His endearment did not go unnoticed by her and she blushed. She leaned forward and said intensely, "We don't marry for love, Ram. You know that. Love is supposed to follow marriage, not the other way around. A marriage is not just about two people. It is about two families. You haven't thought through this at all. You've just got a crazy idea in your head and like a spoiled child, you want it. That's all."

246 · Farahad Zama

"Love is a craze, Aruna. You cannot think it through. Sure, it is supposed to follow marriage. But that doesn't mean that you push it away where it exists, either. Tell me what problems you see and we'll solve them together. Haven't you heard the saying, 'Love makes everything easy'?"

Aruna shook her head. "No. The saying I've heard is that love complicates anything it touches."

"This is one of the reasons that I love you. Nobody can defeat you in an argument."

"I bet you won't be saying that after we've been married for a few years—" she said, before stopping herself abruptly, wishing she had bitten her tongue before the words had slipped out.

"Yes, let's bet on it. I'll buy you a diamond necklace if I'm not saying that on our third anniversary. What will you bet?" asked Ramanujam with a grin.

Aruna shook her head and said desperately, "Ram, please be serious. We cannot get married."

Ramanujam became serious, too. "Aruna, tell me why not," he said.

"Will your family accept me? They are looking for a really special woman to be your bride," she said.

He replied, "You are special, Aruna. I cannot guarantee that on day one there will be no resentment. But I can promise you this—once they see your innate goodness, they will start liking you. Until that happens, I will support you every step of the way. Whatever problems you have, I will make sure that they are resolved. That's my promise, Aruna."

"How can you make promises like that? Look at your sister—she is so beautiful all the time. She looks perfect. I will look so out of place in your house. I'm not sophisticated like her; my English is not as good as hers. You might like my unsophisticatedness now, but in a year or so, it will grate on you. You will look at the wives of your friends and look down on me."

"Aruna, why are you so hard on yourself? A lot of what you call sophistication is just money and exposure. You will pick it up soon enough. You already have more poise and elegance than most of them. Anyway, I hope you don't pick up all of it, because what you think of as sophistication is just worldliness and cynicism," he said.

"In your application form, you said that you did not want a working woman as a wife. I want to continue this job for a few more years, until my sister is married and my family's financial situation is put on an even keel," said Aruna.

"That was my family's preference. I don't mind either way. It will actually be good for you to go out rather than stay at home and watch TV serials all day and put on weight as so many women do after they get married," said Ramanujam.

"Are you sure?" asked Aruna. "I won't be around to cook you a meal when you get home."

"We have a cook at home who's been around since I was a little boy. Even if you wanted to cook anything, I doubt if Kaka will let you. We also have a driver, a full-time maid, and a gardener. The washerwoman comes twice a week to wash clothes at home. Anything else?"

Aruna shook her head at how casually he had mentioned so many people working for them. *The rich are very different from the rest of us,* she thought. She said, "We are a poor family. We live in a one-room house, and if you come to our house, my parents will not be able to treat you the way you are used to. In fact, your car won't even be able to enter our street. You will have to leave it parked on the main road and walk the rest of the way—it is so narrow."

"So I'll walk. Just because I'm rich, it doesn't mean I'm spoiled,

Aruna. You are the one who has a chip on her shoulder about money, not me."

She shook her head and said, "I'm not listening to anything you say, Ram. I said no and my answer is not changing."

Ramanujam stood up. Aruna stood up as well, looking determined. She looked steadily at him, daring him to say something. Before he opened his mouth however, the door opened and Leela walked in.

"Lady, I've finished cleaning the dishes . . ." she began, and then saw Ramanujam. "Doctor babu, is that you?" she asked in wonder.

Ramanujam was startled at being addressed by the servant maid. He looked at her closely and said, "How is your grandson?"

"He is doing well. It's all because of you, sir. Without you, he would have been dead."

"We do what we can, but ultimately, it is all in His hands," he said. "Is he taking those tablets I prescribed?"

"Yes, sir. Those tablets are expensive, but madam helps me buy some of them and I work in another place and they also help me. My daughter and son-in-law manage the rest."

"Yes, they are expensive, but don't neglect them," said Ramanujam.

"You know that my grandsons are twins, Luv and Kush. They used to be identical, but now Kush has fallen behind. Luv is ahead of his brother in talking, doing things with his hands, and other things. Will it always be like this?" Leela asked.

"It is difficult to say," replied Ramanujam. "Remember, we cut open his skull. Brain surgery is a big trauma. It is not surprising that he has fallen behind. As long as he is making progress, be happy. Don't compare him to his brother."

Leela sighed. "You are right, doctor babu. We should just be thankful that he has come through such peril, still alive. Sorry, sir, madam, for interrupting you," she said, and left the room.

Ramanujam turned to Aruna and said, "Is that your last answer? Are you still refusing me?"

"Yes, that's my last answer," Aruna replied.

"I don't believe you. It is enough for me today that you've declared your love. I'm not letting this matter drop. *Hasta la vista,* baby. I'll be back," he said, and left.

Aruna stood at the table, staring after Ramanujam as he got into his car and drove off. *He uses such strange expressions sometimes,* she thought.

Leela came back into the room and Aruna asked her, "Is that gentleman the doctor who treated your grandson?"

"Yes, lady. He is such a good man. He operated on my grandson without taking a single paisa."

"That's not a big deal. You went to King George, which is a government hospital. Of course, he is not going to charge any fee for operating," said Aruna.

Leela laughed. "Forgive me for saying this, lady, but you are a very naive girl. These doctors don't treat you properly in the government hospital unless you go to their private surgery and become a patient there. They will charge you like a normal private patient and then treat you at the government hospital. Surely, you must know that."

Aruna said, "You are right, of course. I know all about it. My father was very unwell for a long time."

Leela said, "It's not just that he didn't charge any money. You know how it is when poor, illiterate people go to these places. We are patronized, treated in a condescending manner. Nothing is explained to us and we are looked down upon. The doctor babu was the only man who treated us as equals. He explained everything clearly in language that we could understand, drew diagrams, and showed us what he was going to do, what we can expect, what the risks were. Forget doctors—even small-time clerks in government offices don't do that."

Aruna stood silent, absorbing what Leela had said. Leela continued, "I am leaving, lady. My work here is finished."

Aruna slowly sat down in her chair, thinking. She saw in her mind's eye all her encounters with Ramanujam. She thought about his earnest promises. Suddenly, as if waking up from a long sleep, she shook herself. Her hand went quickly to the phone and she dialed a number that had imprinted itself on her brain. The phone rang; once, twice, and then to her relief, a familiar voice answered, "Ramanujam here."

"Hi! This is Aruna."

"*Aruna!*" shouted Ramanujam, so loudly that she winced and jerked the phone away from her ear. "Sorry," he continued. "You took me by surprise. What can I do for you?"

"Can you come back? You've forgotten something here," she said.

"Right now? Can you keep it until I come over again?" he asked. "Because you know I will be back."

"No, it won't keep. You better come right now," she said.

"I'm on my way," he said, and hung up.

Ramanujam was back in just a few minutes, but for Aruna those minutes seemed stretched out to many months, as she paced about in restless agitation. Finally, she heard the gate open and in he walked. She stood stiff, quivering with excitement.

He asked, "What have I forgotten?"

Aruna replied softly, "To ask the question again."

"What?" he asked, with a confused look on his face.

"Ask me again, what you asked me earlier," said Aruna, her eyes closed.

After a moment, a slow smile spread across his face and he asked, "Aruna, dear, will you marry me?"

"Yes," she said simply, opening her eyes and scanning his face.

He took one step forward and hugged her tight. Her body stiffened in shock and then yielded softly, molding into his. They remained in an embrace for several seconds and then Aruna gently freed herself. She was embarrassed and refused to meet his eyes.

"I love you," he said.

"Me too," she replied, hesitantly.

"What? I didn't catch that," he said.

"Me too," she said more strongly.

"You too what?" he asked.

Aruna looked at his face finally and saw him smiling widely, and flushed again. "You brute!" she said.

Ramanujam laughed. "Why don't you lock up here and we'll go out," he said.

"Lock up?" she asked, and looked at him suspiciously. "How do you know I have the keys?"

"I . . . I just assumed . . ." he said.

"I *knew* it. All of you plotted behind my back, you meanies."

"For your own good, dear," he replied. "I called them last night after coming back home. Come on now, let's go. We'll buy you shoes and then we can go up the mountain to Kailasagiri and see the sunset."

"Shoes? I already have two pairs. I don't need any more shoes," she said.

"Trust me, dear," he said. "Women *always* need more shoes."

NINETEEN

Early the next morning, the doorbell at Mr. Ali's house rang aggressively again and again. Mr. Ali went to the door and saw an elderly gentleman outside, looking angry. There was a white car parked outside. "What can I do for you?" asked Mr. Ali, opening the door.

The man rushed in and said, "What kind of immoral house are you running? People like you should have their faces blackened and be paraded around town on a donkey."

He was shouting; his face was red and choleric.

Mr. Ali closed the door behind the man hurriedly. He didn't want to promote neighborhood gossip. He told the man, "Calm down, sir, and tell me what this is about. Shouting is not going to help matters."

"How can I not shout?" replied the man. "You have destroyed my family's happiness."

"Will you tell me what you are talking about so we can have an intelligent conversation?" asked Mr. Ali, exasperated.

"I'm talking about my son, whom you led astray. You and that witch who works here must have done some black magic to attract him. We should never have trusted people like you," said the man, his voice rising again.

Mr. Ali realized that the gentleman was Ramanujam's father. "Sir, I realize you are angry, but please keep control of your tongue. Nobody has played any black magic on your son. In fact—"

"Why should I keep control of my tongue? The deputy inspector general of police is a good friend of mine. I will have you arrested. That will teach you to interfere in my family's affairs. What dreams I had about my son's wedding! What thoughts we had about our daughter-in-law, how beautiful, educated, and cultured she would be! How our daughter-in-law's family would be equal in prestige and wealth to ours. Instead, what have we got? A girl who works in a marriage bureau? People will make fun of us. We won't be able to lift our heads in respectable society," said Ramanujam's father.

"Don't threaten me, sir. Aruna is a very sensible girl and, thinking about these things, she refused your son initially. He was the one who kept pressing her until she accepted. And I don't want to hear about how you've lost out because your son has gone off his head. Have that much confidence in your son. Why would he do anything to lower the prestige of your house?"

"Bah!" exclaimed the man dismissively. "Just because your son doesn't listen to you and openly dissents against his mother on TV, you probably think there is no shame in having a child arranging his own marriage. We come from a family with better traditions than that."

"Don't say a word against my family," said Mr. Ali, raising his voice. "My son is fighting injustice and my wife only said what any mother would say when her son is walking into danger. There is nothing wrong with my family."

Mr. Ali took a deep breath and raised his hands in a placatory manner. He said, more softly, "We are not talking about my family. Let us talk about your son's wedding. Don't look down on Aruna or her family. She is a very good girl who will be an asset to you. Her family is no less prestigious than yours. Your son must have already told you that she is a Brahmin. Has he also told you that her ancestors were the royal priests of Rajahmundry? Aruna has read the Vedas in Sanskrit and knows the Puranas. What more culture do you need?"

"Words . . ." said the man.

"Not just words, sir. Aruna is a very good girl, but more important, your son has fallen in love. Have you no regard for his wishes? Respect his choice. Accept Aruna as your daughter-in-law wholeheartedly; your family's happiness lies that way."

"Don't talk to me about my son's happiness. I'm his father and I know better than you where his happiness lies. This is just an infatuation and he will soon come back into line once this so-called engagement is broken and I find a proper bride for him," replied the man.

Mr. Ali asked, "Do you know the Bezwada brothers? They own the biggest sari shop in town."

"Yes," replied the gentleman, the sudden change of topic taking him off guard, as Mr. Ali intended.

"They are originally from a market town near my own village. Many years ago, before they had set up shop in this town, they had a wholesale sari business in the market town. They were not as wealthy as they are now, but they were still very rich. The elder Bezwada brother had a teenaged daughter and she sometimes used to help out in the shop. She fell in love with a handsome Muslim weaver boy who used to supply their shop with silk saris. We don't know how long they were in love with each other, but one day they eloped. She took some money and jewelry from her house, and they used it to evade her father and live on the run for two months. Her father was bereft with grief and used his wealth and connections with the police to hunt them. The police eventually tracked them down when they tried to pawn one of the pieces of jewelry in a nearby town. When they were caught, the girl was brought back to her father's house and the boy was arrested by the police. They alleged that he had stolen the money and jewelry. He was released after a week, but he was beaten badly and his right hand was broken and set wrong so he could never use the loom again. Meanwhile, the girl's father found a widower to marry her to. No matter that he was twenty-five years older and had two children, or that his wife had died in suspicious circumstances—he was rich and belonged to the same caste. On the eve of the wedding, the poor girl drank rat poison and committed suicide."

"Are you saying that my son will commit suicide if this wedding doesn't go through? And anyway, I don't believe your preposterous story," said Ramanujam's father angrily.

"Of course I am not saying that Ramanujam will commit suicide. Your son is older and certainly more sensible than that poor girl. As for the story, the weaver boy was a distant cousin of mine, so I know what happened. All I am pointing out is that the father of the girl acted in what he thought was the correct way. How could he let his daughter marry a poor weaver—and that, too, a Muslim? Most people in his position would probably act like that. But that way lies only misery. We all try to find the best possible bride or groom for our children, but if they go ahead and fall in love, then I think we should back off. We should trust their choice and do our best to make their marriage a success."

"But this match is so unsuitable," wailed Ramanujam's father.

"I don't see why Aruna is so unsuitable to be your daughter-in-law. Unlike that girl I was just talking about, your son is not bringing home a Muslim or a Christian. Aruna is not only a Hindu but also a Brahmin, just like you. She is a mature, sensible girl—not at all flighty or scatter-brained. She comes from a traditional family, and not only will she keep your son happy, she will also look after you and your wife as a proper daughter-in-law should."

"They are so poor. The family probably cannot even afford a decent wedding," said Ramanujam's father.

"What would you rather have? A girl like Aruna who will treat you with respect, or a girl from a rich family who hasn't done a day's work in her life and will find you and your wife boring? A woman like that will probably lose no time trying to alienate your son from you. Is a big wedding more important than the lifelong happiness you and your family will get from a truly wonderful daughter-in-law?" asked Mr. Ali.

The other man shook his head in frustration.

Mr. Ali continued, "Why is money so important to you? Aruna comes from a family of royal priests; her father is a Sanskrit scholar and a retired teacher. Isn't that more important than money? *Shouldn't* that be more important? Were your forefathers merchants that you attach so much importance to wealth? God has given you bountiful riches, and on top of that your son is a doctor who will earn even more money. Why do you need a rich daughter-in-law? She will only bring you money, which you already have a lot of. Somebody like Aruna will bring you respect, knowledge, character; she will uphold ancient traditions. These are the things you can never have enough of. After all, as the Tirukkural says: *'If love and virtue in the household reign, This is of life the perfect grace and gain.'* "

Ramanujam's father was silent. He seemed to be thinking. Mr. Ali took that as a good sign and said, "I can understand that a man in your position has many social obligations and everybody expects a big wedding for your only son. I think I have a solution for that."

Ramanujam's father looked up. "What solution?" he asked.

"Aruna's paternal uncle is a priest at the Annavaram temple. Let everybody know that it is their family tradition that their children get married in a simple ceremony at the temple. Organize a big reception in town—hire a hall in a five-star hotel and invite everybody."

"Is that really their tradition?" asked the gentleman.

"I doubt it, because I just made it up." Mr. Ali grinned. "But who's going to know? Every family's traditions are slightly different."

Ramanujam's father left. Mr. Ali went back inside the house and sat down heavily on the sofa, mopping his brow. Mrs. Ali smiled in appreciation and gave him a glass of buttermilk to drink.

"*What?*" screamed Vani, leaping into the air.

She turned excitedly toward Aruna and held her by the shoulders and jumped up and down. "Tell me more," she cried.

People on the street were looking curiously at the girls, and Aruna felt self-conscious. "Let's go somewhere more private," she said.

It was about eight-thirty in the morning and the two girls had left their home a few minutes before. This was slightly early for Aruna to leave home, but she had left with her sister so she could tell her the news of her engagement.

The sisters went to a nearby café. The early-morning breakfast rush in the café was coming to an end and they found a corner where they could sit without anybody in the tables next to them. The smell of tea, coffee, and sambhar permeated the place. A waiter came up to them and Vani ordered, "Tea, one by two."

As soon as the waiter left, Vani turned to her sister and said, "Come on, tell me. When did it happen? How?"

"Yesterday afternoon. Mr. and Mrs. Ali were out and he came over. He asked me and I said yes," Aruna replied.

Vani stamped her foot. Aruna smiled at the look of exasperation on her sister's face.

"Details," said Vani. "I want details."

The waiter came back with two half-filled glasses of tea, and Vani was silent until he left. As soon as he left, she tapped her finger on the table. Aruna calmly took a sip and Vani looked ready to strangle her.

"He had asked me before, but I refused," Aruna replied finally.

"What? I don't believe it. When did he ask you?" Vani said. "Getting information out of you is like squeezing water out of a stone."

"About two weeks ago. Before I went to uncle's house," Aruna replied.

"But why did you refuse him? I thought you liked him. Hang on! That's why you were all moody and under the weather. I knew it was something like that," Vani said.

"I guess I didn't want to be one of those girls who have a love marriage," said Aruna. "Also, they are so rich that I didn't see how it would work out."

"Silly girl! Any other woman would have jumped immediately if a rich, handsome man proposed to her. His wealth would only make him more handsome," Vani said. "What happened then? Why did you accept this time? Mind you, I think you made the right decision. I can't believe you were actually muddleheaded enough to refuse him. What would you have done if he hadn't asked again?"

"It all seems like a dream now. I guess I'm just lucky that he came over again. Madam found out and had a chat with me. She told me what you just said—that I should have accepted his proposal. I told her that I didn't think he would be interested anymore, but I think they had already arranged to be away from the house when he came by."

"You are lucky to have people interested in your welfare. I guess if you are good, then people around you are good, too," said Vani.

"I don't know about that," said Aruna. "But I'm definitely lucky."

"How are you going to tell naanna? It's lucky that he is a Brahmin. Can you imagine the hoo-ha if you wanted to marry someone outside the caste?" Vani asked, and shuddered.

"I don't think I'd have accepted his proposal if he was not a Brahmin. No matter how good he was. Naanna would have had a fit," Aruna said.

She didn't say that she would never have agreed to marry a non-Brahmin because, apart from causing her parents great distress and loss of face, it would have made it extremely difficult to find a good husband for Vani.

"I have a plan about telling amma and naanna. But I need your help," said Aruna.

"Anything, akka. Tell me your plan," said Vani, leaning forward toward Aruna.

"*What is it, Aruna?* Why are we going into a tea shop?" asked Shastry-uncle.

"I want to talk to you about something."

It was three in the afternoon, and Aruna had told Mr. Ali that she would come in late for work.

A waiter came to their table and Aruna ordered tea. Shastry ordered idlis, steamed lentil, and rice cakes, with no sambhar but with extra coconut chutney. They talked about inconsequential subjects for the next few minutes. Once the waiter had delivered the food and drink, Aruna let her uncle tuck into the idlis. When he had finished one and was about to start on the second one, she asked casually, "What's happening about my wedding, uncle?"

Her uncle looked at her sharply. Aruna blushed under his glance. He said, "Aruna, you are a good girl, not at all like some of the modern girls who seem to think only about boys and fashion. I know how worried you must be about your future to talk so openly about your wedding."

Aruna took a sip of her tea and did not say anything.

Shastry-uncle sighed and said, "You know the situation, dear. Your father has got it into his head that he cannot afford to get you married off. He has never been money-minded before, so I don't understand why he is like this now. I tried to talk to him, but he is being incredibly stubborn."

Aruna replied, "I know, uncle. And I know that you've been trying hard to help me. Thanks very much. I have a confession to make." She tapped her feet nervously on the linoleum-covered floor and, not meeting his eyes, continued, "A man has asked me to marry him and I said yes."

"What?" spluttered Shastry, and choked as a piece of idli went the wrong way.

Aruna jumped up and patted her uncle on the back until he recovered. He took a large gulp of water. His face was red. Aruna came around and sat down.

"You could have warned me. I could have died," he said angrily. "Anyway, what are you saying? I never expected this of you, Aruna. I know your dad is being stubborn, but we'll bring him around. Have you no thought for the family's honor? And what about Vani's future? Which respectable family will accept her into their household if you have a love marriage? I am disappointed in you. You are the last person I expected to do something like this. And what will your father say? Or your mother? A pity that she lived to see this day. It would have been better if my sister had died before seeing this sorry day."

Aruna was upset even though her uncle's reaction was not unexpected. She raised her handkerchief and gave a prearranged signal to a waiter. He left the restaurant. Aruna stayed silent until Vani walked in. Shastry-uncle saw Vani and asked, "Have you heard what your sister just told me?"

"Yes, Shastry-uncle, akka's already told me. And by the way, meet Ramanujam," Vani said.

Ramanujam had followed her in.

He stood in front of the girl's uncle, joined his hands in salutation, and said, "Namaste, uncle."

"Hmph," Shastry-uncle grunted. Vani poked him on his hand. He scowled at her and turned to Ramanujam and said, "Take a seat." He added, *sotto voce*, "You are taking our daughter, what's a seat?"

Aruna heard the mutter and looked at her uncle sharply, but he ignored her.

Shastry-uncle looked Ramanujam up and down, clearly appraising him. Aruna was nervous but she knew that her uncle was a fair man and would hear Ramanujam out. That's why she had introduced Ramanujam to him, and not to her parents.

"So what do you do, young man?" Shastry-uncle asked.

"I am a doctor at KGH," replied Ramanujam.

Vani nudged her uncle again. "His name is Ramanujam," she said brightly.

Shastry-uncle smiled thinly. "Can you tell me about your family? Who is your father? What is your native place?" he asked.

Ramanujam replied, "We are from West Godavary district, uncle. We still have lands there, but my father came here before I was born and we are settled here. My father's name is Narayan Rao and we live in Waltair uplands."

"Isn't that a posh area, Shastry-uncle?" asked Vani.

He glared at his niece and turned to Ramanujam. "What's your caste?" he asked.

"We are Niyogi Brahmins, sir, from the Vashishta gothram," Ramanujam said.

Shastry-uncle turned to look at Aruna, who looked back at him hopefully. She met his eyes for a couple of seconds before blushing and lowering her eyes. Aruna knew that the match was not perfect—Ramanujam's family were Niyogi Brahmins, whereas they were Vaidiki Brahmins. Niyogi Brahmins followed secular professions, whereas Vaidiki Brahmins were priests and officiated at religious ceremonies. But that was a minor issue that could be finessed—at least, she hoped so. She knew that everything else was good, even their gothrams were different, so they were not considered brother and sister, and so could marry.

"Tell me more about your family," Shastry-uncle said, leaning forward slightly.

Aruna and Vani had already warned Ramanujam that he had to impress their uncle if he was expected to take his suit to their father. They chatted for about fifteen minutes. Shastry-uncle found out that Ramanujam's mother's family were from the village next to his own, and that was enough of a connection to place them. The conversation went on and Aruna tried to figure out what her uncle was thinking. Did he approve of the match? She couldn't tell.

Shastry-uncle said, "Aruna's family is going through some financial troubles at the moment, and they cannot afford a wedding right now. In fact, some matches have already come but her father has refused them for that reason."

"I know, uncle. Mr. Ali, Aruna's boss, has suggested a good solution. He says that we should get married in a simple ceremony at Annavaram temple. We can then come back to town and my family can hold a big reception where we can invite everybody."

"That's a great suggestion. Her paternal uncle is the priest there and, yes, it will work very well. But will your family be all right with that?" he asked.

"Yes, uncle. Mr. Ali convinced my dad about it."

Shastry turned to Aruna and said, "Oh! So your boss has met his dad. What do you need me for, then? It looks as if you are managing everything very well without me. After all, I am only your maternal uncle."

Aruna reached out across the table and held her uncle's hand. "Shastry-uncle, you are the most important man in this whole wedding. You are the only one who can convince my dad. I would not dare to go in front of him myself and tell him all this."

Ramanujam said, "My father went angrily this morning to Mr. Ali's house and started shouting at him, saying that he must have been responsible for leading me astray. I didn't know where he had gone, but when he came back, he told me. He was not entirely happy, but he seemed resigned."

"Oh, dear," said Shastry-uncle. "Will your parents be all right about the marriage? Will they treat our Aruna well?" he asked.

"Of course, uncle. I have already told them that I expect them to treat her properly. I will support my wife and make sure that she will be happy."

"Uncle, I've decided that I'll carry on working after marriage and use my salary to help my parents," said Aruna.

"Are you sure, daughter? You might feel like that now, but after marriage you will have other responsibilities. Your priorities will change. Your in-laws might not like it," Shastry-uncle said.

"That's okay, uncle," said Ramanujam. "I think it is good that Aruna will continue working after marriage and not just get stuck in the house. And if she wants to help her family with the money she's earned, who am I to stop her?"

Ramanujam and her uncle got up and left, leaving Aruna and Vani at the table. Just before they went through the door, they heard their uncle ask, "Who did you say your head of department was?"

Aruna turned to Vani and asked, "What do you think? Did uncle like him?"

"I'm sure he did," said Vani.

"I don't think he's made up his mind. Shastry-uncle will go around the hospital and talk to the people who work there, and I don't know what other investigations he will carry out before deciding."

A few days later, Aruna's family were all relaxing after dinner when there was a knock on the door. Aruna opened the door and Shastry-uncle walked in. One look at his face and Aruna knew that he had come to talk to her parents about Ramanujam. She signaled Vani and they both went into the kitchen, leaving the door slightly open so they could hear the conversation in the other room.

After some preliminary conversation, Shastry-uncle said, "I have a match for Aruna."

Her father said, "Not again! My ears have gone ripe listening to you. Shastry, how many times must I tell you? I don't want to discuss the matter anymore."

Shastry-uncle said, "You've told me several times, but believe me when I say this is the last time I will bring up this topic. This time you don't have a choice but to agree to the match I've brought."

Aruna heard her mother say, "Just listen to him once. What's the harm?"

Her father grunted and Shastry-uncle took that as a signal to continue. "The boy is a doctor at KGH. Their family is very wealthy—

they have fertile lands in Godavary district and a big house near the University."

Her father said, "Shastry, now you are joking. Why do you sprinkle salt on an open wound?"

Shastry-uncle said, "I'm not joking, brother-in-law. It's all true. The boy's name is Ramanujam."

Her father laughed. He said, "Why would such people want to make an alliance with a poor family like ours? Is he sixty years old and a convicted wife-beater?"

Vani gripped Aruna's arm. Aruna looked at her and Vani grinned, miming a doddering old man with a walking stick. Aruna's lips twitched but she was too nervous to smile.

Shastry-uncle said, "Nothing like that. He's a young man—twenty-nine years old. He's never been married before and he's tall and good-looking, too."

Her father asked, "Is something wrong with his family?"

Shastry-uncle said, "Why must you be so negative? He comes from a respected family. They are rich but orthodox and not flashy at all. They are Niyogi Brahmins."

"Ah!" said her father. "I knew something would come up."

Aruna's mother said, "That's a minor matter, surely. If the match is as good as Shastry says, we can overlook something like that. After all, they are still Brahmins."

Shastry-uncle said, "You are right. It is a minor matter. I have spoken to several people at the hospital and they are all full of praise for him. I even spoke to the gardener and maid at his house. They've been with the family for over twenty years and they too like Ramanujam very much."

"It's natural, isn't it, for such long-serving servants to say nothing against their master?" said Aruna's father.

"No, that's not true. Servants are the best source of information about their masters. There is nothing they don't know, and usually they are quite willing to talk. Anyway, why do you keep raising objections instead of accepting the match?" said Shastry-uncle.

There was silence for a moment and then Aruna's father said, "You are right, Shastry. You have brought a good match and I am sorry to sound so negative."

"It's done. Naanna's accepted it," whispered Vani in Aruna's ear.

Aruna shook her head. "Nothing's happened. Shastry-uncle hasn't told them the whole story yet," she whispered back.

Aruna's father said, "You know our family's position. How can we go ahead with a match like that? How much dowry do they want? What kind of wedding ceremony do we have to pay for?"

Shastry-uncle said, "They don't want a single paisa as a dowry. And they've agreed for a simple ceremony at your brother's temple. They will organize a big reception later, in town, for all their guests."

Aruna's mother asked, "Shastry, this is the best news you've ever brought me. May this news be true and your mouth always know the taste of ghee and sugar. But how did you find such a good man for our Aruna?"

Aruna leaned forward and peeked through the open door.

Shastry-uncle said, "It wasn't me. Aruna found the match herself."

"What?" screamed her father, standing up.

Aruna winced and drew back. The moment she was fearing had arrived.

"Where is Aruna? I want to hear this from her mouth. I don't believe that I've raised a harlot in my house," shouted her father.

Aruna's knees trembled and she almost slipped to the floor. Vani hugged Aruna and held her close.

Shastry-uncle said softly, "Sit down, brother-in-law. You've raised two good girls. Calm down and listen to me, please."

Aruna's mother said, "Sit down, please. Trust our daughter. Trust that our upbringing was good. Please don't raise your stress levels. It's not good for you."

Shastry-uncle said, "At first, I too did not believe that a well-brought-up girl like Aruna would find her own husband, but the more I have found out about Ramanujam and his family, the more convinced I am that our daughter has done no wrong. Ramanujam is a Brahmin. Aruna has not run away with him."

"That's all good, but how could she?" said Aruna's father.

Shastry-uncle said, "She will have a traditional arranged marriage, and as far as the outside world is concerned, nobody need know anything about how the marriage has come about. You are so worried about your finances, and she has got the bridegroom and his family to agree to a simple wedding ceremony at the Annavaram temple. She has saved you from committing a great sin. A father is not supposed to keep his young daughter in the house without getting her married off."

Shastry-uncle turned to her mother and said, "Sister, you think about it. Aruna's husband will be a doctor, his family owns fertile lands, she will have servants catering to her every wish, she will wear expensive saris and jewelry."

"All that sounds great," said Aruna's mother. "But . . ."

"No second thoughts," said Shastry-uncle. "You don't have to pay any dowry. Aruna will be living in the same town after marriage, not more than three miles away."

"Aruna-a-a!" shouted her father. "Come here."

Aruna freed herself from Vani's embrace and walked slowly into the living room. As soon as she saw her father, she ran to him and fell on his legs. "Sorry, naanna!" she said.

Aruna's father was silent for several seconds. Her mother and uncle looked worried as they waited for the explosion. Vani remained in the kitchen. Finally, her father put his hand on her head and blessed her in Sanskrit, *"Chiranjeeva soubhagyavatee bhava,"* May you forever be a married woman.

Aruna looked up into her father's face with shining eyes. Vani came running out and fell on her knees next to Aruna and held her. Both the girls jumped up and hugged their mother and then Shastry-uncle. Vani couldn't stop jumping up and down in joy. Aruna's mother looked stunned and Shastry-uncle fell back in the chair and mopped his brow.

Aruna turned to her father and put her head on his chest. "Thank you, naanna," she said, with tears in her eyes.

Her father sighed and said, "Don't mind me, my dear. The world is moving on, and I am just an old man stuck in my ways."

TWENTY

"I will not marry Aruna. I don't want to get married at all," said Ramanujam.

"Please don't say that, sir. My daughter will be ruined if she is jilted at the altar. We won't be able to show our faces in society if you reject her now," pleaded Aruna's father.

"I don't think married life is for me. I'm thinking of resigning my job and going off to Kashi to live my life as an ascetic on the banks of the Ganges. There are too many problems and compromises in married life," said Ramanujam.

"Don't think like that," said Shastry-uncle. "If you think marriage brings problems, it also brings great pleasures. Don't reject them without even experiencing them first. My niece will keep house, look after you and your parents in both good health and ill. Why do you want to give all this up and live a cold life as a monk?"

Ramanujam was dressed in a white dhoti—a long piece of cloth tied around the waist, covering his lower body. His chest was bare except for a starched silk shawl over one shoulder, and a white thread looped over the other shoulder and across his chest, waist, and back. He was carrying an old-fashioned black umbrella and a bronze mug with a handle. His feet were shod in wooden sandals and he looked like a monk about to renounce the world. Stopping him were Aruna's father and uncle, acting in lieu of her nonexistent brothers. At a slight distance surrounding them were several guests—all grinning.

Mr. Ali had heard about this custom among Brahmins but had never seen it before. Just before the wedding, a Brahmin bridegroom dresses up as a monk and pretends to renounce all worldly pleasures and live a simple life. It is the job of the bride's brothers and other male relatives to persuade the bridegroom to go through with the wedding.

It was early morning on the day of the wedding, just past seven, and they were on top of the mountain in Annavaram. Behind them, the white tower of the temple, covered in statuary, could be seen. They could see miles of forest stretching out over the hillside. The sun was just out and the light early-morning mist had not yet evaporated.

Aruna's family had all come over to her paternal uncle's house three days ago, and she had been made a bride—her body anointed with oil and turmeric; her hands and feet covered with henna patterns. Ramanujam's father had organized the use of a state government guest-house in the temple town through his contacts, and they had arrived the day before. Mr. Ali and his wife had come along with Ramanujam's family, even though they were guests from the bride's side and were staying separately in a hotel.

Ramanujam was eventually prevailed upon to get married, and the parties returned to their respective houses.

●   ●   ●

Two mature banana plants, each bearing a big bunch of green bananas, had been cut down and tied at the entrance to the wedding hall. Mango leaves were strung between the two banana plants, forming a green doorway, the light green of the long fanlike banana leaves contrasting with the darker green of the smaller mango leaves. Aruna and her close relatives walked into the wedding hall, where a priest was waiting for them. Aruna was wearing a nine-yard red silk sari with a gold border and all the traditional gold jewelry of a bride—earrings, chain, torques around her upper arms, a chain down the central parting of her hair, several bangles on each wrist, and silver anklets with bells that tinkled as she walked. Her hair was braided in a long tail. In the center of the hall, a square raised platform had been arranged with smaller banana plants on the four corners and decorated with more mango leaves. At the center of the altar was a brick hearth. The marriage hall was still empty, and workers were arranging chairs for the guests around the altar. Aruna had come to pray to the goddess Gauri for a successful wedding and a happy marriage afterward. The goddess herself had undertaken severe penances to get the husband of her choice.

Once the bridal prayers were complete, Aruna and her family left the wedding hall. The wedding proper could now begin.

Mr. and Mrs. Ali joined Aruna's family and arrived in the hall.

They heard someone behind them say in a voice that carried, "Doctors, not multinationals."

Mr. Ali noticed that his wife blushed, but stood straighter, looking straight ahead. A small smile played on her face. People milled around until they heard music. Some of the older people sat down, but most of the others assembled by the gate, waiting for the bridegroom's party.

The band soon appeared, wearing bright clothes and turbans, some drummers, some blowing into polished steel trumpets, others into flutes. In the front was a bandmaster, wearing the tallest turban of them all, and waving a baton, directing the popular South Indian film song the musicians were playing. Behind the band was a car decorated so heavily with flowers that Mr. Ali was sure that the driver could barely see out of the windshield. In the car sat the bridegroom and possibly his mother and sister. All the others in his party walked behind the crawling car.

Mr. Ali stood with his wife on one side among the crowd as Ramanujam got out of the car. One of Aruna's aunts broke a coconut in front of him. She then took a hundred-rupee note and waved it around in front of Ramanujam three times and cracked her knuckles loudly on the sides of her head. She gave the hundred-rupee note to a beggar hovering on the edge of the crowd. The evil eye having been thus distracted, Ramanujam was welcomed into the hall along with his family.

All the guests settled down; it was a small wedding and there were only a couple of hundred people in the hall. Mr. and Mrs. Ali found seats in the front row on the side of the altar. Ramanujam and his parents sat cross-legged on one side of the platform, facing west. One of Aruna's paternal uncle's friends and a Brahmin brought by Ramanujam's family officiated as the priests at the wedding. As soon as the bridegroom and the guests settled down, harried along by the priests who were worried that the auspicious time would pass, a small idol of the elephant-headed god Ganesha was brought in. Ganesha is the god of beginnings and no Hindu ceremony begins without a prayer to him. Ramanujam followed the priests in praying to Ganesha for the successful conduct of the wedding and the removal of any obstacles to a happy married life. Once the prayer was complete, Vani and one of her cousins came onto the platform and held a long sari between them, dividing the platform in two and preventing Ramanujam from seeing the other side. Vani stood with her back to Mr. and Mrs. Ali, and they were lucky enough to see both sides of the altar.

Mrs. Ali pointed to a door on the side of the hall and Mr. Ali craned his neck to look. Shastry, the bride's maternal uncle, carried her into the marriage hall and onto the platform in a bamboo basket. Aruna's cousins helped him by holding the basket. Aruna had her head down, but she occasionally looked up at the guests. Her eyes met Mr. Ali's and she grinned at him, enjoying the occasion and the ride in the basket on her uncle's and cousins' shoulders. Mr. Ali smiled back at her, thinking that the ceremony they were watching had probably not changed much in a thousand years.

She was placed in front of Ramanujam, on the other side of the sari-curtain. Her parents sat next to her, and Shastry went and stood next to Vani.

"You'd better not put on any weight," he said, puffing heavily. "I'll be even older at your wedding and I might collapse carrying you."

"I might have a registered wedding, so you won't have this trouble," she replied.

"Silence, silly girl. Don't utter foolish words on this auspicious occasion. Who knows what gods are listening in to grant your wishes?" her uncle said angrily.

Mr. Ali overheard the exchange and smiled. He had met Vani yesterday evening and he liked her sparkiness. Aruna had the same wit, but she was much more restrained, while Vani was uninhibited.

The priests started chanting Sanskrit verses from the Vedas. They called on seven generations of ancestors of the bride and groom to bless the union and grant the couple wisdom to deal with the inevitable problems that arise in married life. As the auspicious moment arrived, musicians in the hall started beating drums and playing the

South Indian flute. The drums reached a crescendo and, at a signal from one of the priests, Vani's cousin let go of her end of the sari and Vani whipped it away, leaving the bride and groom face-to-face. Ramanujam glanced at Aruna boldly, who blushed and dropped her eyes shyly to the ground. A priest knelt in front of them with a bowl holding a paste of cumin seeds and jaggery. Aruna and Ramanujam both took a handful of the paste and applied it on each other's heads.

"Yuck," whispered Mrs. Ali to Mr. Ali. "Their hair is messed up."

"Rustic woman," laughed Mr. Ali softly. "The mixture of the bitter cumin seeds and sweet jaggery represents the bittersweet joys and troubles of marriage."

"Maybe," said Mrs. Ali. "But it still messes up their hair."

One of the priests lit a fire in the brick hearth with sandalwood kindling and ghee.

"Look," said Mrs. Ali, pointing at Ramanujam's sister, who was sitting behind Ramanujam. Her face looked like thunder.

"She looks like she has just popped a peanut into her mouth and it has turned out to be bitter!" Mr. Ali laughed.

"I hope she doesn't cause trouble for Aruna," said Mrs. Ali.

The kindling caught fire and the priests nursed it into a blaze. The drums and flute reached another crescendo, and as the priests called on the blessings of the gods, Ramanujam stood up and, bending down toward Aruna, tied a thread with a gold disk hanging from it like a pendant around Aruna's neck with three knots. Aruna's family's priest handed him another thread with an identical gold disk, and Ramanujam tied it around Aruna's neck like a chain as well.

Mr. Ali, who had never seen a Hindu wedding at such close quarters before, turned to Mrs. Ali. He said, "I thought a mangalsootram was one chain with two pendants?"

Mrs. Ali said, "Leela told me about this. Apparently, one of those threads with the gold coin is given by Ramanujam's family and the other by Aruna's family. Sixteen days after today, the two gold disks will be united on one thread and form the mangalsootram that Aruna will wear as long as she is a married woman."

Aruna and Ramanujam stood up and the priest gave them a garland each. Aruna placed her garland around Ramanujam's neck and Ramanujam placed his around Aruna's neck. Mrs. Ali took out some yellow-colored rice that was tied in a handkerchief.

"Where did you get it?" asked Mr. Ali.

"One of Aruna's aunts gave it to me," said Mrs. Ali.

They joined the other guests in throwing the confetti over the couple.

The drums and flutes stopped. In the sudden silence, the priest tied the ends of Ramanujam's dhoti and Aruna's sari together, and they went around the fire with Ramanujam leading. On round one, Ramanujam asked the God of Fire to witness the wedding and for food to sustain them; on round two, he asked for physical strength so their life and marriage would be successful; on the third, he asked the God of Fire to help them honor their vows to each other and to society; on round four, for a sensual and comfortable life with his wife; on round five, he prayed that he would own lots of cattle, the sign of a rich man; on round six, he prayed for good rains and a long life that they might see many seasons. On the seventh and final round, Ramanujam prayed that he and his wife would always fulfill their religious duties.

Thus with three knots and seven steps, Aruna and Ramanujam were married in front of their families with the God of Fire as holy witness. They were now man and wife. Guests came up to them and gifted the newlyweds with clothes or money or jewelry. Mr. and Mrs. Ali gave Aruna a parrot-green silk sari and Ramanujam a creamy-white silk dhoti. They also gave the couple a half-foot-high elephant made of sandalwood.

Aruna left the hall with her husband. The guests got up and the hall was prepared for lunch.

Mr. Ali started talking to Ramanujam's brother-in-law.

"Where do you live?" asked Mr. Ali.

"Lawson's Bay Colony," Ramanujam's brother-in-law replied.

Before Mr. Ali could ask him another question, Ramanujam's sister glared at her husband and he left hurriedly.

Mrs. Ali joined Mr. Ali. Mr. Ali said, "Oh, dear! Somebody's in trouble."

Mrs. Ali laughed. "You are such a wicked man. You knew it would get him into hot water with his wife if he was seen talking to you," she said.

Mr. Ali said, "I was only trying to butter him up so that he will be friendly with Aruna."

Mrs. Ali rolled her eyes.

"Right," she said, clearly not believing him.

Because Annavaram was quite far from the city and Ramanujam's parents wanted to get back before it was too late, the bidaai, or "good-bye," when the bride leaves home to go to her husband's house, was held soon after a vegetarian lunch. Mr. Ali had asked if he and his wife could leave with them on their bus. They stood outside the marriage hall with Ramanujam and his family, waiting for Aruna to join them.

Several minutes later, just when Ramanujam's father was looking at his watch and muttering about not wanting to go on the mountain roads after dark, Aruna came out. She was wearing a rich red silk sari, woven with gold thread—presented, as tradition demanded, by the bridegroom's family. A golden braid ran along the parting in her hair, with a pendant on her forehead. Earrings, nose-ring, upper-arm torques, a dozen bangles, necklace, long chain, the two halves of her mangalsootram, a wide gold cummerbund, silver anklets, and toe-rings weighed her down. Her mother and sister walked with her, and her father and Shastry-uncle walked behind as she slowly came toward them.

In the background, somebody switched on a tape recorder, and an old haunting tune drifted out:

> *Go, my daughter, to your new house, with these blessings from your father:*
> *May you never remember me, lest your happiness falter.*
> *I raised you like a delicate flower, a fragrant blossom of our garden,*
> *May every season from now on be a new spring,*
> *May you never remember me, lest your happiness falter,*
> *Go, my daughter, to your new house, with these blessings from your father.*

When she reached Ramanujam, Aruna stopped and first hugged her mother, then turned to her sister. Vani suddenly seemed to realize the enormity of what was happening, and her smile disappeared. The two sisters hugged tightly and cried. Their father put his arms around them awkwardly, and after a long minute, they separated. Aruna took a step forward and looked back, like a deer caught in a tiger's stare. One of her aunts joined her, so she would not feel lonely when settling into her new house, and helped her get into the waiting bus.

The reception, held three days later, was grand; more than fifteen hundred people were invited, and almost all turned up. The hotel joined all three of their halls and opened the French windows to the garden to accommodate everybody. Aruna wore an orange sari and more jewelry than she had ever owned in her life. Ramanujam was wearing a long

maroon Nehru jacket with a turban on his head. They both looked re-
splendent as they stood on the stage at one end of the hall, receiving an
endless stream of guests, saying a few polite words to each. The gifts
piled up in a corner of the stage.

The wall behind them was decorated with white, red, and orange
flowers all the way to the ceiling, dwarfing the people standing in
front of it. Exquisite bouquets of roses, specially flown in from Bangalore, were standing in baskets on the table in front of the bride and
groom.

Food stations had been set out in several places around the hall,
so people didn't have to stand in line too long. Waiters circulated in
the hall carrying trays of soft drinks, juices, and water. Mr. and Mrs.
Ali walked around the hall. They met several people they knew; some
people said that the bride and groom looked made for each other.
Most ladies were envious, and a few made catty remarks about a bride
from a poor family making such a good match. Nobody, observed Mr.
Ali, remarked that Ramanujam had been lucky; though if he had not
married Aruna, he would have been married off to some rich man's
spoiled daughter who would not have been half as nice to him as Aruna
would be.

"Let's go into the garden for a bit," Mr. Ali told his wife. "I want
some fresh air."

Mrs. Ali nodded and they made their way through the people toward the French windows. Just as they were about to go outside, Mr.
Ali noticed Sridevi and stopped.

He introduced her to Mrs. Ali. "This is Sridevi, the florist in this
place. She decorated the whole hall with the flowers."

Noticing that she was wearing the mangalsootram and red sindoor
on her forehead, he said to Sridevi, "I see that you are back with your
husband again."

"Yes," she replied. "We got married at the registrar's office a couple of weeks ago."

"How are things going this time round?" he asked.

"These are early days, but it is going very well. Thank you," she replied. "Now that we've moved out of his parents' house and money is not an issue, we don't have any fights."

"That's good. Keep it up," said Mr. Ali.

"I intend to. I haven't forgotten what you told me. I am not actually a guest here. I was closing the shop and just came around to make sure that all the decorations are still looking good," she replied.

"The flower arrangements are fantastic," said Mrs. Ali.

"Thanks. I got this commission thanks to uncle," she said, nodding toward Mr. Ali.

"I know. But you've done a really good job, and I heard that you gave them a big discount," said Mrs. Ali.

"I am basically charging my cost price, because it is your assistant's reception and uncle told me that she was the one who helped find the other match for me. But you know what? I heard so many people talking about the flowers that I think I will get a lot of business out of this," she said happily.

"God makes sure that whatever good we do doesn't go unrewarded," said Mrs. Ali.

They said good-bye to Sridevi and moved on into the garden.

Mr. and Mrs. Ali walked around the lawn among the people. The turnout was truly amazing. They saw many important people of the town among the guests. They overheard somebody saying that even the district collector and the deputy inspector general of the police were among the guests. Suddenly, they heard a voice say, "Saibamma! How are you doing?"

They turned around and saw Anjali—the washerwoman who had

been their neighbor long before and still refused to call Mrs. Ali by name, always referring to her as "Muslim lady."

Mrs. Ali exclaimed, "Hello, Anjali! How are you doing? Which side invited you?" Even though Mr. Ali was too well mannered to show it, he was surprised to see Anjali there. It is not common for a low-caste woman to be invited to a Brahmin wedding.

"My younger son works in the same hospital as the bridegroom, and that's how we got invited. My husband didn't want to come, but I wouldn't miss it for the world. After all, it is not often that we are invited to such grand parties. Hello, babu-garu," she said, turning to Mr. Ali.

Mr. Ali smiled at her in greeting.

Anjali turned to Mrs. Ali and said, "I heard that Lakshmi's son has taken her back. I also heard that you had something to do with it. Is that true?"

"That's right," said Mrs. Ali. "You know that she went to live with her sister after she and her daughter-in-law fell out with each other and her son asked her to leave the house?"

Anjali said, "That's right. I was the one who told you that."

Mrs. Ali nodded and continued, "I decided that the situation had gone on long enough, and went and had a chat with the son and daughter-in-law. I told them that whatever fights they had, a family had to stay together. I told the son that his mother was widowed and that it was his duty to look after her. It took a while, but I convinced them. I then took Lakshmi's son with me and we went to her sister's house. Before her son invited her back, I asked her why she was living with her sister instead of her son. I pointed out to her that she had brought this on herself with her attitude. She had to get along with her daughter-in-law. She might think her son was not being well taken care of or that her daughter-in-law was lazy; it didn't matter. She had to let go.

The relationship between her son and daughter-in-law would be different from the relationship she had with her husband. The people are different; the times are different. Only when she agreed to change her attitude, did I let her son invite her back. It's been over a month now and things seem to be all right."

Anjali said, "That's fantastic, saibamma. You've done very well."

Cheered by the conversation, Mr. and Mrs. Ali went back into the reception hall and mingled with the guests for a while before lining up for dinner. "This is a Brahmin wedding, there won't be any meat here," Mrs. Ali said to her husband.

"You are wrong," said Mr. Ali. "Look over there. That's a nonvegetarian food station."

Mrs. Ali laughed. "I guess the rich do things differently," she said.

While they lined up for dinner, a tall, straight-backed man behind them said, "Hello, sir, madam. Aren't you the parents of Rehman Ali?"

They turned back. The man shook Mr. Ali's hand, and then said, "Namaste," to Mrs. Ali with folded hands.

Mr. and Mrs. Ali looked puzzled. The man said, "You don't know me. I am the superintendent of police for Vizag rural district. I had to arrest your son at Royyapalem."

Mr. Ali said, "Sorry he gave you such trouble."

"We are just doing our job. No problem at all. Anyway, you should be proud of your son. How many people go to any effort to fight for other people's rights?" he said.

Mrs. Ali's face broke into a smile. "Thank you," she said.

Once they finished their dinner, they went onto the stage where Ramanujam and Aruna were sitting down. Aruna tried to stand up when she saw them, but they asked her to continue sitting.

"How are you?" asked Mrs. Ali.

Aruna smiled. "Life is good, madam. Do you know what happened just now? We were both standing, receiving all the people, and he noticed that I was flagging—my smile was strained and I was shifting my weight from one leg to another. He immediately told his father that he was getting tired and would like a break. Isn't that kind?"

Mrs. Ali cracked her knuckles on the sides of her head. "May the evil eye never fall on you," she said.

Mr. Ali said, "We are just here to say good-bye. Enjoy yourself today. When are you leaving for your honeymoon?"

"Tomorrow," said Aruna, her cheeks reddening.

"Great. Have you got warm clothes? Kulu Manali, up in the Himalayas, will be cold," said Mrs. Ali.

"We are not going to Kulu Manali. We've decided to go to a mango orchard just outside Simhachalam," said Aruna.

"What? Kulu Manali is beautiful. And you told me you've never been there before," said Mrs. Ali.

"It was Aruna's idea," said Ramanujam, joining the conversation. He lowered his voice and told them confidentially, "It's actually worked very well. When Aruna said that she didn't want to go for an expensive honeymoon, it finally convinced my parents that Aruna is no gold digger. My father now thinks that Aruna is the best daughter-in-law he could have gotten and even my mum is practically civil to her now."

"No-o . . ." said Aruna, scandalized. "How can you talk like that? Your mum is such a kind woman."

"Darling," her husband drawled, "I know her better than you."

The affection between them was clear to everybody. Mr. Ali knew from long experience that this romantic love would not last more than a couple of years and they would have to forge a different kind to last them a lifetime, but it was still heartwarming to see.

"We'll see you after a couple of weeks," they said to Aruna.

Ramanujam's father came up to them. "Let me see you out," he said.

At the door, Ramanujam's father said to Mr. Ali, "You were right, you know. I don't need more money, I need a good daughter-in-law. It may be a cliché to say this, but thanks to you, I haven't lost a son. I've gained a wonderful daughter."

Mr. and Mrs. Ali left the reception hall and went out of the hotel. Mrs. Ali pointed to the sea nearby and said, "Let's go to the beach. It's been a long time since we've come here."

They walked down to the beach, where the surf was crashing noisily on the sand. The sun had set but it was still quite bright because it was a full moon. Most people had already left, and the vendors were packing up.

As they walked toward the water, Mr. Ali said, "You've been writing a lot recently. Aren't the English lessons all finished now?"

"The lessons have finished," said Mrs. Ali. "However, the lecturer who wrote those lessons in the paper said that the lessons were just the beginning, and that we should read an English newspaper or magazine regularly and write an essay on some topic or other every week to improve our skills."

"Hmmm . . ." he said, impressed, but not really surprised by his wife's discipline.

Mr. Ali sat down on the sand, several feet above the level reached by the highest waves. Mrs. Ali left her shoes with him and went closer to the water, lifting her sari to just above her ankles.

"Don't forget you are wearing an expensive sari," he called out.

She nodded but continued forward.

Mr. Ali started thinking about his marriage bureau. It had been successful beyond his wildest dreams—not just financially, but also so-cially. India was changing and his success was one sign of it. A fly on the wall of his office might think that Indians were obsessed with caste and that nothing had changed in a hundred years. *That's not true,* thought Mr. Ali. Marriage was one institution where caste was still important, but in other matters it was losing its hold. People of different castes went to the same schools and offices; they mingled and became friends with each other. Just a few years ago, people of lower castes, or Mus-lims for that matter, would not have been invited to weddings of upper-caste people. Today, it went unremarked. India was changing and Mr. Ali just hoped he would be around for a while to see the changes. But he groaned at the prospect of the next few weeks without Aruna—it was going to be hard work in her absence.

A particularly big wave rose high above the surface of the water and Mrs. Ali rapidly walked backward, giggling half in fear. The wave crashed back and water rushed rapidly up the beach. Mrs. Ali shrieked, raising her sari almost to midcalf to prevent it from getting wet. Mrs. Ali came back to sit next to Mr. Ali. Together they watched the silver tops of the waves shimmering in the moonlight. In the distance, the silhouettes of a long line of ships could be seen as they waited on the horizon to get into port. A broad beam of light swept across the sea from the lighthouse on the peak of Dolphin's Nose.

Mr. Ali turned to his wife and said, "Call Rehman for lunch tomor-row. It's been a long time since I've argued with my son."

Mrs. Ali looked at him in disbelief for a second. Then tears slowly rolled down Mrs. Ali's cheeks and her face glowed brighter than the surf in the moonlight.

Extracts from Mrs. Ali's English Essays

EXTRACT 1

Visakhapatnam is also called Vizag. On one side of Vizag is the coast and on the other side are green mountains. The population of Vizag is 3.5 million people. When I was younger, it used to be much cooler and Vizag was known as a retirement town, but now the number of people has grown a lot, and every summer it becomes very hot.

There are many tourist spots in and around Vizag. Tribal people live in the forests of Araku Valley. They sometimes come into town wearing colorful clothes to sell brooms, soapnuts, jackfruit, honey, tamarind, and peacock feathers. When I was a little girl, my uncle used to work in the agency that looked after the tribal people. He told me that he used to see tigers when riding in the forest. People don't see the animals anymore. There are also ancient limestone caves there. We once went there and the guide took us inside. It is very silent and cool in the caves, and massive pillars grow from the floor and from the ceiling toward each other.

The temple at Simhachalam is about one thousand years old. It is a very important temple for Hindus. In Vizag itself, there are three hills—the first has a Hindu temple, the second has the tomb of a Muslim saint and a mosque, and the third has a big church. The papers print stories of riots and communal problems in other parts of India, but we never have such problems in Vizag. People of all religions and castes live together without any trouble. I am proud of this.

The Beach Road is very beautiful. The sand dunes (is that the word?) stretch along the road. If you drive for about fifteen miles on this road, you come to the town of Bhimili. The beach here is really special. It is like a big round circle cut in half. If we ever go there, I try to reach it at two in the afternoon. The fishermen's boats come to the shore at this time and you get really fresh fish—vanjaram and chanduva are the best, but I don't know their English names. There is supposed to be a two-hundred-year-old Dutch cemetery in Bhimili, but I have never visited it myself. Some years ago, we were watching a Hindi movie called *Silsila*, which had a song shot in a big field of bright yellow and red flowers. Rehman told me that these beautiful flowers are called tulips and they grow in the country of those people. I looked but could not find this country called Dutch on the map.

EXTRACT 2

Most people in Vizag are Hindus, like Aruna, and speak Telugu, the elegant South Indian language of this part of India. An Englishman named C. P. Brown called Telugu the "Italian of the East."

Is Italian beautiful?

There are many Muslims like me in Vizag, and we speak Urdu. My husband tells me that our beautiful mother tongue, so suited for writing songs and poems, was created in the army camps of the Moghul emperors by soldiers from different countries speaking Persian, Turkish and Hindi. I find this difficult to believe, but sometimes you can see a lovely lotus growing in the middle of a dirty, green pond.

Another thing I find difficult to believe is how English people can get by without words for so many kinds of relatives. Aren't family relations important in England? For example, when an Englishwoman talks about her grandmother, how will her listener know whether she is talking about her mother's mother or her father's mother? Also, we have different words for mother's brother, father's younger brother, and father's older brother, but in English they are all just called "uncle."

I recently read a joke in English that didn't make sense to me. The joke was:

Q: What do you call your son's mother-in-law?
A: Dragon!

How can they make fun of such an important relationship? In Urdu, your son's mother-in-law is your samdhan.

Another rule in India is that you normally do not call people older than yourself by name. So my younger brother Azhar calls me "aapa" (Urdu) and Vani calls Aruna "akka" (Telugu). Aruna and I call them by their names.

This is a list of some words for relatives:

English	Urdu	Telugu
Mother	Ammi	Amma
Father	Abba	Naanna
Brother-in-law	Bhai-jaan	Baava
Older sister	Aapa	Akka
Father's older brother	Taaya	Pedda-Naanna
Father's younger brother	Chaacha	Chinnaana
Mother's brother	Maama	Maavayya

EXTRACT 3

There are supposed to be four castes among Hindus—Brahmins, the priestly class; Kshatriyas, or warriors; Vaishyas, or merchants; and Shudras, or workers. The system, of course, is a lot more complicated than this.

There are subcastes within castes, and subcastes within subcastes. As Muslims, we are not part of the caste system, and until my husband started the marriage bureau, I wasn't fully aware of how complex it all was. Aruna explained to me that the caste system was based on people's traditional professions. Over thousands of years, the system became rigid and hereditary. When I asked her about subcastes, she said that they too were based on people's jobs. She said that we might think that all leather workers were one subcaste of Shudras; but within that, the people who tanned leather were a different subcaste from those who made shoes, and they were again different from people who made saddles.

Among Brahmins, too, those who carry out priestly duties like Aruna's family are Vaidiki Brahmins. They tend to be well versed in Sanskrit. Ramanujam's family are Niyogi Brahmins. These Brahmins do not officiate at religious functions. They are well educated in English and Telugu and are village heads or clerks and accountants.

The most controversial part of the caste system is, of course, un-touchability. The lowest castes, who work in "unclean" professions like handling dead bodies or human waste, are called "scheduled" castes. Hindus from higher castes do not allow the scheduled caste people to come into their houses or even to touch them. In villages, they have to live away from the rest of the people, and there are a lot of restrictions on what they can and cannot do. For example, they cannot use the wells that the other villagers use. Their children may have to sit outside the classroom so that they are away from the upper-caste children. Un-touchability is banned, and the government reserves a portion of jobs and college seats for scheduled caste people, but it will take time to get rid of a problem that has grown over two thousand years. Not every upper-caste person is rich, but most lower-caste people are poor.

EXTRACT 4

I start cooking breakfast between seven and seven-thirty in the morning. When Rehman was a boy and my husband was still in service, I used to start cooking by half past six, but now there is no need to be so early.

We never have the same breakfast two days in a row. If I make parathas one day, I make dosas or idlis the next day. The day after that, I might make upma or pesaratt. To make dosa or idli, I have to soak black-grams for a few hours and wet-grind them into a thick paste the night before, so they ferment. I normally make a chutney as a side dish—coconut and onion are two favorites. Sometimes, I also make sambhar, which is a thick liquid made of lentils, onions, tamarind, and spices. Sambhar can be used as a dip for breakfast or to mix in rice for lunch or dinner. Rasam, on the other hand, is only used for lunch or dinner. It is a thin liquid made with tamarind and spices and used to mix in rice.

In all the years that I've been married, I have made sure that my family always ate a hot breakfast before leaving the house—even if it meant waking up at four in the morning if we had to catch an early train. Rehman used to love his breakfast as a boy. Sometimes I get tears in my eyes when I think of him in some small village—what does he eat? How can food prepared in a hotel, without love, stick to his body? No wonder he is so thin. I wish he would get married soon. I will teach his wife how to make all his favorite dishes, just as my mother-in-law taught me all my husband's likes and dislikes.

When we were younger, we used to eat meat only once a week, and chicken was an occasional treat. Now we have more money and can afford to eat meat more frequently, but as we've gotten older, we don't want to eat rich food so often. We usually eat meat on Sunday. I rarely make a pure meat dish. I mix vegetables and meat—it is tastier that way and cheaper too!

I also make sweets at home sometimes. One pudding that is very easy to make is halwa. This is the method that I use.

INGREDIENTS:

Fine semolina—1 cup (about 200 g)

Sugar—1 cup

Ghee (or unsalted butter)—1/2 cup

Water—2 cups

Cashew nuts—50 g

Raisins—25 g

Cardamom—4 pods

Cloves—4 sticks

Cinnamon—2 pieces

METHOD:

1. Melt the ghee in a flat-bottomed pan on a medium flame and add the cardamom, cloves, and cinnamon.

2. Fry the cashew nuts and raisins along with the spices in the ghee until light brown.

3. Add the semolina and fry along with the above ingredients till the color changes.

4. Add the water to all the above and mix well.

5. Cover the pan and keep on low flame for two minutes. By now, the water should have been absorbed and the semolina cooked.

6. Add the sugar and stir well on a low flame. In a couple of minutes, bubbles start popping through the semolina.

7. Cover the pan and keep on low flame for one more minute.

8. Switch off the flame.

9. Serve while still warm.

This book would not have been possible, but for

My father, who got me into story-writing and always believed that I had a book in me.

My mother, for her paranoid belief that if her children did not study, they would have no roof over their heads and they would starve.

My sister, Nilofar, who gave me the halwa recipe.

Ramachandran-Uncle and Suseela-Auntie, for being wonderful hosts and giving me a view into a Brahmin household.

My friends, and early readers of this manuscript: Tom, Sue, Suchi, and Jasmine, for their comments and encouragement.

James Lynn and the chain of friends who led to Guy Walters, who led to . . .

Jenny McVeigh and Cecile Barendsma, who seem to love my work as much as I do, as all good agents should.

Jenny Parrott and Amy Einhorn, my British and American editors respectively, for their enthusiasm and many ideas.

My wife, Sameera, for supporting me throughout this exercise and taking on even more of the running of the household than usual while I disappeared into the study practically every evening after long hours at work.

My two boys, who think that all writers will be as famous and rich as J. K. Rowling. If only.

ABOUT THE AUTHOR

Farahad Zama was born in Visakhapatnam (Vizag) on the eastern coast of India in 1966. After an (arranged) marriage, his career took him to London on a six-month business trip. Sixteen years later, he is still in London, with his wife and two sons. He works for an investment bank and writes on his commute and sitting in front of the TV after dinner.

2 2 JUN 2009

FICTION
Zama, Farahad

DATE DUE			

GAYLORD·M2